BARNEY POLAN'S
GAME

Also by Charley Rosen:

Fiction

Have Jump Shot Will Travel (1975)

A Mile Above the Rim (1977)

The Cockroach Basketball League (1992)

The House of Moses All-Stars (1997)

Non-Fiction

Maverick with Phil Jackson (1976)

Scandals of '51: How the Gamblers Almost Killed College Basketball (1978)

God, Man and Basketball Jones (1979)

Players and Pretenders (1981)

BARNEY POLAN'S GAME

by CHARLEY ROSEN

A Novel of the 1951 College Basketball Scandals

SEVEN STORIES PRESS
New York

In the U.K.:
Turnaround Publisher Services Ltd., Unit 3, Olympia Trading Estate, Coburg Road, Wood Green, London N22 6TZ U.K.

In Canada:
Hushion House, 36 Northline Road, Toronto, Ontario M4B 3E2, Canada

Library of Congress Catologing-in-Publication Data

Rosen, Charley
Barney Polan's game / Charley Rosen
p. cm.
ISBN 1-888363-56-8
1. Polan, Barney—Fiction.   2. Basketball players—United States—
Fiction. I. Title.
PS3568.076473B3 1998
813'.54—dc21   97-24273
                                                              CIP

Dalton Trumbo quotation from his acceptance speech on receiving the Laurel Award from the Writers Guild of America on March 13, 1970. Trumbo accepted the award, feeling that it offered a chance to summarize his conclusions about the blacklist.

Book design by Adam Simon

Seven Stories Press
632 Broadway
New York, N.Y. 10012

Printed in the U.S.A.

9 8 7 6 5 4 3 2 1

To Daia, for her beautiful sanity.

To Dan, for his honesty, his patience, and his meticulous integrity.

"...it will do no good to search for villains or heroes or saints or devils because there were none; there were only victims."

—Dalton Trumbo

Chapter One

August 14, 1950

—BARNEY POLAN—

God, I love my paunch, all this beautiful pink flesh, solid and undeniable. Like truth. Like justice. Like success.

Patting my belly, I've often said to an admiring postgame audience at Toots Shor's: "I figure my bumper here must've cost me a couple of thousand bucks. Damn right. That's twenty-five years of drinking beer. So this round's on me."

Even though sportswriters are supposed to be impartial, I'm a Brooklyn boyo and Dodger fan through hell or high water, so my beer is Schaefer. In bottles or from the tap, but never in cans because of the coppery aftertaste. Damn right. Yankee fans "ask the man for Ballantine." Giants fans drink Knickerbocker, strictly pisswater.

I'm proud to be just an old-fashioned guy who values purity and quality. That's why there's always a Cuban cigar between my crooked yellow teeth, small leathery-looking cheroots that smoke like long-burning fuses. With my sporty blue eyes and stubborn chin, with my cigar, my trademark soiled felt hat, and even the blasted blood vessels that lace my nose, I look like what sportswriters are supposed to look like.

The difference is my talent. I'll admit to being a witty and energetic writer, able to compose inspired Brooklynese with overtones of Shakespearean irony. Damn right. Even the Broadway wiseguys treat me with respect. Years ago, using the local dialect in an exquisitely ambiguous fashion, the great Jimmy Cannon of the *New York Post* dubbed me "The verse of the peepul."

Verse...voice. Get it? Fucking Cannon's a genius!

The athletes on my beat praise me for honoring an off-the-record etiquette. Whose beeswax is it anyway if a certain outfielder is a boozer? Or if a certain college football coach cheats on his wife? Certainly not John Q's.

I'm proud to be a minor celebrity in all five boroughs. Sure, the photo of my smiling puss atop my thrice-weekly column in the *Brooklyn Sentinel,* "Sports A-Plenty," is twenty years old, and I've carefully avoided being photographed since then (ever since I became prematurely bald and itchy-headed). But the hat always gives me away. Publicly I swear up and down that the battered gray felt I always wear is the very same topper in the old photo. In truth, since the inside sweatband always rots after four or five years, I've gone through five hats since then, each one meticulously stained and aged on the fire escape outside my bedroom window to resemble its predecessor.

"I go for a man who wears an Adams hat!"

These are only two of my most guarded secrets: my scabrous baldness and my Dorian Gray hats. Fortunately I'm able to ease my conscience in many ways. After all, my old man is bald as an egg, and heredity ain't nobody's fault. Right?

The champion of the underdog, that's me, too. A notorious sap for a sob story, an easy mark for any old punch-drunk boxer or punchless second baseman down on his luck.

So who doesn't love Barney Polan? Nobody, I tell myself as I remove the top of a red-plaid cabana outfit (that Sarah got me years ago for my thirty-third birthday) and defiantly expose my wondrous bumper to the hot summer sun. (Besides my father in the Beth Abraham Home? Besides my crazy Uncle Max in Coney Island? Besides the ballplayers I rag for their errors? Besides Giants fans?) Nobody, that's who.

Even so, deep within some intravascular black-blooded chamber, the truth gnaws at me and I can't fool myself. More and more, my hats seem to suffocate my brain, my cigars raise tiny blisters on my tongue, and maintaining my universal goodwill is a strain, a mental hernia. Sometimes, with my costume and my stale dialogue, I feel like a restless actor trapped in a long-running play. Sometimes I yearn to quit the newspaper and move to a secluded cabin in Oregon or Montana, where I'd cook my modest meals over an open fire, use "Sports A-Plenty" as toilet paper, and write a fat, poetic novel to make William Faulkner weep. (I'd write about my childhood in the streets of Brooklyn. About my crazy friends and their cruel rites of passage. About my parents. About good and evil. About love. Of course I can do it. Damn right. Red Smith never wrote a novel.) And sometimes, for reasons I don't understand, I feel like running naked through the streets, screaming and spitting curses at the sky.

Now, where the hell is the fucking pool? Eagle-eyed sportswriters aren't supposed to wear spectacles, so I have to squint mightily to read the nearest signpost:

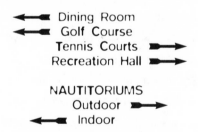

WELCOME TO LEVY'S BY THE LAKE

      ◄── Dining Room
      ◄── Golf Course
      Tennis Courts ──►
      Recreation Hall ──►

NAUTITORIUMS
Outdoor ──►
◄── Indoor

Ambling past the tennis courts, I squint again, this time in disgust. The tennis courts are aswarm with players and pretenders all smartly dressed in neat white outfits. "Out!" they shout at one another. "Deuce!" and "My ad!" Line drives are thwocked. Pop-ups are pinged. A chorus line of leathery middle-aged women rehearse the proper strokes with the club pro. All this against fields of green asphalt square-angled with crisp white lines.

This is considered a sport? With no cursing and no spitting and no scratching of the crotch? Instead of one-to-nothing the score is 15–love, and 3–2 is 40–30. Imagine a 3-2 pitch, two out, bases loaded, score tied in the bottom of the ninth, the Giants against the Dodgers in Ebbets Field. Imagine Red Barber announcing to the fans, *"Silence, s'il vous plaît."*

Let that snob Red Smith write odes to half volleys and overhead smashes. Tennis anyone? Not anyone I want to know.

The vast hotel grounds are teeming with guests, mostly vacationing Jews up from the city. A few golfers stride purposefully to and from a distant course wearing knickers and plaid stockings. Rapt honeymooners lost in time stroll hand in hand. But mostly family groups complete with *mishpocheh*, perhaps a *zaideh* in a wheelchair, and always the obnoxious, caterwauling children. (It's hard to like children, they're such a pain in the ass, so helpless and yet so demanding. I've almost convinced myself to be thankful that Sarah and I were childless. Almost.) In midweek only an occasional single prowls the white-stoned pathways and spacious green lawns.

Tucked snugly under my left arm is today's *Sentinel*, a scarce commodity up here since it's a forty-five-minute drive into the nearest one-horse town (Monticello). Up-to-date newspapers are particularly valuable for yesterday's major league box scores and today's pitching matchups, the results at Belmont and Aqueduct, as well as today's racing form.

Meanwhile I'm sweating so heavily that my cigar is drenched and falling apart. Pttu! Surreptitiously I spit the slimy tobacco into my palm, then toss the mess into a nearby bush as I finally approach the

"Outdoor Nautitorium," the hotel's most popular summertime venue. And the pool is certainly the grand centerpiece, nearly long enough for waterskiing. Rude gangs of children jump in and out of the pale blue water, shrieking and splashing, pausing only to pee in warm green currents. Three old women in rubberized bathing caps navigate the shallows with dainty, fearful steps. Most of the old folks are schmeared and laid out upon wood-slatted lounges to sizzle in the sun.

A hefty young tomato in a blue bathing suit shouts across the pool to a small exuberant child, "Don't run, Michael! You'll fall and break your neck!"

On the far side of the pool and connected by a common wall to the "Recreation Hall" is a large wood-shingled pavilion filled with elegant wrought-iron furniture where other guests play impassioned card games. There's also a noisy crowd on the shuffleboard court, where Mickey Nightingale, the hotel's longtime resident *tummler,* entertains the middle-aged ladies. "Simon sez to put your right thumb in your *tochis* and your left thumb in your mouth!... Oy, look at the missus here. Your thumb, *tateleh,* not your pinky.... Simon sez, girls! No, no, that's close enough. We don't want to get raided by the police! That's right.... Now, Simon sez switch thumbs!... Heh! You're all disqualified except Missus Fishbomb here...." The sound of the ladies' half-hysterical laughter, shrill and clucking, makes me think there's a fox in the henhouse.

Red-shirted attendants of both sexes are everywhere—fetching drinks, dispensing towels, arranging chaise lounges, tables, and chairs, constantly adjusting the tabletop sun umbrellas.

Among the cardplayers in the pavilion I recognize Georgie Klein, a small-time bookie from the Bronx who frequently has useless information to sell. With his protruding Adam's apple, Klein looks like he's just swallowed a doorknob. Also Jimmy O'Hara, a second-string clerk in the Manhattan D.A.'s office whose long bony nose reminds me of a can opener. There's a cut-man named Joe Leibowitz. And Flatfoot Ferdie, a runner for some two-bit mobster. Plus other suggestive silhouettes dimmed by the shade, the familiar sporting crowd and attendant wisenheimers. The game is always seven-card stud and the stakes are a-dollar-and-two. Georgie is dealing.

Eyebrows are raised as I cross the near horizon, and cordial greetings are shouted.

"Hi ya, Barney."

"Good to see yiz, Barn."

"Howdy, boys."

"Hey, Barney," Klein pipes. "What's the spread tonight?"

"The only spread I'm interested in tonight," I say with a sly grin, "is the horseradish on the pot roast."

The cardplayers laugh in sparkling good humor and I favor them with a smile in the shadow of my hat brim. Then I turn away to scout out a poolside lounge chair in the shade.

"See you later, boys."

"See ya, Barney."

Already stretched out on adjacent lounges there in the sunshine beyond the deep end of the pool, Johnny Boy Gianelli is talking to his young wife, Rosie, but I pretend not to see them. Not to see old Gianelli's narrow chin jabbing and thrusting at the young woman like an accusing finger. Or his thin lips sucking on his ill-fitting false teeth. Jeez! A rich man like that, owner of a construction company in cahoots with the Black Hand. You'd think he could afford a better set of choppers.

According to the police blotter, Gianelli is sixty-seven years old—yet he still has a full head of gray hair. (Better gray than none.) Even Gianelli's twitchy little Charlie Chaplin moustache is gray, and bushy gray eyebrows shade his pebble-colored eyes. Gianelli wears a white terrycloth cabana outfit and a floppy straw hat, also rubber thongs that show his blue-lined and gnarly feet.

Gianelli's wife, Rosie, is a shapely dame in her early thirties whom the old fart rescued years ago from the chorus line at the Copa. Sitting next to Rosie and blatantly ogling her tits is Ray Paluski, Jr., six-foot-three-inch high-scoring frontcourtsman for the Redmen of St. John's, a Jesuit college in Queens. Junior averaged 11.3 points per game in '49–'50, pacing the Redmen to a 14-and-8 record. Actually a disappointing season for St. John's.

The persistent rumor is that young Paluski is porking Rosie.

I turn away just in time to ignore Paluski giving me the high sign. As an upstanding and righteous purist, I don't approve of scandalous behavior.

Speaking of which, here's Senator Joe McCarthy's face on the front page again, goddamned Irisher, always making trouble for the Jews. Sure, he talks about "Communists" and "the Red Menace," but he's really just another vicious anti-Semite. What's his latest shtick? Waving around pieces of paper—"proof," he says, that the State Department is riddled with Communists and Communist sympathizers. Aha! It's this "sympathizer" business that gives him license to find subversives everywhere he wants to look. And he's got everybody scared, including Truman. Anybody who looks cross-eyed at McCarthy is accused of being "soft" on Communism.

Oy, so much bullshit, so much confusion. Weren't the Communists instrumental in establishing labor unions? Damn right. I wouldn't have a pension in my old age without them. And didn't the Russkies fight the Nazis? So now what? This one's supposed to be guilty. That one's supposed to be innocent. What the fuck do I know about politics?

All I know is that, according to the Constitution, everybody's innocent until *proven* guilty—and then they're guilty forever. Until then, leave me out of it.

All I know is that the good guys won the war and that eventually the good guys always win.

All I know is that Hitler killed six million Jews, and cocksuckers like Joe McCarthy are trying to finish the job.

All I know is that today's installment of "Sports A-Plenty" is a gem. My theme is baseball—"The Phillies are running on empty." Get it? Phillies... *Fill*ies... empty. Anyway, Philadelphia can't possibly win the pennant because their big hitters (Del Ennis, Andy Seminick, Willie Jones, Granny Hamner, and Mike Goliat) are right-handed and therefore susceptible to the Dodgers' right-handed pitching. Also, only Robin Roberts and Curt Simmons are established pitchers, and how long can the Phillies' ace reliever, Jim Konstanty, get hitters out with the slop he throws?

Have no fear, the Bums will prevail.

Hold on. Who's this gangly Negro teenager, dressed in the hotel's red uniform, hustling up to me with a huge smile on his face. The tall boy is stooped as he carries a thick rubber body pad under his long right arm. He looks vaguely familiar—his ebony skin glistening in the relentless sunshine, the tight smile pressing his puffy lips into a thick red line, the thin white scar above the left eyebrow, and the eyes, the huge round eyes, fawn-eyes brimming with such sweetness and innocence that I suddenly feel fraudulent and hopelessly corrupt.

"Anywhere in particular, Mister Polan?" the boy asks. "I could angle you toward the pool or toward the sun or in the shade. You want an umbrella, suh? Or something cold to drink? Whatever you say, Mister Polan, suh."

I hate being catered to, being waited on. Such ruthless benevolence giving the false impression that I'm a helpless boob. Besides,

Negroes always make me feel guilty, for what I don't know. "Over there's good," I say, pointing toward a dark corner with good angles on both the pool and the pavilion. "And, when you get a chance, could you please bring me a bottle of Schaefer? A bottle, not a can."

"Yes, suh," the boy says, and effortlessly aligns the body pad on the designated lounge chair.

"Wait a minute," I say with sudden remembrance. "Haven't I seen you play someplace? I never forget a face."

"Yes, suh," the boy says, boldly rising up to his full six-foot-three-inch height. "I'm Royce Johnson from Seward Park High School down on Grand Street. We won the P.S.A.L. city championship last March in the Garden and I had thirty-one points. You wrote in the paper that I was the best high school player you've ever seen. But, believe me, Mister Polan, you ain't seen nothin' yet."

I'm glad the kid is a braggart. Now I can feel superior to him again, even as I move clumsily to settle into the chair. "Oh, yeah. Now I remember you. With the behind-the-back dribbling and the quick set shot."

The boy hovers over me, beaming brightly. "I got a jump shot, too, that my coach wouldn't let me use."

"So what're you doing here, Royce? Working, huh?"

"Working the pool and helping in the kitchen, yes, suh. Coach Goldberg got me the job for fifteen dollars every Monday and lots of free food. I'm gonna go play for City College next year."

My smile is tight and full of wisdom. "Coach Goldberg won't be too happy about your behind-the-back tricks. The Ol' Coach, he hates show-offs."

"No, suh. Me and Coach Goldberg already got us a understanding. I'm just gonna be proud to play for him and I'll do whatever he wants and don't do whatever he don't want. But after a while, once he learns how good my game is, then I know he's gonna give me the ball and turn me loose."

"I like to see such confidence in a young player," I tell him with practiced sincerity. "Good." Then I pause long enough to let the boy scoot off to get the beer. "Very good."

Actually I'm mildly surprised at the hotel's progressive stance in having a Negro work so out in the open. The young fellow, Royce Johnson, must be quite the hoopster.

Checking my sightlines, I lean back into the cushioned lounge, looking forward to seeing the kid play tonight.

Of course I'd much rather see the Dodgers play tonight, but not in Cincinnati in August. The Dodgers' current road trip includes three games in Cincy, four in Chi-Town and three in St. Louie. No thanks. Sixteen summers of sweltering Midwest roadtrips was quite enough. Sixteen years as beat writer for my beloved Bums.

I can still recall the names, uniform numbers, and essential stats of every player. The stars: Del Bissonette, #25, hit .336 in 1930. Babe Herman, #4, hit .330 in 1943. And the benchwarmers from Johnny Hudson to Al Glossop. Hey, a few of the old-timers are still hanging on. Joe Hatten. Hugh Casey. Rube Walker is now a coach. The Brooklyn Dodgers were my first love and I'm convinced that their newest star, Jackie Robinson, makes them God's team too.

Back in 1925 when I started at *The Sentinel* as a copyboy, I would've given a trillion-to-one odds against a *shvartzer* ever playing in the majors.

As of this very morning the Dodgers are still two and a half games ahead of the Phillies, and Robinson is hitting .324, with seven homers, sixty-seven runs scored and nineteen stolen bases.

Even when I was a kid, I always studied the stats, reading *The Sporting News* like a sacred text. In the many pressrooms and hotel bars of my acquaintance, I'm the official adjudicater of most sports arguments:

"Who was better, Barney? Ducky Medwick when he was wid the Cardinals or wid the Dodgers?"

"Medwick hit three points higher lifetime with Brooklyn, but he won a World Series with Saint Louie. You figure it out for yourself."

"Hey, Barney? Who won the Davis Cup last year?"

"Ask me next if I fuckin' care."

Thankfully I don't spend much time in pressrooms or hotel bars anymore, and these days I can pick my assignments to suit myself. Sometimes in the spring I'll take the train to Philly or Boston. Perhaps slum at the Polo Grounds when the Dodgers are out West. Another option is a periodic visit to the Bronx to report on the lordly Yankees.

My columns appear on Mondays, Thursdays, and Saturdays, forty-eight weeks a year, making 1,296 columns since 1941 (*The Collected Woiks?*). I remember well my very first column, a spring-training celebration of Mickey Owens's great hands behind the plate. (Six months later, in Game Four of the World Series, the Dodgers had a 4–3 lead in the top of the ninth inning when the Yankees' "Old Reliable" rightfielder, Tommy Heinrich, apparently struck out swinging to end the ball game. But the ball also eluded Owens, Heinrich was safe at first, and the Yankees rallied to win, thereby assuming a commanding 3–1 lead in the Series. In my postgame appraisal I now declared that Owens was always a defensive liability and that his was "a name to all succeeding ages curst.")

From Canarsie to Bensonhurst, from Coney Island to Park Slope, baseball is a sanctified ritual. According to a tag line that I use at every opportunity, "Life is a metaphor for baseball."

Truth to tell, I used to be mightily bored in the long off-season. "I don't like hot stoves," was my judgment of winter, "because I once burned my ass on one." And what else was there? Six-day bicycle races have gone the way of vaudeville. What about ice hockey? The N.H.L.?

Naw. Just a bunch of dumb Canucks on skates who wear suspenders under their uniforms. Wee? Wee?

The National Football League is a bad joke because too many people know about the fixed ball games. And I absolutely detest the professional basketballers. "The Basketball Association of America," or "the National Basketball League," or "the National Basketball Association," or whatever the hell their name is this week. With forgettable franchises like the Anderson Packers, Pittsburgh Ironmen, Providence Steamrollers, St. Louis Bombers, Toronto Huskies, Tri-Cities Blackhawks. Gypsy teams in a gypsy league. Mercenaries.

Winters were painfully long and empty until just a few years ago when I discovered the several joys of college basketball.

Legend has it that Ned Irish, a twenty-nine-year-old sportswriter for the *New York World-Telegram*, had been assigned to cover a basketball game in Manhattan College's tiny gymnasium early in 1930, in the hardscrabbling heyday of the Depression. The gym had been filled to overflowing with fans, and Irish had torn his pants while fighting his way inside through an open window. Irish became convinced that college basketball was ready to go big-time. Accordingly, on December 31, 1931, Irish produced the first college basketball program in Madison Square Garden, an S.R.O triple-header involving six New York colleges, to raise money for the relief of the unemployed. Before long, Irish was promoting similar events for his own profit. Functioning now as vice president of Madison Square Garden, Inc., Irish has become the impresario of college basketball. His crowning achievement was to inaugurate, in 1938, the annual, and always lucrative, National Invitational Tournament in the Garden. He expanded his operations into arenas for hire in Buffalo and Philadelphia. By 1950 Irish could offer a touring college team at least a six-date package, the chance to play their way across the country and back without ever seeing a campus.

Look at all the money generated by college basketball just from the gate receipts and beer concessions. Paydays for everyone from ushers to cleanup crews. For the athletic directors and the coaches. The neighborhood bars and restaurants. "Sis Boom Bah" and "Boola Boola." Damn right.

In my columns I've always made certain to laud the undergraduate cagers because they play strictly for the love of the game. College baskets is the only amateur sport worth watching. Vot den? The rowers? Pole vaulters? Polo players? No, thanks. Only college basketball warms my blood in the wintertime.

Only five months ago, in the N.I.T.'s championship game, the sons of immigrants and the grandsons of slaves miraculously upset the University of Kentucky's top-ranked basketball team, the blue-blooded legions of Adolph Rupp, by 82–59. There it was in black-and-white. On March 5, 1950. Truth and justice proved by a single headline—C.C.N.Y. COPS CHAMPIONSHIP.

Oh, here's one more reason why I suddenly love college basketball—in 1925 I earned a Bachelor of Arts degree with a major in journalism from the College of the City of New York. So, if God were to grant me the power to decide, I would never trade City's miraculous N.I.T. title straight-up for even a Dodgers World Series championship come September. Definitely not. Not even if it meant sweeping the Yankees. Another secret I'll have to keep out of my column.

Naturally there's a seedy side to the college game, and I've heard all the rumors of point shaving and dumped ball games, mostly from disgruntled bettors. My own sources never report anything except pissant stuff—college players playing in money tournaments under false names. Varsity coaches skimming their players' meal monies. I constantly receive all kinds of "inside info" from the old-time bookies in several National League cities. Rumors of occasional funny point spreads and unseemly fluctuations. Nothing to worry about. I figure that most of the bookmakers of my acquaintance are so used to setting odds for basketball games that they're often clumsy and capricious when quoting one of the newfangled point spreads. Two-and-a-half? What? Plus or minus $8\frac{1}{2}$? Jeez, a smart college coach with *real* inside info could make himself a fortune.

Aha! There's the real proof that everything's on the up-and-up. Except for Sidney Goldberg at C.C.N.Y. and Henry Carlson at Rhinegold U. in Yonkers, the other area college coaches are poor men with lean bellies. And except for the lads at Harvard, Yale and Princeton, I've never seen an undergraduate cager with money to spare. Hey, look at the home-relief kids on C.C.N.Y.'s championship squad: Otis Hill. Barry Hoffman. Phil Isaacson. None can even afford a shine on their shoes.

The defense rests.

Besides which, the American sports public, the writers, the athletes, the coaches, and even the gamblers have learned a painful lesson from the Black Sox Scandal in 1919. Say it ain't so, Barney. Damn right.

Growing up on Ditmas Avenue, only a subway stop from Brooklyn College, I was especially distraught at the newspaper accounts of a sinister turn of events that began early in 1945: The Manhattan County's D.A. office happened to be tapping the telephone of a pawnbroker whom they suspected of receiving stolen goods, when quite by accident, the wiretappers discovered that the supposed fence was also involved in fixing a college basketball game. The sonofabitch! In my expert opinion the conniving pawnbroker's deed was unforgivable, comparable to a shyster swindling a widow out of her savings, or a pederast let loose in a kindergarten.

Surveillance was stepped up and the full plot was quickly uncovered. Five members of the Brooklyn College basketball team were implicated along with several local gamblers. Each player had already been paid a thousand dollars and was promised another two thousand if he "laid down" in an upcoming game against Akron University. It was also learned that one of the Brooklyn College ballplayers wasn't even a registered student. (Fucking 4-F chickenshit bastards!) The gamblers were arrested, the ball game was canceled, and the players were expelled in disgrace.

In "Sports A-Plenty" I went slightly overboard in calling for a public ceremony wherein all the participants would have "666" branded across their foreheads. But surprise, surprise.... I received bundles of letters supporting my suggestion and none in opposition.

An ambitious graduate of St. John's, John Morley was (and is) the district attorney. His official judgment was that the "Brooklyn College betting scandal involved only a neighborhood crowd," and I was easily convinced.

Eventually New York City's lawmakers amended the civil bribery bill to include gamblers who made bribe offers to amateur sportsmen, and the matter was forgotten by nearly everyone.

Of course, several notable individuals did speak out in warning. Most prominent among them was Forrest "Phog" Allen, the basketball coach at Kansas who had learned his Xs and Os from the game's founding father, Dr. James Naismith. Allen predicted a gambling scandal that would "stink to high heaven." But most knowledgeable observers felt that Allen was merely bellyaching because his own teams hadn't been up to snuff in recent seasons. In any event, no further bribery schemes were uncovered, even as gate receipts at the college doubleheaders increased and jubilant alumni continued to fund basketball scholarships by the dozens. One of my subsequent columns featured a spokesman for a national coaches' organization who chastised Allen for showing "a deplorable lack of faith in American youth and a meager confidence in the integrity of coaches."

Rumors of peace. Rumors of war.

In the meantime, all things considered, as far as I can tell, as far as I want to know, college basketball is as kosher as a rabbi's wife.

And there's one last reason why I'm so loyal to college basketball: Red Smith continually rails against the "pituitary goons" who play "roundball." Well, fuck Red Smith and everybody who looks like him. Damn right. I can write rings around that snooty bastard.

Closing my eyes, I can feel the sun's gentle pressure on my face, on my glorious bumper. And I yearn for simpler times. For the grandfatherly guidance of FDR. For the days when G.I. Joe saved the world. Back when the Russkies were dauntless allies. When a tune from Walt Disney set the time:

> *Whistle while you work*
> *Hitler is a jerk*
> *Mussolini is a meanie*
> *But the Japs are worse*

When good versus evil was always a solid bet.

These days I often feel much older than my forty-eight years. Old enough to breathe an ancient sigh. I wish I were home in my tiny apartment in Brooklyn Heights. With a bottle of Schaefer at hand. With the radio tuned to the far-off Dodger game. The electric fan strategically positioned over a trayful of ice cubes so that a frosty breeze blows in my face. All this while I indulge in my most secret of passions:

Only in the private 100-watt illuminations of my apartment am I secure enough to freely devour the Shakespearean canon. In fact even more than my collection of autographed baseballs, my most treasured possession is an oversized replica of the *1604 Folio,* which cost me a handsome $550. Every *s* is printed as an *f,* and I love reading the soliloquies aloud. *"Tomorrow and tomorrow and tomorrow. . ."* And *"life"* is like the Boston Celtics' Kleggie Hermsen, *"a poor passing player."* In one infamous column after the homestanding Dodgers swept the hated Giants in a three-game series in June 1941, I foolishly wrote this: "To paraphrase Shakespeare, 'Ah, Ebbets Field were paradise enow.'" My lowbrow readership was aroused as never before or since. One irate letter from Red Hook excoriated me for providing a bad example for the schoolchildren by using "pig Latin." Another letter claimed that only Yankees fans read Shakespeare and that I should be exiled to the Bronx. Chastened, I henceforth kept my Shakespeare *en cathedra.*

In spite of my obvious blessings, I do have a short litany of annoyances: Giants fans, Yankee fans, and the latest National League pennant race. The Soviets stealing plans for the A-bomb. The hair clogging the bathtub drain. But by far my most persistent, most agonizing problem is finding a suitable topic for my next column, then the one after. . . . New ideas and fresh slants three times every week, *"until the last syllable of recorded time."* Sometimes I feel like the merest of hacks.

Mostly, though, I feel weary: Of being divorced and childless. Of consuming too many solitary dinners of canned beans and condensed tomato soup. Maybe I should try getting married again. That spinsterish-looking dame in research has a nice smile and a nice set of headlights. . . . Maybe I'll have a kid this time. Barney, Junior. . . .

I must have dozed. There's a crisp white towel folded on the end of the lounge pad and a bottle of Schaefer set on a tray beside me, the bottle still moist, the beer now warm. Taking a hearty swig, I notice another familiar face: Otis Hill, high-scorer for C.C.N.Y.'s unlikely N.I.T. champs, one of two Negroes on the team. In the fall Royce Johnson will make three.

Sitting otherwise unnoticed at the farthest lip of the pool, the broad-faced Otis wears greasy white pants, a T-shirt, and a brown-stained apron. The young man sits in the shade, his pants rolled up above his ankles, barely dangling his naked brown feet in the water. Otis glances around quickly, carelessly, then leans over and cups a handful of water to splash into his dark face.

That's when my attention is rudely snagged by a loud greeting from Ray Paluski, Jr. "Hey, Scoop! What's the good word?"

The late-afternoon sun is shining directly through Paluski's crewcut, casting a fierce halo around the young man's head and shoulders. On his bare chest, Paluski wears a gold crucifix suspended from a gold chain. (The goyim with their magic chinning bars.) Junior's basketball sneakers—black canvas U.S. Keds—are laced loosely over bare feet. His blue cotton swimsuit is decorated with a large white anchor on each hip. He also wears a floppy straw hat identical to Gianelli's.

The kid is a royal pain in my ass, mindless and arrogant, forever busting my chops. Yet in spite of myself I can't help admiring his swagger, his carefree optimism and boundless vitality. (How come I can't remember ever being that young myself?) And the two of us do have an historical connection. I was just a cub reporter in the late twenties during the heyday of "Big" Ray Paluski's illustrious career at St. John's, back when Junior was just a gleam in his father's eye. Ray and I got to be friends, real friends, for a while. I remember when he brought the little shaver to a Dodgers game, and the next time I met Junior he was almost full grown and already a big-shot cager for St. John's Prep.

Junior certainly does resemble Big Ray—both of them six-foot-three-inch shooters with the same bold, high-cheeked face, the square jaw, the same blunt surfaces thrusting fearlessly into the winds of chance. Junior is slicker, his gray eyes more restive, but Big Ray played much better defense.

Standing over me, Junior is considerate enough to position himself so that my eyes are in the shadow of his hulking body, but speaking sharply, I say, "Don't call me Scoop."

Junior merely shrugs his shoulders and shows his naked palms in exaggerated innocence. "Why not?" Then he craftily rotates his torso just enough to make me blink in a flash of sunlight.

I change the subject. "So how's your dad?"

"He's okay, I guess," Junior supposes, moving again to cast me in his shadow. "Dad says he doesn't want me to break his scoring record, but I say tough shit for him. I'm a senior next year and co-captain. Next season belongs to me. You heard it here first, Scoop. And the season after that? If the old fart's lucky, I'll throw him a free ticket to come see me play at the Garden with the Knicks."

"That's the right team for you, all right. The N-I-X."

We both laugh. Despite his breezy self-assurance, I'd say that Junior has about as much chance of playing in the N.B.A. as a one-legged man has of winning an ass-kicking contest.

"Dear old Dad knew you'd be up here tonight, and he told me to tell you he wants to talk to you about something important."

"Well, you can tell him for me that my phone number hasn't changed in twenty-nine years. The only thing that's different is that these days he's a hotshot wheeler-dealer or something. Tell him the only thing that's really important is some inside info."

"About the market or the races?"

"Now, you leave your old man alone," I say with all the sudden dignity at my disposal. "He worked hard enough, so let him enjoy a few hobbies."

"Yeah. Good old Dad. I ain't seen him face-to-face since the Fourth of July up here. . . . He had a dame with him. Some blonde twat. I forgot her name. He was sniffing her all over like the fucking old goat he is."

Then he sees my copy of *The Sentinel.* "Hey," he says. "Is that today's? Let me see it, will ya? How many hits did Ted Williams get? I had a six-hit pool."

"None. He was oh-for-four."

"Against Houtteman in Briggs Stadium? You're shittin' me."

"Here, read it yourself."

"Naw," he says. "I'll take your word for it." But he does take notice of McCarthy's picture and the front-page headline: REDS IN STATE DEPT? Then he shakes his head and says, "The guy's a genuine American hero."

"You're talking about Joe McCarthy? He's a genuine troublemaker, is what he is. I just wish he'd leave well enough alone."

"You don't know what the fuck you're talking about, Scoop. The fucking Communists don't believe in God, and wherever they come to power, what's the first thing they do? Kill the priests, rape the nuns, and turn the churches into whorehouses."

"I still think that McCarthy should keep his yap shut unless he has definite proof that somebody's guilty. That's what justice is all about. A lot of innocent people have already had their lives ruined by his loose talk."

"Don't make me laugh, Scoop. Justice has nothing to do with it. If you get caught, then you're guilty. If you don't get caught, then you're innocent."

Scratching at my belly, I once again change the subject. "So how's your summer going?"

"What could be bad? Fifty bucks a week plus meals and a single room. So I organize volleyball games and coed softball games, you know? So I run around with a whistle and I pitch and I make sure everybody hits the ball. And I sleep through breakfast and I drink lots of beer and I fuck the young wives during the week while their husbands are working in the city and fucking their secretaries. What could be bad?"

Noting the slight roll of flab above Junior's blue bathing suit, I say, "You don't look like you're in such good shape."

"In good enough shape to kick Sammy Goodrich's ass tonight. That fucking snotty bastard, he thinks his shit smells like Chanel Number Five. You stayin' to see the game? We play Kutscher's staff after supper."

"That's why I'm here." Then I reach out to playfully pinch at Junior's waist, but the young athlete nimbly jumps away.

"Hey, Scoop! Watch your hands! What're you, a fruit?"

Unfortunately my laugh is also well known, a guttural braying sound. "Haw! Haw! Sammy Goodrich is always in tip-top shape. He's probably been doing roadwork every day at six in the morning. He's gonna run your fat ass ragged."

"What're you so worried about how out of shape I am? Huh? You got a bet on the game? What's the spread, Scoop? Kutscher's plus two-and-a-half?... Naw, that ain't the real spread."

"Oh, yeah? So what is the real spread?"

Junior clenches his wide face into a loose-lipped mischievous smile. Then he leans forward in close conspiracy. "Keep it under your stinkin' hat, but the only spread that counts is the feast that Cookie's gonna make for us if the total score of both teams ends up in a nine. Get it? Let's say we beat 'em thirty to twenty-nine? Cookie wins a bundle and we eat like kings. Thick juicy sirloins he got for us. Not those shoe leather skirt steaks he makes for the dining room.... Or say if we win by thirty-seven to thirty-two—"

"I get it. Nine the hard way."

"Easy as falling off a log, Scoop. 'Cause me and the guys, we got the right kind of experience."

Junior laughs too heartily to suit me, and besides, I don't care to hear such talk, even in jest.

"Believe me, Scoop. Goodrich's playing with a bunch of high school kids that can't score with a pencil. We'll kill 'em."

"Hold on! You got a high school kid playing with you too. Right? Royce Johnson? Says he's going to City?"

"Yeah. Royce Johnson. But hold on, Scoop, the fucking kid can really play. Shit, he's a six-foot-three point guard. He's a fucking revolution. You think Cousy and Bobby Davies have some fancy passes? This kid makes 'em both look like they're playing hip-deep in sand. Watch him close, Scoop. The kid has eyes in back of his head. He always sees and he always delivers. I'm just wondering why the kid's going to City. I'll bet you dollars to doughnuts that Goldberg must've sold the poor nigger the biggest load of bullshit this side of the slaughterhouse."

Already in the sun too long, my proud paunch is beginning to feel hot and tight. I should've brought some schmear. Wiping my sweaty face with the towel, I wonder if my hat is really "stinkin'."

"Too bad Goldberg doesn't allow any fancy stuff," I say. "He's gonna ruin the poor kid and put his freewheeling game in a straitjacket."

"Goldberg!" Junior spits the name like he's loosening a shred of cigarette tobacco from his lower lip. "What I want to know is how's the ol' fogey gonna control all those niggers? Otis is already getting too uppity and out of hand. That's why we're gonna kick City's ass next year."

"Not a chance, Junior. They didn't graduate anybody except Musberger."

"You'll see."

We can barely hear the normal pooltime squalling and chatter, but our heads snap around in perfect unison as someone shouts, "Ray! Ray!" It's Gianelli, on his feet, his wife clinging to his arm, about to take his leave.

I look back at Junior to say, "You still fucking that sleazeball's wife?"

Junior shrugs lightly like a little boy who's just been accused of doing something he considers inconsequential, like not flushing the toilet or not closing the refrigerator door. "Why not?" he asks. "She's a free hole."

"That still don't make it right."

"It's okay," Junior insists. "I wear rubbers.... Hey, the dame's nuts about me. I can't help being so good-looking and sexy. I'm the top banana."

"And what'll happen if that greaseball catches you? If you're lucky, he'll only have your balls cut off."

"Relax, Scoop. The old man doesn't know shit from Shinola. Believe me, Scoop...."

Gianelli calls out again, more stridently this time. "Ray! Come on, huh? Sometime today!"

"Hey, Scoop. Gotta go. See ya at the game."

Then youngster bounds away, leaving me to say, "Don't call me that," to nobody.

—ROYCE JOHNSON—

Hell must be just like this: The smell of burning flesh, the pots of boiling oil and boiling water. Everywhere I look, pieces of meat are bursting into flames. And the heat beats at me like a blood-red drum.

And the waiters, rushing through the clatter and the smoke like lost souls, carrying trays piled high with Jew food, *blintzers,* and what the hell kind of fish is *go-filter?* The thick yellow chicken soup bubbles up bones, and I can't help shuddering. Jew food. I wouldn't wash my dirty socks in that stuff. *Borsht. Ka-nishiz. Kishkiz.* And those crazy rules I can't keep track of: These dishes for tonight. Those for tomorrow. Milk doesn't go with meat. And that little rabbi guy who comes snooping around and we have to hide the silverware.

There's the boss, a forty-year-old white guy name of Cookie. He's a skinny motherfucker, all grizzly and unshaven, with piggish red eyes. He looks like some fancy-man chef in that high stiff white hat of his, and he's the king of this fucking hellhole. Me, I don't trust a skinny cook.

"Goddammit!" Cookie is screaming. "Who put all the fuckin' salt in the fuckin' gravy? Idiots I have working for me! Fuckin' idiots!"

I work at one end of this long bustling room, scrubbing pots and pans in two huge sinks. Far away, at the opposite end of the kitchen, the two big swinging doors—IN and OUT—are shouldered open by the waiters. Through the crack between the doors I sometimes catch glimpses of the guests. Rich people, old people, somebody's grandparents. And always the kids, spoiled brats, whining and mewling. I'm allowed into the dining room only when broken glassware needs to be cleaned up—and even then only from Sunday dinner to lunch on Friday.

Every Monday afternoon I send Ma $8.50. She writes me, says to save more for myself, but I don't. Next week I'm going to send her nine dollars.

"She says it's burned," an elderly waiter moans. "She says she wants pink in the middle."

"Fuck her!" Cookie roars. "I'll give her something pink in the middle! Go trim the fuckin' edges and serve it to her again! She won't know the fuckin' difference!"

Me, I work stubbornly, in good spirits, scratching the burned and scalded surfaces with large pads of soaped steel wool. My gray work clothes are drenched, the apron, the pants, even my precious pair of U.S. Keds, as wet as if I'd just climbed out of the pool. Man, I'd love to take a swim in that big ol' pool just once in the daytime instead of sneaking around in the dark. Anyway, I've got no real reason to complain about anything. That's because I'm positive that I'm a basketball player destined for greatness. First I'll be an All-American, then an N.B.A. All-Star, and someday I'll be immortalized in the Basketball Hall of Fame. Guaranfuckingteed. That's why what I do, or who I am, off the court isn't really important. For me, reality is defined by baselines, endlines, timelines, and referees' whistles. All the truths I need can be found on scoreboards and game clocks. So what if I have to call fat white men "suh"? The poor bastards—running one fast break would probably kill them.

Meanwhile the fires rage and the cheese melters glow redly. Okay, so my fingernails are all broken, my fingertips wrinkled and bruised and stuck with tiny splinters of teased steel. I can't feel the pain because my hands are numbed by the hot water falling endlessly from the spouts. It's no big deal. I do my chores as quick as I can, speeding up time with my own two hands, bringing tonight's ball game closer faster. My heart's set on scoring twenty points tonight, especially against the great Sammy Goodrich.

That loud shattering noise behind me must be Otis dropping another glass. Better him than me.

"Fuck!" Otis yelps, and his huge body shakes with rage. "That's another four fuckin' cents they'll dock me!"

Otis tends the trio of machines that washes and dries the plates, glasses, and silverware, loading and unloading the clinking bins and racks and stacks. Sometimes when the work slows down, Otis can snatch a smoke while all three machines automatically rattle and clang. But not now, as a relay of busboys carries large plastic tubs of dinnerware back and forth, both clean and soiled.

One of Otis's huge hands grips another wet glass, his square face on the verge of misery, his thick lips curled into a perpetual sneer. In the sickly yellow light Otis's wide brown eyes look tight and jaundiced.

"Fuckin' machine," Otis says. "It don't rinse right and Cookie always blames me and they bleed my paycheck four cents at a time. Man alive, Royce. Who said Lincoln freed the slaves? Not ever no nigger ever said it."

Otis flexes his chin toward the floor. "Watch your step, boy," he says. "That glass'll cut right through them old worn-out sneakers of yours."

For a moment Otis tries to smile, but then he grabs the glass as though it was a hand grenade. Will he place the glass in the appropriate slot, or hurl it to smithereens against the wall?

Cookie suddenly bellows in our direction: "I need more fryin' pans! Goddammit! What's the fuckin' holdup back there?"

Alarmed, I redouble my efforts, scratching with my ruined fingernails at several scorched pieces of fat at the bottom of another large pan.

"She wants a what? Goddammit! A cheese omelet. Tell her she got the wrong fuckin' meal!"

"Fryin' pans! Where are the fuckin' fryin' pans?"

"She says there's a fuckin' nigger hair in the fuckin' chicken soup!"

"Goddammit!"

Me, I work harder, faster, bringing the promised tip-off closer, quicker. The hot water pinks my palms, the steam sears my eyeballs.

Otis leans forward to light a cigarette on the gas jets beneath the vats of chicken soup. "Slow down, boy," he says, surprisingly calm. "No need to kill yourself."

"But Cookie said he needs the frying pans."

"It don' matter none. He'll just use the dirty pans over again. Fry the horseshit burgers in the same pan where he just fried the cowshit burgers."

Slackening my pace, I look up at Otis, a six-foot-five-inch 220-pound powerhouse. The newspapers call him the "Mini-Mikan," and he's my hero. That's the truth and I'm not afraid to say it. Otis's name has been all over the papers for the last three years, and who could forget Marty Glickman's play-by-play of the N.I.T games on the radio?

"Here's Otis Hill with a step-back two-hander...! Spinning high and far...! And it's good! Like Nedick's! City College now leads by four...."

Until this summer I hadn't played against anyone nearly as good as Otis Hill. The two of us play one-on-one sometimes after lunch, and every session is a revelation. I'm learning how to protect my dribble with my off hand and how to spin dribble with tighter efficiency. Otis is also showing me how to employ my elbows, hips, and shoulders strategically. "An elbow in the right spot, boy, is just like a Christmas present. It's better to give than receive."

As much as I want to make a good impression, I always feel intimidated by the big man. Chewing so much on my thoughts, trying so hard to find the right words, that I rarely say anything interesting in Otis's company. Anyway I'm not really worried, because my game talks as fancy as Shakespeare. I'm not saying that I always understand everything Otis says, but I treasure what "O" once told me about my game: "You're good, boy. Real good. Too good for your own good."

The highlights of my summer employment are the weekly ball games in the hotel league. So far we've beaten Grossinger's, The Pines, the Nevele, and Brown's, and lost only to Kutscher's at their place. Our record is 4-and-1 and we're in first place, even though we never practice. Ray Paluski is our self-elected team captain and his motto is "I ain't practicing in the off-season." At night, when the air is cool and Otis and me want to light the outdoor basketball court and play one-on-one until dawn, Paluski is usually off the grounds and carrying the light-switch key in his pocket. Otis believes that Paluski doesn't want any of the players to be in better shape than he is.

There's also good hooping every Sunday, when Otis and me are joined by Lyndon and James from Ellenville for ferocious games of two-on-two. Lyndon and James earn thirty-five cents an hour working part-time from dinner on Friday to Sunday's late breakfast. Those nights Otis and me have to share our bedroom with the two weekenders. It's a cramped converted storage room in the basement situated directly beneath the kitchen. The hard mildewed cot doesn't bother me anymore, but I never sleep well, what with the nighttime rats scrabbling just overhead, eating the kitchen floor, eating the ceiling, poised to jump down on my face while I sleep.

Otis laughs when I complain about the rats. "Rats got to live, too," he says.

Still, counting the money, my room and board, and my friendship with Otis, this is the best job I've ever had. Add in all the happy hoop-time and I figure I'm out-Jewing the Jews.

"What-chu lookin' at, boy?" Otis asks me during a short slack time, his upper lip curling as he greedily inhales cigarette smoke.

"Nuthin', O. I'm just doin' my job. Just earnin' my money."

"Money," says Otis, snorting smoke through his wide, flat nostrils. "This here ain't money. This here is shit for the birds."

"Then how come you're here?"

"'Cause it's the off-season and I'm broke, that's why. The rest ain't none of your concern anyway. Shit. I already dun tole you, boy, where the real money's at."

I shake my head. "No, suh. That kinda stuff ain't for me. Coach Goldberg told me about the Knicks already bein' interested in me and he promised—"

Otis spits something lumpy into the chicken soup. "I don' care what the fuck Goldberg dun tole you. That boolshittin' motherfucka! With his fancy ways and his phony accent. Like he was born in London or somethin', 'stead of fuckin' Delancey Street. Goldberg don' give a half-a-shit 'bout you, boy. Lookit… if he heard any coins ajinglin' in your pockets, he'd try to sell you the Brooklyn Bridge."

A bell rings and Otis tosses his smoking cigarette underfoot. Then he leans to unlatch the ringing machine, careful to avert his head when the blast of white steam is released.

"I guarantee you somethin', boy," Otis says. "All summer he's your best friend in the whole world. Then when practice starts in October? He won't even remember your fuckin' name. And that ain't no lie, boy. Lookit. I played for him for three seasons already and you know what he still calls me? Big Boy. Ain't that the shit? Big Boy. If I wasn't wearin' a basketball uniform with a number on my back, shit… the old boolshit-ter wouldn't even recognize me. All's he care 'bout is only two things… Number one is his bank account. Number two is winning lots of ball games. *He* wins, but *we* lose. You'll see for yourself soon enough, boy. Then you'll be happy to rig up a ball game just to stick it to him. Everybody's doin' it. And so will you."

I shake my head again. "Not me."

Look here, I can accept Otis's mean streak and the grudges he carries. That's part of what makes him such a great ballplayer. But how can I believe the crazy things he always tells me about crooked ball games and easy money from gamblers?

I'm no dope. In my spare time I'm reading *Thirty Days to a More Powerful Vocabulary* and I use the words whenever I can. I've also been around the block a couple of times, so believe it when I say that playing basketball is an unmitigated joy, a full-speed and headlong celebration of everything that's beautiful and free. How could I ever imagine Otis playing to lose? Especially when he always plays so hard in the hotel league and also the half-court runs against the brothers from Ellenville? It must be some kind of inside joke or something.

"Fuckin' imbeciles! What's this? The fuckin' debatin' club? I want those fryin' pans, chop chop!"

—BARNEY—

There's a subdued clamor in the dining room, the silverware and glassware jingling politely as Levy's hearty midweek crowd of two hundred guests attacks their food. Sounds of oral delight, stuffed squeaks of laughter, intermittent coughings and grepses. Every dropped and shattered glass is hailed with applause and sarcastic cheers.

"Bombs away!"

"Mazel tov!"

"Bombs over Tokyo!"

The long, low-ceilinged dining hall is "air-cooled," and I can almost hear the low rumbling of underground machinery. The noise is enough to give me heartburn. I'm a finicky eater and always uncomfortable in restaurants, whether in Boston or Chicago or Philadelphia, or even here in the Jewish Alps. But a free meal is a free meal and, besides, I can't get my fill of Cookie's pot roast. All it costs is a line or two in "Sports A-Plenty" of lavish praise for Levy's cuisine. If it's for free, then it's for me.

Even the car I drove up in from the city is a freebie, a beige 1949 Henry J sedan, commandeered from the sales department, with **BROOKLYN SENTINEL** scripted in large white letters on both front doors. And what would I give for an otherwise unaffordable car of my own? For a brand-new Cadillac, say, all black and plush with power to spare. A lifetime of free plugs and small lies? For a big-ass Caddy? At least that. Damn right. Ah, the joy of getting something for virtually nothing.

After leaving the pool and returning to the car for clean clothes—

khaki pants and a blue polo shirt—I proceeded to a little-used staff bathroom in the basement of the Recreation Hall. Using wet wads of toilet paper, I wiped my armpits, my pate, and my crotch. I didn't need a shave, but I did sprinkle myself with some cheapo cologne I found on the edge of the sink—"Harlem Shower." Sometimes my resourcefulness amazes even me.

Whenever I've deigned to dine at Levy's, I've always been placed at the table of honor, a roundtable off in the far corner, barely hidden behind a brace of artificial shrubs, where old man Levy used to take his meals before dying two years ago of sudden heart failure. A table set for ten.

Jimmy O'Hara is already there, the benchwarmer from the D.A.'s office. Georgie Klein, the bookie, is noshing one of the onion rolls for which the hotel is justly famous.

Additionally two young men are also on hand, college basketball referees, now disguised in civilian dress and accompanied by their wives. Both refs stand up to shake my hand, but I finger-flick the brim of my hat and nod my head in half-assed salutation. Because the existence of referees (and umpires, too) is strictly a necessary evil, I don't want to know their names. Damn right. They're nothing but frustrated G-men and lawyers, tinhorn fascists, wearing convict stripes, hiding behind a whistle. Look at those two sniveling specimens. Their noses are so far up my ass that if I farted I'd blow their brains out.

Like Wild Bill Hickock, I insist on sitting with my back to the wall. Accordingly I find myself positioned between O'Hara and Klein.

"Hi ya, Barney."

"Howdy, boys."

"We was just talking about tonight's ball game," says Klein as I wiggle my ass onto my seat. "No, no, Barney. There's no line on the game or nothing like that. I ain't so desperate yet. But listen to what I got cooked up."

The wives study their menus and their husbands lean across the table toward Klein.

"Some guys are just horny to bet," Klein explains. "Just like some guys are horny for dames. Present company excluded of course. So I set up a score pool and I got ten guys lined up to pick a number from one to zero for a hunnert smackers a pop. That's a thousand in the pot, right? So what do I do? I only give 'em nine-to-one odds. Follow me? No matter who scores what, I score a hunnert bucks. Yessiree. A little vigorish for the wheels of progress."

Snatching the siphoned bottle of seltzer from the center of the table, I squirt myself a glassful. I drink quickly, then belch grandly behind my linen napkin.

While I'm consulting the menu (I don't know why, since I always order the same things), I'm distracted by somebody moving. I glance up, expecting to find the waiter, seeing instead two more tablemates settling into chairs directly opposite me. Johnny Boy Gianelli and his wife, Rosie. Shit. Who invited him?

"Gentlemen," Gianelli says as he aims agreeable nods around the table. "No, no. Don't get up.... And ladies."

"Hi, Johnny Boy," says the younger ref.

"Evening, Mister Gianelli," the other ref effuses. "Missus Gianelli."

"*Bon appétit,* everybody," Gianelli says, and I get by with a mumble and a small smile.

Gianelli is richly attired in a white linen suit, the jacket worn over a red silk shirt open at the neck. Rosie wears a flaring white skirt embroidered with small red roses and a matching halter that boldly exposes her shoulders. She has a distinctive, catlike face, her cute little nose pulling on her upper lip to make her appear astonished and vulnerable. I've never seen such clear blue eyes on a bimbo. But Rosie's bosoms are her fortune. Her abundant cleavage is too much for me to ignore and she smiles sweetly as our eyes lock. Embarrassed, I look away, pretending that what I'm really doing is depositing the wetly mashed end of my cigar butt into the nearest ashtray.

When was the last time I got laid? There was that skinny whore in Boston. Another one in St. Louie. Twice, then, in the seven years since Sarah divorced me.

"What're you having, honey?" Rosie asks her husband.

"What else!" Gianelli says eagerly. "Steak. Cookie always has a thick sirloin special for me. What about you, honey?"

"A piece of flounder, maybe."

The matter settled, Gianelli folds his menu and looks brightly at O'Hara. "So, boy wonder. What's the latest news bulletin from City Hall? The D.A. found Judge Crater yet?"

O'Hara uses both hands to brush back his short-clipped black hair before pointing his *goyisher* pudgy nose across the table at Gianelli's face.

"It's business as usual," O'Hara says. "Morley's still fishing around for an issue that'll launch him into the governor's mansion when Dewey's through. His latest brainstorm is to crack down on the gold smuggling in the jewelry business."

Klein is impressed. "Very clever," he says. "The jewelry business is run by Jews, most of them Hasids, so there's very little political risk in pulling their beards. Much safer, say, than going after the numbers runners and the whole gambling syndicate. Or the kickbacks and short-cuts in the construction business. Or any of the other rackets run by organized crime."

But Gianelli won't take the bait. He merely laughs lightly, then speaks with his mouth full of bread without ever spewing forth a single moist crumb. "Well, this is off the record," he says, turning his head quickly, trying to catch my interest, "but I certainly wish the D.A. the best of luck."

Jesus, this guy's gonna make me puke. I wonder what would be an acceptable excuse for me to get up and go. (I have to see a horse about a man. I think I left the headlights on, the motor running, my balls in the bathroom.) That's when the waiter appears, a wimpy little college kid with glasses and a shit-eating grin, oh so polite, already angling for a big tip.

"I recommend the flounder tonight," the waiter says nervously. "And also the braised beef ribs. And of course Levy's is famous for our broiled chicken."

As ever, I order the borscht and the pot roast, with "a dollop" of horseradish on the side, oil and vinegar on my salad, and a bottle of Dr. Brown's Cel-Ray soda.

O'Hara orders the eggplant stew and feels compelled to justify his choice. "I love eggplant," he says, aiming his nose my way, then pausing as though he'd just made a dramatic pronouncement in the courtroom. When I fail to respond, O'Hara quickly delivers his punchline: "Eggplant is the missing link between the plant world and the animal world."

After the waiter departs, Gianelli says, "So," and moves his hands below the tabletop to loosen his belt a notch in anticipation of a grand meal. "What a fine group we have here tonight. Good company always aids digestion."

I never take my hat off in public—not at a restaurant, not even at a ball game during the playing of "The Star-Spangled Banner." (Just salute like a soldier-boy and nobody gets offended.) With my hat on, I can incline my head just enough so that the brim hides Gianelli from view. Because I've already ordered my meal, it's too late for me to escape, but just looking at that high-rolling creep is enough to give me heartburn.

Before Johnny Boy became president of "Gianelli Construction—From Design to Finish," he was a gin-runner and general hard-boiled yegg—seventy-six total arrests, everything from assault to fraud, with only one conviction (ten dollars for speeding on the Whitestone Bridge).

"The sunshine," Gianelli is saying. "That's why we're here. Leaving the hustle and bustle of the city behind. The water, the country breezes. A good meal. Then watch a nice basketball game. I mean, what could be better? Right?"

"Right," the older ref echoes, nodding earnestly like a demented pigeon.

"So," Gianelli ruminates. "I drove up here in my brand-new Cadillac with the Dyna-Flow transmission. It's terrific. Like sitting in my living-room chair. Coming all the way up here to see this Royce Johnson maybe matched head-to-head against Sammy Goodrich. I figure that Goodrich is playing with a bunch of kids and he needs a much more structured game to play his best. But who knows? Every game, it's a new story. Perhaps that's also why the dean of the press box has graced us with his presence. Eh, Barney?"

Looking up, I produce a neutral grin.

Gianelli answers his own question and poses two more. "Of course. Of course. . . . And if I got a little action on the side? Who gets hurt?"

"Not me," says Klein, and everybody laughs except me.

"Since Georgie here wouldn't make me a quote," Gianelli continues, "I got the Kutscher's boys plus three-and-a-half from a guy in Ellenville. Klein, you stinker. Trying to ruin my fun."

Klein smiles with artificial enthusiasm. "Nothing personal, I assure you. So long as the vigorish flows gently to the sea."

"And I also let Georgie here talk me into betting a C-note on number three for the total handle. I mean the total score. What a racket you got, kiddo. But what the hell? Pardon my French, ladies. A little action on the side makes a game more meaningful to me. You know? And Rosie here, she likes to watch them young boys running around in their shorts."

Another nearly unanimous round of hearty laughter.

Gianelli enjoys playing *mein host*, and he even turns his charm on the referees, saying, "So what do you guys do for an honest living? I mean, I heard that refs only get pin money, right? Even in the Garden. What's the going rate? Ten bucks a game?"

"Some guys get up to twenty," says the younger ref. "My real job is I'm a high school English teacher in Bayside, Queens."

O'Hara is amused. "Say, maybe at halftime you and Barney here could entertain the fans by quoting the Bard."

Gianelli smiles at large. "I wasn't never too good at English," Johnny Boy says. "I always did better at arithmetic.... Three-to-one. Eight-to-five. The daily double. Things like that."

Gianelli looks around the table to acknowledge the appreciative giggles and grunts, but I yank a handkerchief out of my pocket and pretend to blow my nose. This is fucking ridiculous. I should've driven into Monticello for a pastrami sandwich at Kaplan's Deli.

"And what about you?" Gianelli asks the other ref. "What do you do in the real world?"

The other ref reddens and says, "I sell life insurance. Hey, by any chance is anybody in the market for some?" His wife pokes his ribs and gives him a dirty look.

Then the same easy smile from Gianelli. "How about you, Barney? You got enough life insurance?"

This time I can't help staring briefly into Gianelli's eyes, two small shiny stones that reflect dull wisdom but infinite patience. Instinctively my vision shifts to the foothills of Rosie's mountainous tits, then I say, "I don't believe in life insurance because the insurance company bets that you'll live, you bet that you'll die, and all the time you're rooting for them. Insurance is not my style. I don't want to be worth more dead than I am alive."

Gianelli laughs softly. "There's all kinds of insurance.... Right, Georgie? What's the kind of insurance you need? Deadbeat insurance?"

"Laying off my bets is the only insurance I need."

Gianelli next focuses a quizzical glance on O'Hara, who says, "The law is my insurance."

"I shall not want," says Gianelli. "Amen."

The waiter approaches, groaning under his heavily laden tray, then carefully distributing the plates like he was handling explosives. My meal looks scrumptious, but one of the refs' wives is upset. "Hey," she yips at the waiter. "I ordered the kasha varnishkes, not the kugel. What's the matter? Don't you speak English?"

At this point our cozy dinner party is joined by another latecomer. Sidney Goldberg, Himself. The Ol' Coach is resplendent in white pants with a sharp crease, a dazzling Hawaiian shirt, and blue alligator shoes. Beneath his neatly trimmed mane of gray hair, the only incongruity is a chronic light blue five o'clock shadow that darkens both cheeks and his dimpled chin. Goldberg thinks his chin looks like Cary Grant's. I'd say it bears more of a resemblance to a baby midget's ass.

Goldberg's journey through the half-crowded dining hall was accompanied by light applause, which he graciously acknowledged with a slight wave of his right hand. Now another waiter materializes out of nowhere to ease back a chair and then slide it forward under Goldberg. "Well, well," Goldberg says, suffering fools with benign patience. "Looks like we have splendid company for dinner."

"Here to watch your new boy play?" O'Hara suggests.

"And whom might that be?"

"That Johnson boy from Seward Park."

His aristocratic brow wrinkling in mild confusion, Goldberg says, "Actually that isn't the case at all. Heavens, no. We're here to imbibe some of Cookie's excellent pot roast, then motor over to Goshen to observe the trotters run. We see a sufficient number of basketball games over the course of a season. If the Coach wants to see a freelance, ragtag game, why, the Coach can go to the nearest schoolyard."

Sidney Goldberg had been an All-American basketball player at City College, the best set-shooter of his generation and a war hero to boot. I'd observed and admired much of Goldberg's later career with various barnstorming teams, even his stint with the Cleveland Rosenblums in the long-defunct American Basketball League, and I'd certainly appreciated his skills and craftiness. Too bad the Ol' Coach is so obnoxious these days, with his hoity-toity affectations and his imperial pronouns.

Whenever I cover a C.C.N.Y. ball game, my postgame interviews of choice are with the players rather than with the Coach. So far I've managed to keep my dislike of Goldberg out of print. So far.

"The trotters, you say?" Klein asks with a doubtful frown. "C'mon, Coach. Everybody knows that the trotters are crooked. How many horses have you bet on that broke in the stretch?"

"We never bet," Goldberg says. "Our only interest is in studying the breeding lines of the horses and admiring the skills of the drivers. No, we never bet.... My, my, the Coach is feeling quite peckish."

The frazzled waiter rushes up to take Goldberg's order of pot roast. Since alcoholic drinks are verboten in the dining hall, Goldberg neatly slips the waiter a twenty-five-cent piece for "a little sherry in an iced-tea glass."

Imagine my disappointment when my pot roast turns out to be too dry and the borscht too thin. After Goldberg's food and drink is served in record time, the younger ref proposes a toast:

"To college basketball. Where dreams come true."

"Here, here," says O'Hara.

The older ref says, "Bravo."

And Gianelli has a point to make: "You know something, Coach? I unnerstand that you Jews practically invented the game in the East Side settlement houses, what with all the give-and-go and all that fancy weaving. But I'm here to tell you that the Pisanos are taking over. That's right. I mean, look at Hank Luisetti from Stanford College with the one-hander that he can shoot on the move. It's the new wave, Coach. Tell me it ain't."

Goldberg ponders his glass of sherry. "The one-handers are too wild," he says gravely. "Shooting off of one foot puts a player way off balance, unable to go forward and capture a rebound or get back on defense. In fact we think that Luisetti is an aberration, a once-in-a-lifetime phenomenon. Layups, hooks, and set shots, those are the only decent shots the Coach's boys are allowed to take."

Despite the unsavory pot roast, I've eaten too much and my belly feels bloated and about to burst. I need a Bromo-Seltzer. I need a nap. Maybe that's why I'm feeling contentious. "I beg to differ," I say in Goldberg's general direction. "The game is constantly changing. In the pros, Jumpin' Joe Fulks scores big with a one-hand *jump* shot. And look at George Mikan. The modern-day pivot man is unstoppable."

"Bah," says Goldberg. "The Original Celtics would have easily defeated the Minneapolis Lakers. Mikan just sits there like the Statue of Liberty. Unquestionably the big man can murder you if you permit him to catch the ball in his preferred sphere of influence. But with Mikan, everybody in the gymnasium knows exactly where the ball is going to wind up. When the Coach was playing, why, we would have rendered someone like Mikan virtually harmless. How could Mikan ever play defense against a five-man weave? He never could have guarded Joe Lapchick. Never. Joe would have driven right around him with little difficulty. We would have tired Mikan out by forcing him to run the floor. That's still the way to beat the Lakers."

Even my horseradish is too bitter. "The Original Celtics beating the Minneapolis Lakers?" I hear myself saying. "I hate to say this, Coach, but you're way off target."

Goldberg sneers at me as if I were a roadside beggar. "And how many National Invitation Tournaments have you won, Mister Polan?"

"You don't have to be a chicken, Mister Goldberg, to eat an egg."

Goldberg shrugs and turns to his meal, daintily slicing his pot roast into bite-size pieces before eating the first one. "Delicious," he says for the ages.

After taking a slow sip of my Cel-Ray soda, I reach for another onion roll to sop up the pot roast's meager gravy.

"Ooo," Rosie says. "That's that celery soda, ain't it? Could I have a little sip?"

"Sure."

I pass her my glass, but as she squints her eyes away from the lively effervescence, her makeup flakes off into my glass.

"Well," she says, pausing to run her tongue around the inside of her mouth. "It tastes better than what it sounds like. You know what I mean?"

—ROSIE GIANELLI—

I mean, I can play Judy Holiday with my eyes closed. Dumb and silly, but truthful in an artless way. Jeez. Anything is better than sitting here listening to this boring sports stuff. I'm interested in the players, not the spectators.

There's that fat-assed Polan staring at my tits. Jeez, what a bunch of duds.

Just to create some excitement, and under the guise of reaching for Johnny Boy's hands, I deliberately knock over a glass of water, which crashes to the floor. Immediately the diners at the nearest table begin to applaud and someone shouts, "Mazel tov!"

Johnny Boy stands up and raises his clenched fists high above his head in mock triumph, effectively taking the rap for me.

"Thanks, honey," I say when he sits down.

Thanks for nothing.

Goldberg's table manners are impeccable—after elegantly chewing and swallowing each meaty morsel of his pot roast (which appears to be much juicier than mine), he carefully wipes his lips with a napkin. "The only team that approached the Original Celtics in their mastery of fundamentals," he announces, "was the Saint John's team of the late twenties. The so-called Fantastic Five which featured Raymond Paluski. That was most likely college basketball at its very finest."

"They were fantastic, all right," Klein says with a fish-eyed look. "Saint John's is a Catholic school, but the starters were three Jews, a Pollack, and a Lutheran."

"What d'ya expect?" O'Hara chides. "Five priests?"

"None of those aforementioned players could ever have gained admission into City College," Goldberg says stiffly. "Their high school grades were inferior."

Just then Royce Johnson appears wearing a clean apron, handling a broom and dustpan. I have a smile ready for him, but he looks expectantly at Goldberg, who blithely ignores the boy sweeping and disposing of the broken glass.

After Royce has gone, the younger ref turns toward Klein. "Cleveland still eight-to-five tonight with Feller?"

"Yep."

The ref pauses, suddenly aware that his question has been overheard by everybody. "Okay," he says, blushing. "I'll take Cleveland five times."

"You got it."

Gianelli takes immediate notice. "I hate betting odds. I mean, point spreads are more accurate. More scientific. That's why I'd rather bet on college basketball games."

Klein disagrees. "Nah. Betting on basketball is too boring. So it's City College versus Rhinegold. Here or there. Plus five-and-a-half or minus three-and-a-half. This way or that. Big deal. Betting baseball is more challenging because baseball is harder to dope out. The different ballparks make more of a difference in baseball. The pitchers change. Cleveland at Detroit. Feller versus Houtteman is different from Garcia pitching against Newhouser. The short porch in the Stadium. The wall in Fenway. The lefty-righty matchups."

I've also got an opinion: "I think that betting on anything is a sign of arrogance. When a bettor makes a bet, what's he really doing? A bettor is saying that he can predict the future. Whenever he wins, he's godlike. When he loses, he blames the refs. Or he says this player or that player was shaving points."

"Gentlemen," Goldberg says, his pot roast neatly devoured. "The Coach will not sit here while the lads of City College are mentioned in the same conversation as illegal point shaving. And post time approaches as well. So I'll bid a pleasant evening to you all."

Another smattering of applause accompanies Goldberg on his way out of the dining room.

"Well," says one of the wives, "that was rude of him."

"Relax, lady," says Klein. "The Ol' Coach is entitled."

—RAY PALUSKI, JUNIOR—

Check it out. There're lots of reasons why Levy's never loses at home. First off, there're the four thick support poles planted deeply into the black asphalt playing surface only a foot out of bounds, one for each basket plus the two lightpoles. Sure the poles are padded, but the canvas padding always sags and, just two weeks ago, some poor shmuck, a guard from Grossinger's, ran into a light pole and busted up his arm. Players unfamiliar with the court usually start tiptoeing around whenever they're near the boundary lines. Here're some more home-court advantages: The only water fountain is next to our bench. The dented halfmoon backboards that make bank shots risky, even on layups. Also, the rim of the westernmost hoop is actually nine feet ten inches above the playing surface. To the east the distance from floor to rim is the regulation ten feet. Okay? But this here is why I'm such a fuckin' genius: During most of July and August, any low-angling sunset casts a fierce brightness behind the westward backboard, a glaring halo to blast a shooter's eyes. This effect will last anywhere from ten to twenty-five minutes as the summer progresses. So what do I do? I make sure to consult the daily weather charts in *The Farmer's Almanac* before I schedule our home games, and I make sure we're already warm- ing up facing east before the visiting team arrives. And if the bad guys make a fuss and want to switch baskets? Then I just put on a puss like they're the ones who're being the assholes. Hey! What d'ya mean switch baskets? All our fans are sittin' over here. So now they gotta get up and move? Hey, we got some pregnant women sittin' here. Hey, my uncle's got a broken foot. Hey, my granny's in a wheelchair. Hey, this. Hey, that.

Right? So anyway, tonight's game is set to begin at exactly 7:47 P.M.

As usual I've got every angle covered.

With the poles, the blinding sunshine, and the well-fed referees, I figure the spread should be Levy's minus $10\frac{1}{2}$, maybe even $11\frac{1}{2}$. I wonder who's the bozo that gave Johnny Boy $3\frac{1}{2}$?

So anyway, what the fuck do I care? It's no skin offa my ass.

Here I am, sitting on the front bench and leaning over to tighten my sneaker laces while the rest of my teammates are already on the court practicing their running layups. (And look what Scoop has done, the asshole. He's put the newspaper near the water fountain, with the page folded over to his stupid fucking column.) Jesus, I hope nobody else but me notices my gut bunching over the top of my shorts as I bend forward to tie a double bow.

Here comes Sammy Goodrich, sweating like he's already run a marathon and looking for a drink of water. "You don't need to warm up?" he asks me.

"Well, I figure that each of us has only got a certain amount of shots that we can make in our careers, so I try saving mine for the ball games when they count the most."

He laughs as he splashes water into his face. "I consider myself lucky whenever a shot goes in."

I stand up in a hurry like I've been goosed. "You'll need plenty of luck to beat us tonight."

"Probably so. Say, is this your paper? I haven't seen a fresh newspaper in about a week. Can I take a look?"

"Sure," I say, then I quickly tuck in my stomach and join the layup lines.

—SAMMY GOODRICH—

What do we have here? Barney Polan on the Philadelphia Phillies. What a fucking rag. They should print this on toilet paper. And here's McCarthy's ugly mug again. God bless America. It's all so ridiculously obvious. To keep the military budget sky-high, the public is brainwashed into believing that Communists are plotting violent revolution—so McCarthy finds a Red in every closet. If the public was more concerned with home-relief chiselers or racial discrimination, then that's what McCarthy would be screaming about.

Of course, my father had McCarthy pegged right from the start. But I have to be careful. I can't let the truth make me bitter like it's done to him.

Fuck me! I wish my mind would shut the fuck up and let me enjoy the fucking ball game!

—JUNIOR—

$\mathbb{B}$esides me and the two niggers, the Levy's roster includes Jim Clancy, Artie Brennan and Nick Giambalvo, third-string varsity players for St. John's, all capable and savvy players. Add a couple of high schoolers from the Bronx who couldn't play dead.

For the occasion I wear four pairs of thick socks and my outdoor sneakers, Spalding Double-L's with the concave soles to prevent sprained ankles. I always prefer playing indoors on a soft, bouncy, slidey wood surface because outdoor asphalt courts release the day's heat slowly and the softened tar sucks at the bottoms of your sneakers. But whatever the surface, my game plan is always the same—shoot first and never ask questions. Fuckin' A. My primary goals here tonight are to make sure that Cookie wins the points pool and that I avoid injury.

Like I say, I never miss a trick.

—BARNEY—

$\mathbb{M}$ ounted along each sideline, the low metal bleachers can accommodate a hundred spectators, and the sparse crowd rattles around trying to get comfortable. As both teams warm up, several of the older men and women sit nearly motionless, stunned by so much sunlight and by having eaten so much food. One of the younger women complains that the metal benches are dirty, and the children chase each other along the baselines, swinging themselves around the poles.

"Michael! Stop running! Michael! You'll trip and break a leg!"

Most of the cardplayers and the racing buffs sit up behind the home team's bench, drinking rum and Coke from plastic cups, and the kibitzing is relentless. The wise guys who laugh the loudest always have the least money.

"Yo, Footie," says Carmine DeRosa, a thick-shouldered ex-pug with two cauliflower ears who works part-time breaking heads for Gianelli. "That was some bet you made today in the fifth race. Five hundred bucks across the board on the even-money favorite. I tell you, Footie, you're a gambler's gambler."

"What's it your business anyway?" Footie says back. "I won a hunnert on the fucking race. What'd you win. Hunh? The only winning tickets you ever get are the ones I throw away by accident."

"Ha! Ha!"

"Heh!"

"That's okay, Footie. You're still the king of the fucking chalk eaters."

My preference is to shun the courtside seats and situate myself precisely seven rows up, straddling the timeline and facing both team's benches. Here at Levy's, my favorite seat turns out to be on the topmost row with a sturdy well-bolted fence behind me. Unfortunately I find myself once again claiming a space between Klein and O'Hara.

While I quietly belch into the privacy of my right fist, O'Hara slicks his hair and reconnoiters the crowd for unattached dames, and Klein sits to my left, smirking, his pockets full of money. Gianelli and Rosie are parked three rows down and off to the right, perfectly situated for me to track the twilight gathering between Rosie's breasts.

As the team's captains (Junior for Levy's and Goodrich for Kutscher's) confer with the refs at the center jump circle, O'Hara reaches over and gently taps my shoulder.

"Just wanted to say thanks for those tickets, Barney. Box seats right behind the Dodgers dugout. I'll tell you, me and my boy sure had ourselves a whale of a time. You remember Jimmy Junior, don't you, Barney? I introduced the two of you when we happened to meet in the bathroom at a Giants-Dodgers game last summer at the Polo Grounds. Remember?"

Of course not, but I say, "Sure, I remember. Cute little tyke. About belt-high and the spitting image of you."

O'Hara beams. "That's him! And I'll tell you, Barney, you made me a hero in the eyes of my kid, and that's something I'll always be grateful to you for."

Dismissing O'Hara's effusive prattling with a regal wave of my right hand, I say, "It was no big deal, O'Hara. Just a quick phone call to cash in a favor somebody owed me."

Then what do you know? O'Hara starts squirming around in his seat like he's got the heebie-jeebies. Uh-oh. Maybe he's coming down with the drizzling shits, so I slide away from him, trying to remember if he'd eaten the pot roast.

"Um, Barney," he says slowly, reluctantly. "There's something else that I... I mean, my kid's been pestering me... I mean, you know *Happy Felton's Knothole Gang?* Before every game in Ebbets Field, when a couple of kids play catch or something with one of the Dodgers players and the kids get autographed bats and balls and sometimes even gloves and it's all on the TV?"

But I don't respond, not a nod nor a blink, enjoying O'Hara's intense discomfort.

"Anyway, Barney. Like I said, my kid's been pestering the bejesus out of me. You know how kids can be. So... do you think there's any chance you could get him on? The show? *The Knothole Gang?*"

"I dunno," I say coldly. (This O'Hara guy has some fucking nerve. What'll he want next? A pass into the Dodgers locker room?) "That's a toughie. I'd say it's a long shot at best."

O'Hara is still as twitchy as a long-tailed cat in a roomful of rocking chairs. "Oh, I understand," he says. "I really didn't expect... I mean, I had to promise my kid that I'd ask. You know?"

Nodding vaguely, I return my attention to the basketball court, but O'Hara has one more question: "Who're you rooting for, Barney?"

"I don't give a rat's ass who wins," I say with a pontifical smile, and I look around to see if anybody else is listening. "What I'm rooting for is triple overtime."

—JUNIOR—

The opening tip-off is controlled by Otis, leaping high above the six-foot-seven Sammy Goodrich and tapping the heavy leather ball over to me. Then I toss a long downcourt pass to where Royce is racing toward the basket unopposed. Catching the perfect pass in perfect stride, Royce moves gracefully hoopward for a right-handed lay-in, the ball shining in the sun like a golden coin.

It's the only set play we have and it always works.

2–0, favor of the good guys.

As the game proceeds, the inexperienced Kutscher's players hurl wild shots and foolish passes into the boiling eye of the sun, and before I even break a sweat, we're up 10–2 and they call a time-out. (So much for Gianelli's $3\frac{1}{2}$-point line. Jesus! I should've gotten down a bet somewhere.)

All I say in our huddle is this: "Good hustlin' out there, you two." (Meaning the niggers.) And this: "Let's just keep doin' what we're doin'." But my unspoken strategy is to encourage the two niggers to run their brains out while I settle for an occasional back-door layup and sometimes a set shot coming up behind the fast break. And I must admit that I sure do like playing with Royce because the kid always takes a look in my direction. Too bad it's too late for him to choose St. John's.

On defense I want no part of Goodrich with his tricky left-handed moves. Goodrich was Rhinegold U.'s leading scorer in '49–'50 and a bona fide second-team All-American. Scoop once wrote that Goodrich was "the perpetual man in motion." So I just sic the young nigger on the kike, and Levy's leads 16–6 after the first quarter.

The score is recorded with chalk on a handheld blackboard by one of the waiters, a stoop-shouldered doofus who's both thrilled and terrified by his awesome responsibility. The poor jerk spins slowly like a top, calling out the numbers for the hard of hearing and constantly moving in a cloud of white dust.

I can hear Carmine DeRosa shouting, "Hey, Footie. Is that your son there keepin' the score? You fuckin' chalk-eatin' jerkoff."

—ROYCE—

I hate this stupid uniform—the jersey made of some washed-out red-ribbed material that gets heavier the more I sweat. The numeral "7" on my back and the name "Levy's," cut out in peeling white strips of felt, in front. The shorts are tight around the crotch, and my movements are also restricted by the built-in cotton hip pads. Even so, I'm at the top of my game from the get-go.

I'm having fun guarding Goodrich, but I'm also a little disappointed because he's guarding Otis instead of me. Sure, Goodrich never stops moving, forever faking and spinning, wielding his elbows like rapiers, holding my shorts to gain a half-step, even stepping on my toes. But Goodrich's hard work is mostly ignored by his shot-happy guards. Once in the first quarter and twice in the second, Goodrich manages to beat me to offensive rebounds and he scores the chippies. Otherwise his guards are shooting from the hip and he rarely touches the ball. Strange thing, though—the guy never says anything. Not "Good defense, kid." Not "Nice play." Not a word. Not even when I line up beside him along the foul lane while Otis is shooting two, hacked in the act. "Hot," I say cheerily, "ain't it?" Instead of talking, he shoots me a look like I ain't worth shit. What the fuck is wrong with the guy? Is his jockstrap too tight? Did his pet dog just die? Is his girlfriend pregnant? Well, fuck him. Nobody's gonna spoil my fun.

The visitors' only offense comes from the kid that Junior's supposed to be guarding, a thick-legged sharpshooter popping sets from the first edging of shadow along the baseline. What else is new? Fatso couldn't guard a fire hydrant.

...Leaping high to snatch one of Fatso's bad passes, my feet never touch the ground as I throw a jump pass like Otto Graham, a pass that ends up in the outstretched hands of Otis. A fan screams, "Stuff it, Otis!" But Otis takes a last sideways step and gently lays the ball off the iron backboard and through the iron ring.

Otis never dunks the ball during ball games because he says it's "bush league" and might provoke some form of retaliation—a blind-side elbow, or a knee to the thigh. And besides, the chain nets could easily tear a dunker's hand to shreds.

The game unwinds too quickly, but I keep the ball on a string, dribbling behind my back at every turning, even tossing an under-the-asshole bounce pass to Junior open on the wing.... Here comes the shot...! And it's good!

Hallelujah! The game belongs to me.... All right. The fat white boy wants the ball again. Here it is, Fatso. Make another one of them rickety old-timey set shots and I'll deal you another ace soon enough. As always, I tear through the game with a joyous heart, running each fast break like I'm breaking out of jail.

—BARNEY—

I like that new kid," Gianelli shouts over his shoulder to Klein. "Where's he from?"

"Seward Park High," says the bookie, always eager to please.

Gianelli nods impatiently.

"Grand Street," says Klein. "On the corner of Division."

At half time the Levy's staff is ahead by 29–13.

During the short intermission each team caucuses in the darkness while Mickey Nightingale does a standup routine at center-court: "Hey, Missus Nussbaum. You like swimming? What say you and me go into a couple of dives together?" He also plays games with the kiddies: "Simon Sez to put your hands over your mouth.... Simon Sez to stay that way until Sunday." When the teams are ready to retake the court, the *tummler's* finale is his trademark song:

"All the people smell like onyx,
'Cause there's no hot water in the Bronix."

Nobody reminds me to laugh, so I don't.

Cookie shows up early in the third quarter, looking snappy in white linen pants, white-on-white dress shirt, sleek blue blazer with gold buttons, red bow tie, and straw hat.

The sun has vanished, the asphalt is cool. The hissing yellow lights. The frosty silver starshine.

By now all structure is gone from Kutscher's erstwhile offense and it's every man for himself. Meanwhile the Levy's team is playing bull's-eye at the friendlier basket. "Hooray!" Cookie says when the score reaches 33–16.

—JUNIOR—

We're up 40–23, and I'm content to run only between the keyholes. Let the niggers run all the way from baseline to baseline. So what if I sometimes find myself huffing and puffing and running the wrong way down fast-break street? I'll still score in double columns because I write their checks, so the refs always whistle me to the foul line, where I'm 85 percent effective.

But the crowd gets excited only when Royce shows some trick dribble. They cheer his every score—set shots, layups, even a driving left-handed hook. Hey! What about me? Here's a one-hander from twenty feet that cuts the net! But my only reward is a polite patter of applause. Fucking idiots. What do they know about who really owns the game?

After three periods our lead is 46–27.

This is when I get down to business, making or missing easy shots and throwing slick passes that either connect or miss by mere inches. Everything depends upon the score. I've also saved my personal fouls for the stretch run, dashing around the court like a mad scientist, calculating and recalculating points-per-minute.

"Hey, Junior," Otis says in passing. "Stop hogging the ball. Let Royce hold it."

"No, no. I got it, man. I got it."

Fortunately the refs are easy to fool:

"Eddie! He's holding me! Eddie! Don't let him do that!"

"Tweet!" Eddie says. "Number six green with the hold. Junior shoots one. Line 'em up, boys."

Finally, with three seconds left in the ball game, the score is 57–32 and Royce is dribbling out the clock in the backcourt. I can relax and take a deep breath. Another job well done. Another ball game under my control. I'm a genius! A fucking mastermind!

Then suddenly that fucking fruitcake Goodrich comes hustling into the picture, swiping at the ball but whacking Royce's arm instead.

"Tweet!" says Eddie the ref. "Foul on Goodrich.... Number Seven here shoots one. Line 'em up, boys."

—ROYCE—

$\mathbb{M}$e, I love to shoot free throws. The old-timey way that my father taught me—dangling the ball between my knees with two hands, thumbs on the laces, then dipping and lifting the ball slowly, shooting underhanded, flipping my thumbs to impart the last spin, then the ball rising, then falling like a shooting star, and the chains barely jumping when the ball slides through. So far tonight, I'm 5-for-5 from the foul line and 7-for-10 from the field. This last second foul is an unexpected miracle, a chance to score twenty points, well worth the fresh bruise on my arm. But before the ref can hand-deliver the ball to me, Junior signals for a time-out.

Otis is disgusted, mumbling to himself, "What the fuck is it now?" Then Otis walks slowly toward the bench while Junior beckons me into the center-jump circle.

Meanwhile the bleachers rattle as most of the fans dismount. Several players from both teams congregate near the scorers' table.

"What're you doin' later?"

"Probably going to the club."

"Who's playin'?"

"Jerry Vale? Jack E. Leonard?"

"Who cares as long as there's plenty of dames."

Junior speaks to me at midcourt, the two of us alone, while everybody else heads to the bench. Even so, he talks with his hand shielding the side of his mouth like we're in a crowd. This crazy white boy's got something up his sleeve.

"You played a great game, Royce." Patting my back like I'm a fucking dog. "I mean it, man. But the thing is...you gotta miss the foul shot."

"Say what?"

"Am I stuttering or something? I said you gotta miss the fucking foul shot."

"Hey, man, whatever you're doing is your own business. Just leave me out of it."

"Take it easy, man. No need to get excited. Hey, hey, Royce, man. Just picture this, will ya? Just picture a big juicy sirloin steak smothered in onions. How do you like your steaks, man? Medium rare? Well done?"

"I ain't hungry."

Just then Otis approaches us in time to overhear Junior say, "Hey, Royce. I ain't joking with you. Forget about the steak, all right? You just gotta miss the shot."

I expect Otis to step his way into the circle and tell Junior to fuck off. But Otis just laughs lightly and walks away.

"What's all this about?" I want to know. "Some kinda point-spread boolshit?"

"What're you? Stupid? We're already up by twenty-five. Point spreads don't go that high. No, it ain't got nothin' to do with no point spread."

"Well, whatever it is, I ain't missing no free throw. Watch carefully, man. I'm gonna dedicate my twentieth point to you."

"Listen up, nigger. Either you miss or somebody's gonna be breakin' your fuckin' kneecaps with a baseball bat."

Now I want to punch his face and watch the blood splash over his fat belly. But I got to be cool. "You and what army?"

"Not me," Junior snarls, reaching out to touch a pointed finger into my chest. "Some pros'll do it. Tough guys who don't play around. Understand?"

I slap at Junior's outstretched hand, but miss. "Get the fuck away from me, man," I say. "I ain't botherin' you. Shit. I'm the one that's keeping your fat ass in the game, throwing you passes soft as your mama's tittie."

"You fucking moolie! Don't you ever say nothing about my mother!" Junior reaches out again to poke my chest, but this time I jump back so quickly that he stumbles slightly. We can both hear Barney hee-hawing from the sideline.

Then Junior shows me a cruel smile and wild, red eyes. "I promise you, nigger boy," Junior says slowly, "you'll never play basketball again. Too bad. Hell, you might never walk again. But, what the hell... America's a free country. You go ahead and suit yourself." Then he walks away.

Me, I can't seem to get comfortable on the foul line. Is the ball too heavy? The raised laces too slippery? That fucking cracker, what's he talking about, break my kneecaps... boolshit.... Twenty fucking points is what's happening.

Then I look toward the bleachers where Gianelli sits in a front row talking to a large man who has two heavily scarred ears. I know that cat, Carmine De-something, a rough customer. Oh, shit!

And that's why my hard-spinning free throw falls short, banging off the front rim and rattling the chains.

Chapter Two

October 14, 1950

—HENRY CARLSON—

I'm not one to make a big to-do about it, but as a pilot in the Great War, I personally accounted for forty-nine "kills" and survived twenty-one crash landings, including three in enemy territory. I was awarded several medals and citations for valor under fire, including a Congressional Medal of Honor. From time to time, when Barney Polan has nothing better to write about, he revives the old war stories and calls me King Henry, the Lion-Hearted.

These days my life is more about old men's lost dreams than anything else. But the sights and sounds still bang around in my memory. Gut-shot teenagers dying in screaming agonies. Mustard-gas victims coughing up bloody pieces of lung. Blasted limbs and headless torsos.

Basketball is not war.

In war, people die. In basketball, you win some and you lose some, and nobody dies.

I was born on Mott Street nearly fifty-one years ago. My father, a ragpicker from Kraków, and my mother, a seamstress, are both long dead. May Jesus bless their immortal souls. Amen. I have a younger sister, Emily, married to a minister and living in Rapid City, South Dakota. But I never had the time, energy, or inclination to marry. There was always a ball game to play, or coach, or scout. Who needs a wife anyway? The student manager of the basketball team does my laundry gratis, I eat out every night, and can my pecker really tell the difference between the inside of a vagina and the inside of my left hand?

But wait a minute. Let's take a time-out here.... Who the heck am

I trying to kid? I can barely look a woman in the eye without my attention dropping to her breasts. Then I get guilty and ashamed and tongue-tied. The truth is that I was always afraid of women. Afraid of their light-footed grace, their passion and their patience, their secret tunnels and chambers of delight that can magically transmute scum into life, their roundness and softness. Afraid of their otherness. Afraid of the little boy that I become in their presence. Afraid of how easily they can see into my heart. Women always seem to know more than me about everything and anything. Except basketball!

And so, every morning I thank God that my life is safely bounded by man-made sidelines and endlines, by whistles and buzzers, and by the sureties of the scoreboard.

My motto is, "You've gotta love it, or else you're gonna hate it." And my job, my profession, is the love of my life:

Rhinegold University features a modest cement campus on twenty-one acres with no lawns, no dormitories, and only seven trees. The current student body numbers about three thousand, most of whom diligently pursue prelaw degrees. All of the classrooms, labs, faculty offices, and the library are housed in five white-shingled four-story buildings. In lieu of a cafeteria there's a popular Jewish deli across the street. A dusty baseball field occupies the western end of the campus, adjacent to a parking lot. In deepest left field there is a small gymnasium that barely seats fifty spectators in a single row of folding chairs and was originally designed in 1913 to accommodate only intramural activities.

After the Great War, however, Rhinegold's student body was suddenly increased by several hundred returning veterans (including me, class of '22), and by 1920 a new athletic facility was desperately needed. At the time the cost of a new building was estimated at $2.1 million. An easier alternative was to rent an old, stolid red-brick gymnasium owned by the Yonkers School of Dentistry that was situated on Main Street only ten blocks from the Rhinegold campus. The original rental was twenty G's per annum, which automatically increased after ten years to thirty G's. It's a snug little building whose high-vaulted windows are caked with grime and admit only gray hues of sunlight. A smoky haze lingers in the rafters, occasionally dropping spots of charred sunshine onto the basketball court. And I'm familiar with each of the building's secrets: the basement valve that controls the radiator in the visiting team's locker room, the loose floorboards under the east basket. The tighter rim. The crooked one.

There was no varsity basketball team when I attended Rhinegold, but I was the captain of the Students Basketball Club. Immediately after I graduated, the nine holdover members of the S.B.C. petitioned the college administration to establish men's basketball as an intercollegiate sport. The initial budget was one thousand dollars, half for uniforms, balls, and referees' fees—and five hundred for the coach. And I was the obvious choice to become the once and future coach of the Golden Lions, a nickname of my own choosing. The previously nameless gym was subsequently christened The Lions' Den, and we won twelve of fifteen games in our first season.

Since then our home court has been a considerable advantage for the Golden Lions: 219 victories against only 7 losses. Count 'em. Unfortunately 3 of those losses were to City College teams coached by that rootin'-tootin' asshole, Sidney Goldberg. On the road, Rhinegold's record is a mediocre 124-and-129.

The roll-out bleachers in the Den seat just one thousand fans (S.R.O. is 1,800) at a buck each, paltry arithmetic that limits our guarantee for visiting teams to only $750. These days, with sellouts so common in Madison Square Garden, home games are increasingly difficult for me to schedule. City College hasn't played in the Lions' Den since 1939.

"The Coach doesn't want his boys playing there," Goldberg told the press. "Some of those floorboards are harder and some are softer, and Coach Carlson's teams have their own court too well scouted to make for a fair contest. As long as the coaching situation remains unchanged at City College, we will only consent to play the Rhinegold team either at our home gym or at the Garden."

That's Goldberg for you. The fucker can sure talk a blue streak, and he can coach some, too. But he always refers to himself in the third person, like he's God talking about one of his very own archangels.

In any case, the Den's narrow court is perfectly suited to my celebrated mania for pressing defenses. The 1-2-2 full-court press is my specialty, the dreaded Diamond Trap. But I also preach the intricacies of 1-3-1 presses, both full- and half-court. Also the 2-2-1, a.k.a. The Box, plus a 1-2-2, 3-1-1—a frenzy of innumerable defenses. Better put on your track shoes when you come to play us here.

I love everything about coaching at Rhinegold, especially the kids. They have such a fragile innocence. The "police action" in Korea menaces their future. But for the time being, their biggest worries are term papers and math exams, getting laid and getting drunk. Theirs is a hard-won innocence because guys like me risked our lives for it, even died for it. Theirs is a meaningful innocence that must be protected.

And so I meet their parents at the ball games and their girlfriends, too. They invite me to their weddings and send me Christmas cards.

Sammy Goodrich may be the only kid I've ever coached that I don't like. I'm not saying that I hate him. Not at all. In fact I love the hard-ass way he plays. And I feel bad for him that his mother died when he was a boy. And even though Sammy always has a kind of frozen look on his face, I'll bet the kid feels awful that his father never comes to see him play. Or maybe I'm wrong. Maybe the kid doesn't really give a shit.

For sure, I've coached several shy kids before, kids like Sammy who always sit by themselves whenever we travel. But this fucking kid doesn't even talk to his teammates.

Wait a minute. Time out.... As much as I hate to admit it, the truth is that I think I'm afraid of this frigging kid because he knows more about basketball than I do. Ain't that a bitch!

Sometimes, during a ball game, he'll sigh or even shrug when I call a play or make a substitution, like he knows I'm screwing up. And sometimes I get so flustered by his disapproval that I'll change the play or rescind the substitution. But that doesn't work either, because he also has certain sighs and little shrugs that hide his laughter. Not that the kid actually says anything disrespectful. "Yes, Coach." "Sure, Coach." "Whatever you say, Coach."

And, really, what am I actually afraid of? That someday Sammy will start shouting in the middle of a ball game, during one of our time-out huddles in the Garden, screaming so that everyone in the building can hear him, "Hey, everybody! Henry Carlson doesn't know shit about basketball! He can't tell a fucking X from a fucking O! Take away the home-court advantage and Henry Carlson is a patsy! A fool! A total fraud!"

Look, I've been coaching long enough to know how to handle an occasional looney-tooner. Besides, he's a senior, and before you know it he'll be gone and forgotten, just another fart in a windstorm.

The main reason why I've survived so many seasons is my adherence to a personal and professional code of behavior:

First off, I'm a gentleman. I've never received a single technical foul, not as a player or as a coach. My feeling is that the good calls and the bad calls even out over the years. Besides, the refs are only trying to do their jobs. By now, of course, none of the refs wants to go down in history as the first to ruin my clean slate, so I do get away with more ref-baiting than other coaches. But what good is an advantage if you don't use it?

Secondly, I try not to be a pig. My salary as varsity coach and athletic director is $16,450, certainly more than I need and probably more than I deserve. The college also pays my life insurance premiums (my sister, Emily, is the beneficiary), health care, and buys me a new Studebaker every two years. As athletic director I'm solely responsible for the budgeting of all four of Rhinegold's varsity sports: baseball, tennis, squash, and basketball (which turns the only profit). The basketball program generated nearly $125,000 in the '49–'50 season, including $115,000 from three "home games" at the Garden (defeating Colgate and Santa Clara and losing to City College). I also administrate the equipment budgets, and that's where most of my private savings account comes from.

And what's the to-do anyway? Items that are budgeted at 100 percent cost, I purchase at 60 percent and divvy up the difference with the salesmen. Hell, yes. Since all the other A.D.'s do something similar, why shouldn't I?

Thirdly, I try not to be a prick. Like Sidney Goldberg, who laughs at me and calls my players "basketball bums." That rat bastard Goldberg, now with an N.I.T. championship to prove he can walk on water. Meanwhile, here's my lifetime record against the Old Coach:

@ The Lions' Den — 8–3
@ C.C.N.Y. — 4–6
@ the Garden — 0–4
TOTAL — 12–13

Also, the Golden Lions have appeared in seven of the ten N.I.T.'s to a measly combined record of 2-and-7, which prompted Jimmy Cannon to write this: "In foreign wars against quality foes, King Henry's legions become chicken-hearted."

Every brave man is a coward to himself. And "The Bomb" scares me shitless. I have recurring nightmares of star-sized fireballs that melt cities. In the daytime I still flinch whenever I hear an aeroplane buzzing overhead. Is it one of ours or theirs?

The H-bomb. The Superbomb.

Even the Russkies have one, courtesy of the Rosenbergs, the traiterous kikes. A device that can obliterate New York City, leaving a fiery crater where Madison Square Garden used to be. Making yours truly glow bluely in the nuclear darkness that seems to be imminent. Just the other day, didn't Max Lerner write that we're only two seconds away from nuclear midnight?

Even so, I'm eager for the newest season to begin, because I sincerely believe that the latest edition of the Golden Lions will be the best ever. Varsity basketball practice commences at three o'clock tomorrow afternoon, and Rhinegold's season opener is only six weeks away—the featured second game of a doubleheader at the Garden against City College. And before the bomb blasts the earth into oblivion—Jesus, save me.... Please, God.... Mary, Blessed Virgin and all the saints.... Save me from the living fire—before the flaming clouds mushroom into God's heaven, just once let me beat Goldberg at the Garden.

It's nine o'clock on a rainy Sunday morning and I'm dressed for comfort in a blue rumpled suit, feeling bright and chipper, happy to be safely ensconced inside my beloved gym amid a small select crowd gathered to witness Rhinegold's annual Tryout Day. On the court 154 high school seniors are dressed in various uniforms, each with a paper number pinned to the back of his shirt. The players are being conducted through their several tasks by my assistant coach, Sandy Pickman, a roly-poly man who wears a plain gray sweat suit and whom I trust. Sandy's an all-right guy with a good feel for a ball game, and he likes lording it over the players whenever he can. The miracle is, that with his baked-potato face and the paltry salary I pay him (five thousand dollars plus all he can steal), he has such a beautiful spouse. God bless him, Sandy must be a swordsman in the sack.

"Make those layups!" Pickman shouts. "Hey! Number eighty-six! Use your left hand."

I sit high above the action on the top row of the bleachers, directly above the timeline and facing south. Barney Polan is seated beside me, clad in his standard working outfit—cigar, soiled hat, brown gabardine slacks, and a green V-neck sweater. Each of us has a notebook open on his lap.

For a time neither of us speaks as the building echoes with bouncing leather balls. Then Pickman's whistle shrills and the round man shouts, "All right, boys! Odd numbers line up here! Even numbers over here!... Spread out now! All right! Here's the drill...."

Over the course of the morning and early afternoon, me and Pickman will choose the twenty best players to participate in a ball game later this evening. At stake are two precious basketball scholarships that'll be available for next season, scholarships funded by the Rhinegold Roundball Boosters Club.

Scattered throughout the bleachers are a dozen other coaches, eager young men from small-time schools in the metropolitan area— St. Francis, Wagner, Adelphi, Hofstra, St. Peter's, Iona—scouting in competition for my castoffs.

Sure, the whole operation's kind of dehumanizing, almost like a slave auction. But what the heck? I may have a more relaxed perspective than most coaches, but I'm still competitive. Ultimately I do get paid to win ball games, and like I said, I love my job. Coaching basketball is better than working, and also better than not working.

"I guess Sammy Goodrich is your big hero again this year," Barney asks, his pencil poised.

"He's a good clean kid," I say. "The best player I've ever coached."

I glance at an auxiliary basket beyond the main court where the team's student manager fetches rebounds as Sammy rehearses his left-handed jump shots. The Golden Lions' star player wears neutral gray sweatpants, plus a gray sweatshirt with RHINEGOLD U. crudely stenciled across the chest in square yellow letters.

"His senior year," I say, "will be Sammy's best ever."

Meanwhile Barney consults his notes. "And the only starter who graduated was the center. Greg Dobbs. But you've got a six-ten freshman center from Jersey City named... let's see... Carl Elliot. What's his story?"

"The kid's a project," I say. "He's big and strong and mean, but right now he's too uncoordinated to chew gum and clap his hands at the same time. Hell, Barney. You know what I always say about freshmen: The best thing that happens to freshmen is that they eventually become sophomores."

On the court several of the Golden Lions hopefuls are dashing up and down from baseline to baseline, alone and in various combinations, everyone with a number on his back. Here by invitation only, they perform spot-shooting drills on the side baskets, also 3-on-2-on-1 full-court drills, ball-handling exercises, then desperate games of 1-on-1 between like-sized players.

Even as I chat with Barney, I lean over an opened looseleaf binder and write occasional numbers with a stubby pencil. "Well," I say blithely as I cross out another set of digits (#29, who crosses his feet on defense). "Here's another bubble burst."

—BARNEY—

Clearing my throat, I shift my cigar to the opposite corner of my mouth. I certainly don't want to spend all day here in the wilds of Yonkers. I'd rather be home still sitting shivah for the Dodgers. Imagine...despite Jackie Robinson's late-inning heroics, Brooklyn's pennant hopes were terminated by that excrutiating loss in Philadelphia on the last day of the season. The Dodgers lost in extra innings, but were tragically undone in the top of the ninth when that rag-arm Richie Ashburn threw Cal Abrams (such a nice Jewish boy) out at the plate. And why, God, are Jews so agonizingly slow afoot? For instance, Hank Greenberg and Moe Berg. In the World Series I'd secretly rooted for the Yankees to beat the upstart Phillies. And yet the Bronx Bombers' 4–0 sweep had been meager consolation.

"Let's talk about your schedule, Henry. You open up at the Garden against City...."

While the 154 hopefuls do some mindless running en masse, Pickman clambers up the bleacher steps toward us. (For Chrissake! It feels like a fucking earthquake.) "Hi, guys," Pickman says, his round face always smiling. Then he bends forward to whisper into Henry's nearest ear. "Scolari didn't show, boss. That's Number Seventeen. Neither did Morissey. Scratch Number Thirty and also Number Five. That's Gary Baum, the big clumsy kid from Taft."

Henry grunts softly. "I'll betcha Goldberg's got Morissey sewed up. Ain't that a bitch?... Anyway... here, I wrote some numbers down.... Numbers One-ten through One-sixteen. Seventy-five. Thirty-two.... You can send these guys home. Keep a sharp eye on Numbers Eighteen and

One-twenty-three. Those're the kids from White Plains."

Pickman lurches back down to the court and blows his whistle again. "Thanks, boys," he announces. "We really do appreciate your efforts here today. And the following boys can leave with our appreciation. One-ten, One-eleven, . . ."

Up in the stands, Henry nods for me to resume my questioning. "Sorry, Barn. Business before pleasure."

"Absolutely," I say. "So, we were talking about opening up against City at the Garden. I know that you're also scheduled to play them at their place in January. But am I correct in assuming that the game at the Garden is the one you want most?"

Henry laughs lightly. "Everybody wants to win in the Garden."

I agree. "The Garden of Earthly Delights."

"Hell, yes," says Henry. "But if I had my druthers, I'd just as soon not ever play at the Garden. If not for the colossal jackpots I never would. Too many Broadway characters lurking around. Too much betting going on. Even the hot-dog vendors can quote a point spread. Too many bright lights. . . . This is all off the record of course."

"Of course."

Pickman's whistle bleats and the rotund assistant makes another grand pronouncement: "The resta you boys can go take a water break."

The eager survivors hustle off court and into the nearest hallway.

"When I'm running the show," Henry says proudly, "my players never get water breaks. Drinking water while you're playing gives you the cramps."

I shrug to hide my impatience. "What else can you tell me about your team?"

—HENRY—

Barney Polan is a nice enough guy, always friendly and easy to talk to. Trouble is, like all sportswriters Barney thinks that watching so many basketball games has made him an expert. Actually my favorite sportswriter is Red Smith. I appreciate his eloquent prose and his dignity. But I do enjoy reading "Sports A-Plenty," for its odd mixture of unwashed ideas and pretentious language. Out of the goodness of my heart I'm willing to enlighten (and confound) Barney with an inside look at the theory and practice of pressure defenses.

"The whole idea of the press," I say, "is to force your opponents into making decisions much quicker than they're used to doing and much quicker than they want to do. When you play us here in this gym, then it's time to put on your track shoes and hustle until your feet bleed. If a visiting team won't pay the price, why, then, we've got 'em. For example, what the Diamond Trap is specifically designed to do is this..."

Barney is writing copious notes, and I take his industry as a mark of respect. Hell, yes. I always like dealing with Barney Polan. He's nothing like those young punks nowadays. Always asking pointed questions. What are so-and-so's high school grades? How's what's-his-name's sore ankle? Always probing for privileged information.

Not like the old days when the writers only wanted coaches to phone in the scores and the high-scorers. Back then it was anything goes. I still chuckle whenever I recollect Toby Williams, a burly six-foot-two-inch rebounder I tried recruiting in 1928. Williams opted to enroll at New York University, where he soon became academically ineligible. No problem. Even though Williams was still enrolled at N.Y.U., I paid him five dollars a game to play for Rhinegold's varsity. The name in the scorebook was Marshall Timms, who tallied 10.2 points per game as the Golden Lions won four of five games to start the season. (An expenditure of $6.25 per victory. Quite a bargain.) Later that same season Williams regained his eligibility at N.Y.U. and scored twelve points in a losing effort against Rhinegold in the Den.

Hell, yes. Everybody was doing it.

Even the sanctimonious Ol' Coach once played a nonmatriculated night student for two full varsity seasons. It was no big deal. And despite our mutual enmity, neither of us would ever rat on the other. After all, we both grew up on the Lower East Side. Some of the local coaches even had relatives who came over on the same boat. A closed fraternity of coaches, each of us trying to metamorphose Xs into Os.

"…There's an automatic trap at every crossing and the back man triangulates the ball and the passing lanes…."

"Yeah, Henry…. I understand…. It's automatic…right. Now, about the City game…"

—SAMMY—

My left foot moves forward, stepping into my jump shot. *Swish!* Here comes a perfect bounce pass from the student manager, whatever his name is. *Swish!* Always stepping with my left foot, my left arm moving pistonlike, my fingers curling as I softly release the ball. *Swish!* The ball is an extension of my body. *Thunk!* That one's too hard right. Bring in that left elbow. Torque the left hip. *Swish!* Always stepping just so to jump start the shot machine. *Swish!* Shooting is a matter of intelligence and willpower. *Thunk!* Just like life. *Swish!*

Poppa was a sewing machine operator, a piece-worker in the garment district. A gray-eyed, leansome six-two, he towered over his contemporaries. Good old Morris Goodrich, one-half of a traveling Mutt and Jeff routine. When asked, "How's the weather up there?" he'd spit and say it was raining. What a card he was. Even at home Poppa was a laff riot. "Why do Jews have such big noses? You give up? Because the air is free."

Mama was usually Poppa's best audience. Millie, with the puppet-lines around her mouth and the blond whiskers on her chin. She was small yet zaftig, perhaps five-foot-one, 150 pounds, a homely woman, her hazel eyes always appearing wounded, offended. Her hair was colored the yellow of an old man's teeth. "Morris," she'd marvel, "you're a regular comedian. You always made me laugh, Morris. I think that's why I fell in love with you."

When I was two, I was as big as a four-year-old, confounding everybody's expectations. "What?" said Uncle Simon. "Such a big boy and he's still in diapers?" As I grew, I suffered gnawing pains at night in my knee and ankle joints.

Poppa always kept his distance, but Mama loved to hug me. "You, I can always talk to," she'd say. "My cute little *boychik*. Sammeh-leh, my only child. Come over here, you, and give to your mother a great big hug."

Otherwise, Mama was a quiet, serious woman, proud of her cooking (her specialty was kasha varnishkes) and her sewing (darning socks was her joy), and everybody always swore "you could eat off Millie's floors." Mama always said she was proud to be a housewife, and to help make ends meet, she sometimes worked part-time as a switchboard operator in the International Ladies Garment Workers Union office downtown on Lexington Avenue.

Mama and Poppa had much in common: laughing, dancing cheek-to-cheek to fox trot records, eating Chinese food ("Chinks"), and listening to the opera broadcasts on WQXR.

As far as anybody knew, we were a happy family, and I always laughed uproariously at all of Poppa's jokes.

And I kept growing. "*Kayn aynhoreh*," Poppa would say with a broad wink. "Such a big boy from such a little woman? Tell the truth, Millie. How tall was the mailman?"

We lived in a series of gray brick tenement buildings that stretched side by side along a one-way street in the East Bronx—1775 Fulton Avenue, Apartment 9, third floor in the back. "Stay out from the basement," Mama told me, always nagging. "And you should also stay off from the roof. Too low and too high is *nicht* good." Better I should go clean my room and read something "useful." For my eighth birthday I was presented with a copy of Jack London's *Iron Heel*.

That's because Morris and Millie used to be card-carrying Party members in the thirties (wasn't everybody?), who advanced the

Revolution by distributing pamphlets at subway stations and bus stops all over the Bronx. Years later a romantic light still gleamed in their eyes whenever they proudly displayed their battle scars to friends or relatives.

"This is from when the fascist bastards attacked the buses in Peekskill when Marian Anderson sang there. That's how we first met. Remember, Millie?"

"I should forget so easy? They broke a bus window with a brick right where me and Morris were sitting and the same piece of glass cut us both. The same piece of glass. Look. I got here a matching scar on my arm. Look."

They lost their zeal after the Soviets signed the infamous nonaggression pact with Hitler, and they let their Party membership lapse after the war. In fact I always suspected that what Poppa called "Stalin's ideological betrayal" was one of the roots of my father's increasing bitterness and unhappiness with his own life. Gradually Morris and Millie even lost interest in protests and revolution, in politics and justice.

Yet Poppa maintained his scorn whenever politicians made speeches on radio or TV. "You wanna know the truth, kiddo? The truth is that democracy is a dirty lie and a crock of shit. Look it, what's the difference if I vote for this crook instead of that crook? It's just like Henry Morgan says on the radio. When you vote, all you're doing is encouraging them. You should listen to him sometime, kiddo. I love that Henry Morgan. He's clever and he's got heart. Me, I'm only clever."

Every advertisement Poppa ever saw was another crock of shit: Certain cigarettes were claimed to aid digestion, but they actually caused lung problems. Automobiles were death traps. Toothpaste corroded tooth enamel. "The whole culture is a crock of shit. You hear, kiddo?"

Poppa also fancied himself a poet, even though he'd written only one poem, "Ode to Autumn," which he'd invariably be called upon to recite at family gatherings, reading with a slight literary lisp:

So silently has another equinox slowly turned the world—
gray leaves twirling flying already dead
Only a few blazing flowers to survive the frosty curtain
of nightfall
Runny noses
winter cough
Sturm *and screen*
The fearsome nocturnal sigh of an oil burner coming alive
The hawkwind whipping my face
Wild ducks arrowing southward and blackly under sere gray
clouds of doom
Vitamin C and thermal underwear
Snow tires and tired batteries
Politicians scheming with dull lies and
shiny smiles
Earnest citizens pulling disconnected
levers
behind black curtains

So silently does death come upon us—
dancing our imaginary lives macabre upon
the crumbling edge of despair
Turning the earth to stone
Spring seems so far from here —
escaping like a warm tailfeather of a dream from a
cold and rheumy morning

Even so—
some joyful someday
shall the barren heart-stones of winter
suddenly burst forth into luminous blossoms

Afterward Aunt Bessie would always cry, and Poppa's brothers would sigh and say, "It's beautiful," or "So lovely." Everybody would demand to know why such a wonderful poem hadn't been published, and Poppa would explain: "In a cigar box under my bed, I've got in it over a hundred rejection letters. From *Reader's Digest* and *Collier's*. From poetry magazines and newspapers from coast to coast. Even from the *Jewish Daily Forward.* Form letters, I got. 'Dear Sir or Madam.' And why is this so? Why can't such a masterpiece find its way into print? Because this *farkuckta* country is anti-intellectual. Because this *pishechtz* culture caters to the lowest common denominator. That's why."

Then he'd tell a joke and everybody would laugh. "Why did the *faygeleh* cross the road?... Because his *shmeckle* was stuck in a chicken."

So, despite his funny one-liners and hilarious routines, Poppa was a bitter man. Imagine, such a talented writer hemming skirts and cuffing pants. Behind his soft laughter, his teeth were sharp and hungry. He vowed not to submit any more poems until "Ode to Autumn" was published.

Mama's grandpa had been a rabbi in the old country, but her only concession to Hebraic culture was to cook chicken soup, boiled chicken, and chicken fricassee every Friday night after she lit the *Shabbes* candles and whispered the prayers to herself.

"Women," Poppa said to me with a smirk. "So superstitious. So emotional. It's because of their period. Women."

About religion Poppa said this: "Religion is the gefilte fish of the masses." When I asked him about being Jewish, Poppa said, "You know what kind of Jews we are, kiddo? Gastronomical Jews."

When I was eleven years old, Mama died of sudden heart failure. Standing at the stove, stirring a steaming pot of kasha varnishkes, she silently collapsed and died.

The funeral took place two days later. I can still remember the hungry grave, so deep, dark, bottomless. Also the familiar graveside mound of freshly spaded earth.

Hey, you guys! Let's play King of the Hill!

The mourners wept without restraint. Neighbors and friends. Co-workers and fellow travelers. Relatives. There's Aunt Bessie, Mama's only sibling. There's Poppa and Simon and Nathan and Heshie, the brothers Goodrich.

Inside the chapel Uncle Nathan wouldn't let me join the line for a last peek at my Mama before the casket was nailed shut, nailed by a big *shvartzer* with a heavy hammer. *Wham!* Uncle Nathan led me away toward the gleaming limosines. "*Tacha,*" Uncle Nathan said, "you should remember better what she looked like, your darling mama, before she died."

"Shah!" Uncle Heshie said. "You're scaring him, Nathan, more than he's scared already." Uncle Heshie was always my favorite uncle, because of the tattooed anchor on his right bicep, and because it was Uncle Heshie who taught me that a dime is worth more than a bigger, thicker nickel. Then Uncle Heshie turned to me, saying, "Your darling mama is only sleeping. You hear, Sammy? She's only sleeping."

Uncle Simon was the eldest and always had the last word, his thin moustache twitching like a rat's tail. "For a *long* time she's sleeping," Uncle Simon said. "For a *very* long time."

Poppa had nothing to say. Not yet. Now and again, he'd stiffly pat the top of my head. Sometimes he patted too hard and I winced. Neither father nor son ever cried in public.

Oy-oy-oy.

The gravesite was situated at the farthest southwestern corner of a stone-sprouted field of green, The Gates to Zion Cemetery, in the Bronx. Nearby an old woman cloaked in black placed a pebble atop a small weathered tombstone. A long fly ball away, over there by the fence, a solitary man stood in front of a larger headstone. He was dressed in heavy garments, an Hasidic Jew in his team's famous road uniform, reading silently from his backwards text, ducking and weaving to avoid a knockout punch from the Master of the Universe.

Oy gevalt iz mir.

Meanwhile, at the foot of the open grave, the attendant rabbi, with his sharp nose and slick silver hair, incanted the traditional fill-in-the-blanks one-prayer-fits-all in a whining tremolo. "Bah hah bah hah Mildred Nussbaum bah hah Mildred Goodrich bah hah bah hah The International Ladies' Garment Workers Union bah bah Number Two-thirty-one bah hah bah hah *adonoi eloheinu....*"

And those same brawny *shvartzers* played out the thickly woven straps that lowered the coffin into the bottomless hole.

"Gently," said Uncle Simon. "Gently, *boyes.* Gently."

How eagerly I grasped my uncles' easy comforts, hoping that some day, in a very long time from now, we'd all gather here again within the Gates of Zion to celebrate Mama's reawakening. Then would our bitter grief turn sweet as she'd tell us of glorious dreams and truths.

But the rabbi sneaked a glance at his wristwatch. And the *shvartzers* began shoveling spadefuls of the King's Hill down into the pit, the clumps of earth thudding against the coffin, the small stones banging and bouncing. I was cold and frightened. What if they woke her too soon?

Poppa finally had something to say. Even through his tears, he winked wetly and, swallowing a sob, said, "Tell me, somebody. What was the name of the first Jewish Indian?"

"Please, Morris. Not here. Not now."

"Give up?"

"Don't be a jerk, Moishella."

"Morris. Don't."

"His name was Sitting Shivah."

At age thirteen, I'd somehow grown to a plump six-foot-three, obviously some kind of ancient peasant mutation, and the day after my bar mitzvah I went to the schoolyard and celebrated my own rite of passage by suddenly snappping a brisk left hook into the snout of Butchie, the neighborhood bully.

Whapp!

That made me a neighborhood hero.

"Hey, Sammy. You wanna be on my punchball team? You could play shortstop and bat cleanup."

"Sammy? You wanna bite of my salami sandwich?"

With Poppa not getting home from the garment district until nearly six o'clock five nights a week, I was free to roam the streets after school, playing whichever sport was in season, competing with power and reckless courage but little skill. Mostly, we played handball, box ball, stickball, and punchball. Off the field, we played seven-card stud for nickels and dimes.

We played basketball infrequently only because Freddy Manfredi was the second tallest kid in the neighborhood, only five-ten, and I could easily overpower him.

"Hey, Goodrich. Don't fucking push me, ya big stiff. I ain't afraid of you."

"Fuck you, Manfredi. Just call the fucking foul, you fairy, and let's play ball."

Basketball provided the perfect arena for me to exorcise my secret rages. Only football was more physical, but who was crazy enough to want to play football?

"Football ain't a contact sport," Manfredi used to say. "It's a collision sport."

I was a straight-A student without breaking a sweat, and I was decidedly unpopular with my peers because of this. Not that I gave a shit about them either. When I was in the eighth grade I was reading Russian novels and also getting interested in philosophy. For a time I considered myself to be the gadfly of David G. Farragut Junior High School and answered every question with another question. "Sammy, what were the causes of the Industrial Revolution?" "Miss Silver, what were the causes of the causes of the Industrial Revolution?" I was a wiseass, all right, but I thought and therefore I thought I was.

I first started to take basketball seriously when I was fifteen: During one of my long, brooding, solitary walks, I followed the sound of the bouncing ball and came upon a "steady run" in the wintertime locker room of a public swimming pool in a Negro neighborhood just fifteen blocks from Fulton Avenue. It was a full-court game played between portable baskets on a cold stone floor. Wandering in out of sheer curiosity, I was instantly welcomed. "Lace 'em up, big fella. You got next with me."

The game was presided over by "Bill," rumored to have been a Harlem Globetrotter in his distant youth. It was a fierce and honorable game in which the shooter was the only player who'd ever dare admit to being fouled, and everybody else rebounded like gangbusters. Cowardly hoopers were derided as "bitches" and worse.

"Only a pussy would call that a foul, man. Not even the white boy would make that call."

And the "bloods" would laugh loudly at their own private jokes.

I loved the company of those joyful warriors who played with such sheer aggression and compassion. Smelling from booze on Saturday mornings. Laughing away everybody's mistakes. "Keep on shooting, Mister Good-and-rich," Bill would urge me. "You throw enough shit against the wall, some of it's bound to stick." But at the time I couldn't master the fine art of shooting a basketball—it seemed to squirt out of my hands like a gigantic watermelon seed. "Young Mister Good-and-rich," Bill would exclaim with a laugh. "I don't believe you could piss in the ocean."

After long, lonesome sessions in the playground I ultimately perfected the jump shot and I went on to play varsity basketball at Polk High School. The coach was a math teacher whose only advice was "Bend your knees, boys. Bend your knees." Nevertheless, by my junior year, I was an All-City player and wooed by powerhouse college coaches. St. Louis University offered me one hundred dollars a week for watching the grass grow on the football field. Ohio State, Dayton, Florida State, California, and other schools from exotic locales also bid for my services. But these schools were all so far away from here and populated with six-four jumpshooters with crewcuts, and sheep-fuckers and blue-eyed blonds, and where everybody loved church socials and hayrides and hated New Yorkers, especially Jews (and where could I get a good egg cream or pastrami sandwich?). Besides which, I had to find myself here before I could lose myself somewhere else, and this is where I was.

Okay, I understood the basic vanities, and even cruelties, of capitalism, and I recognized the truth of Poppa's version of the American way of life. But his naked negativity was too sterile even for me. Moreover, Communism was a fraud because its operating premise was the inherent goodness and unselfishness of the human race. What a joke. Did I even know anybody who was inherently good and unselfish? Sure— Superman, Captain Marvel, and Flash Gordon. Also, the atomic bomb had vaporized more than the cities of Hiroshima and Nagasaki—it had also annihilated ideals. After the mushroom cloud and the firestorm, could anybody still believe in God? In morality, love, guilt, or innocence? Wake up, everybody, and smell the burning flesh. And what did the Nazi atrocities prove? That victims are the only true innocents.

So where did that leave me? Attracted by the vague possibility that somehow one could move beyond guilt, beyond victimhood, to bravely forge a new kind of innocence, one that is tough and pragmatic.

All of this internal combustion sounded good, even if I wasn't completely sure what I really meant by it. Was I crazy? Or was I incurably sane? I talked to myself in terms of "quixotic possibilities," which I believed were sufficient to sustain me as I grew into the rest of my life.

After Mama died, Poppa became even more sour. He still told his jokes: "What's invisible and smells like worms? Give up, kiddo? It's a bird's fart." And we still laughed together, but our laughter had become too easy, too cheap, too perishable, and it couldn't soothe our pain. A quick smile still played on Poppa's face, but his cold gray eyes never showed joy.

And Poppa never came to see his son play. "Basketball," the old man said, "shmasketball."

Except for basketball, high school was boring. None of my classes engaged my interest. Mostly, I stared at girls' bodies.

And who were these enchanted creatures? Girls. Women. I was desperate to discover what they knew.

That's why I learned enough astrology to boldly initiate a conversation. "Hi there, beautiful. What sign are you?" And I memorized the daily horoscope listings in the *New York Post* so I could sound halfway authentic. "A Capricorn, eh? Well, you may be a traditionalist in some respects, but you're also quick to make use of new ideas if you think they can be turned to your advantage, right? What the stars are saying to you today is to seize whatever new opportunities come your way.... So what are you doing tonight?"

A Taurus named Arlene Erlich was my first "piece of ass." She was an otherwise pretty pony-tailed blondie with a thick scar that fused her congenitally cleft lip. She was sweet, somewhat dim-witted and she never laughed at my fumbling efforts to fuck her. Still, after all my adolescent fantasies, actual sex was a considerable burden to me. "Was I too quick, Arlene? Tell me the truth, is my penis too small?"

"No, of course not. I love dicky-wicky."

But I was intimidated by Arlene's ravenous cunt, afraid of her rollicking orgasms. Anyway, after two months of delirious suckings and fuckings, Arlene jilted me for a first-year law student at Columbia.

I felt betrayed by Arlene's defection, so even though I was excited by the prospects of more sex, new love, and the idea of finding a soul mate, I was more afraid of being rejected again. So I spent a lot of time by myself, reading Proust and Joyce, rereading the Doester, listening to FM jazz stations, playing solitaire. And because I was so fearful of rejection, I was cool to all friendly overtures. Would any of "them" have been so nice to me if I hadn't been such an outstanding basketball player?

Often it was easier to examine *Playboy* with my eager penis enclosed in the Merry Fist.... Oh! Such succulent tits and cunts and asses.... Oh! Oh! Oooo!

Say there, Miss January, was it good for you too?

I felt trapped inside myself, formless and confounded. Where was life? Real life? Playing basketball was fun, but it was too easy, and it was only a game after all.

Midway through my senior year at Polk H.S., I decided to accept Coach Carlson's offer to attend Rhinegold University on a "free-ride-full-boat-with-plenty-of-money-under-the-table" basketball scholarship (even though Carlson was obviously a blowhard and the Rhinegold campus was stunted and ugly). Maybe I did this just to prove something to my father. Maybe to offer myself as a sacrifice to him. What the fuck did I (do I) know about anything? And where could I ever fit in in this absurd, bloodthirsty, sweet-toothed culture? How could I help bring about the glorious revolution, the golden dream of freedom, without blighting my life as it had blighted Poppa's life? And why did I think it was *my* responsibility to try?

So all I had left was basketball after all, the only love that would never betray me. The ever-changing angles, the instantaneous opening and closing of opportunities, the decisions on the run, the one-on-one and burn-on-burn, and hopefully a reprise of what I felt during those wonderful runs with the bloods in the locker room of the swimming pool where ten players played one ball game and the playing counted more than the score. Maybe that's where I'd find God and love and peace of mind and a true sense of myself.

Thunk!
Thunk!

God, I'm glad to be out of that fucking place, that mausoleum disguised as a gymnasium. The silver rain is delightful, refreshing my spirits, as I jog lightly along the sidewalks, barely stretching my long springy legs, my calves like steel springs, my feet made of vulcanized rubber, bouncing off the unforgiving concrete surface, leaping over windblown scraps of newsprint, over discarded candy bar wrappers, a petrified dog turd, carefully timing the traffic lights, green for "Go," green for envy, green for springtime. Long green, like the two twenty-dollar bills from Henry Carlson tucked into my socks.

Faking left, I cut to the right around the passersby, mostly church-goers who wave at me with friendly intentions. Everybody in Yonkers knows the perpetual-motion man—my 16.2 points per game average, my forbidding defense, my familiar joggings and sprintings between the Lions' Den and the college. Such a big, strapping lad, always working so hard.

Men, women, and children are dressed in their Sunday best, yet I focus on their feet. Hip. Hup.... A hard fake left twenty paces away from the black Florsheims, just to see if I can make them flinch. Hip. Hup. Faked into a panic, the Florsheims kick each other. Hup. And it's too late—I've already gone right.

Behind me I can feel their faces turning to watch my back, my ass, my flying heels. All six feet seven inches of me. Thrilling at my passing presence. Gaping. Glory be, the circus is in town.

An old lady in widow's weeds refuses to be fooled by a long- range fake left, and as I pass her by, she looks up with her palms hiding her eyes from the sun, squinting in wonder. Then a white poodle on a long leather leash barks in my direction. A sharp jab step left-and-right and the foolish dog jumps for cover. Near the corner of Platt Street, an old man cringes as I run around him. Children laugh and point. "Look, mom! Look at the giant!"

It came as no surprise when, the day after my first varsity ball game (seventeen points, eleven rebounds, and five assists), three of my teammates—Gary Edwards, Chip Landers, and Charlie Bloom—invited me to join them in doing business with Johnny Boy Gianelli. Fortunately another teammate, Jerry Burrell, had already supplied the details while sitting next to me on the long bus ride home after a preseason scrimmage against C.S.I., the College of Staten Island. Jerry hoped that when "the boys" cut me in, perhaps I'd be able to finagle him a piece of the pie, too. "Everybody's doing it," he said.

In truth I adored the idea of illegally fixing ball games for many reasons: I'd seen how my teammates had gone about trying to lose that first game (won at last only because of my own irresistible excellence)—the foolish passes thrown off of each other's feet, chests, and heads. The clumsy fouls and palsied shots. The fumbled rebounds and banana-peel flops on defense. (How could anybody not realize they were dumping?) I knew that I could do the job with grace, with skill, with cunning. Yes, I could be a spy, a double agent, paid handsomely with invisible money. I also wanted the chance to prove that everything Americans believed in was a lie.

Nevertheless I had to be careful, so I assumed a self-righteous, indignant tone and refused my teammates' offer.

That's because I was convinced that Gianelli and his stable—including the saps at C.C.N.Y., St. John's, and who knew where else—would eventually get nabbed. There were too many players under Gianelli's control, too much danger of loose talk, too much money foolishly spent, and too many drastic fluctuations in the point spreads as the local bookies frantically tried to lay off Gianelli's outsized bets. Gianelli's entire setup was just too precarious. If one pebble fell, then the whole building would collapse. That's why I decided to conduct my business through the back door. Dealing with a pissant like Georgie Klein is annoying but a much safer bet.

Veering left, I kick an empty beer can into the street, where it's quickly mashed by a passing bus. I'm loosey-goosey and always ready to play. I've even worn an extra pair of socks to save my feet from the stubborn sidewalks and I'm sweating freely inside my yellow-lettered sweat gear. Running through the familiar downtown streets of Yonkers on a gleaming autumnal afternoon, I am beyond the law, beyond redemption, and therefore totally free.

When I reach the perimeter of the Rhinegold campus, I turn up the jets just enough to stoke more heat into my thighs. My aim is to run the 2.1-mile circuit in fifteen minutes flat. So I run in place until the minute hand on my Bulova wristwatch reaches the nearest corner-point moving upward toward noon. I know it's silly, but I love the watchband circled tightly around my left wrist, the leather amulet of a warrior.

So I run with deliberate swiftness around the wrought iron fencing, past the various gates and driveways, still running easily here where the Sunday sidewalks finally belonged to me. Gliding. Bounding. Slowing to a walk when the course is finally run, I continue walking until I stop sweating. And the Bulova's message is ambiguous.... Was it fifteen? Or fifteen and a half? Or even sixteen minutes? These are important differences of speed and heat, of energy and courage. Only a stopwatch could ever reveal the truth. Yes. I'll buy one tomorrow morning. Yes. My dirty money is always wisely spent.

—ROYCE—

Me and my ma—her name is Mae—live in a three-room railroad flat four floors above a Chinese hand laundry on the west side of Harlem. The rent is eight dollars per month and gray water falls from the faucets. My bedroom is the last room in the line, separated from the bathroom by the kitchen and then the living room, where my ma sleeps on a foldaway bed. The apartment isn't much, but it's clean and we feel safe living here, so don't be feeling sorry for either of us.

My ma is thin and sharp-boned, and her dark almond-shaped eyes are always bright and lively like she doesn't have a care in the world. She was brought up in rural Mississippi, Jim Crow country, but she's proud of her African features—her full lips and glossy midnight-brown skin. Maybe she looks fragile, but she's tough enough. She'd started working full-time as a washerwoman at the age of ten back home in Booneville. Life's been hard for her, nigger-hard, and I respect the serious side of her nature. The only joke I've ever heard her tell is about how so many years of rubbing clothes against washboards have rubbed out her fingerprints.

Ma's Sunday shift in the laundry room at Harlem Hospital always wears her out. Tonight, while she was at work, I did the peeling and slicing, so it took her only a few minutes to fry the potatoes and the burgers for our supper. A slow, quiet meal. As ever, she asked me about my studies. "I'm doing fine, Ma." We also discussed my upcoming practice schedule because on Monday, Wednesday, and Thursday evenings, Ma attends night classes at Baruch College down on Twenty-third Street to study typing and Gregg shorthand, and I'll have to warm up the dinners she'll leave for me. "Don't worry, Ma. I'll be okay." On Sundays, I do the dishes and she goes to sleep right after dinner.

Except when my daddy is home and they've both been drinking, Ma is a notoriously light sleeper. She's accustomed to the traffic sounds from the street, so she sleeps right through them. Only the house sounds disturb her. She swears that years ago she was once awakened by the sound of "Roycey pissing his diapers."

Me, I sleep on an army surplus cot. My feet protrude over the hard edge, and the small space cramps my long limbs. For comfort I have a chicken-feather pillow. For warmth, a pair of G.I.-issue brown blankets.

At one time the small walls around me were painted a glossy white. Now they're dull gray and mottled with green water stains. Scotch-taped to uncracked sections of the walls are various newspaper clippings. There's a photo of Otis Hill soaring to grab a rebound in heavy traffic. Also several headlines:

SEWARD PK. SCHOOLBOY CHAMPS

—— **BEAVERS COP TITLE** ——

CITY COLLEGE N.I.T.'S BEST!

The crook of a wire clothes hanger is thrust deep into a crack above the closet door, the wire frame bent forward to form a crude hoop. My ball is a grapefruit-size roll of sweat socks, and my aim is true even while lying back on my cot. A perfect shot causes the cotton ball to fall against a closed folding chair strategically positioned to rebound the ball toward my knees, close enough for stretching one-handed catches. Only rarely do I have to climb out of bed to retrieve a missed shot. And every shot decides a ball game at the final buzzer.

What else is here? An old dresser, a bureau, a lamp, and a freshly painted silver radiator. Nice and cozy. Better than that shit-hole I lived in up at Levy's.

There's even some four-legged critters in my room to keep me company and add some excitement. I put two spring-triggered mousetraps out every night but haven't caught anything in over three weeks. Tomorrow I'll change the bait from cheese to bacon.

The other companions of my small yellow darkness are the solitary cockroaches that roam the walls and floors, scouts in advance of huge nighttime armies that feast on their own shit and live forever. I always bang on the wall before entering my room, giving the convocated roaches a chance to disperse. Actually, I really don't dislike the cockroaches. They're not filthy-looking like the mice. Sometimes I imagine them in their shiny brown armor, like tiny warriors.

Oh, man. I've got to pee, but there's no way I can tiptoe to the bathroom without waking Ma and stealing the sweetness from her dreams. So I remove the empty milk bottle from under my bed and relieve myself. Ahhh! So what if a few drops splash onto my fingers? I won't be jerking off tonight anyway—not with tomorrow the first day of practice. Lena Horne will wait for me.

I have a small General Electric radio that I bought for $1.25 from the Salvation Army store to pull in Marty Glickman's broadcasts of all the basketball games (both college and pro) played in Madison Square Garden. (*"It's Good! Like Nedick's!"*) But my prize possession is a windup Victrola, a gift from my father, that sits on the top of my low-lying dresser.

My daddy (his name is Kelsey) is a bebop saxophone player, currently riding a first small riff of success. This means that now, more than ever before, Daddy is on the road. Boston, Detroit, Philadelphia, D.C., Chicago, even a two-week trip to Los Angeles. Despite the fact that

Daddy regularly drinks away most of his wages, he's always welcomed back by Ma. The two of them love to party, to make love and drink and entertain friends.

Daddy was home most often when I was a young boy. A brawny six-foot-three himself, Daddy sympathized with my growing pains, and his impulse was to forgive my awkwardness. "That's okay," he'd say when I clumsily blistered my fingers on hot pot handles and noisily dropped objects that always broke—glasses, dishes, bottles full of milk.

Used to be he'd take me to the park and we'd play catch with a real Spaldeen, or sometimes we'd go over to the schoolyard and he'd teach me how to hoop. Jump shots, set shots, running hooks, clever dribblings, and underhanded free throws. When I'd lose my concentration and get tired, he'd challenge me: "We ain't goin' home, son, till you make three shots in a row three times from the top of the key. Three with your feet set, three going left and three going right." I'd complain and sometimes even weep when a shot rimmed out and I'd have to start all over. But I loved my daddy and he loved me back.

Daddy never practiced his horn in the apartment. "The acoustics ain't too cool," he'd say. When he tried practicing on the roof, the neighbors squawked, so he took to going to the park and practicing there. Sometimes I'd tag along with him, watching and listening in great admiration as he blew his way through various chord changes and other mysterious exercises. He'd laugh at me sitting there with my mouth open. "Don't you ever even think of being a jazzman," he once told me. "It's a good enough life for a broke-down old fool like me, but you've gotta do better." He was a sweet man back then and I used to miss him when he was away.

Imagine my surprise when I came upon him one day in the kitchen, sitting with his horn in his lap and big sloppy tears falling down his face. "It ain't nothin'," he said. "Leave me be." But I just waited silently till he finally relented and opened up his heart.

"The thing is, son, that I just ain't good enough on this here instrument. I mean, I'm a solid professional and I can read real good, and I'm always right on time, and I always work hard. But the one thing I don't have is enough imagination. That means I have to figure out and rehearse all my solos, you know? There ain't no life in my ax, man, and the truth is killin' me. What I'm best suited for is a second- or even third-reed man in a big band, playin' all them riffs and such, but there hardly ain't no big bands no more, exceptin' Stan Kenton, who's a lightweight, and Woody Herman, who's way outta my league. The thing is, ever since Charlie Parker breezed into town, he's been blowin' the rest of us all to kingdom come. Makes me feel like a plumber."

I told him that he sure sounded fine to me, but he wouldn't be so easily consoled.

"The worst thing," he continued, "is that this Parker cat is on the needle. I mean, we all smoke up some muggles from time to time to get in the mood, you know? But the needle, man, that's a whole other story. And all these cats are sayin' that if you wanna play as good as the Bird then you gotta ride the flying horse like he does. But, man, I don't want to. And it's all getting so confused and complicated, 'cause the junkers ain't hiring the straights for no gigs. . . . I don't know, son, if it's worth it no more. But there isn't anything else I can do to get by."

He looked at me eye-to-eye and then he felt embarrassed, so he shooed me away.

By the time I was twelve, I was already six-foot-one and thought nothing of cutting school to hoop it up in the playground. Playing basketball was the most fun in all the world. But there was a serious side, too. Even in the most deadbeat game, each basket was crucial, proving my worth as a hooper and as a human being. This is how much

I took basketball to heart, and I'm not ashamed to say it:

It was a windy October morning, a Tuesday, and the welfare eagle would fly as soon as the mailman came. Meanwhile the wind swept through the park, chasing the dead leaves and yesterday's newspapers. A dozen black men lounged around on one section of bench. They shared a battered copy of the *Daily News*, which they all read from back page to front. They also circulated a bottle of wine and a joint. Their lips danced with laughter, taunts, and schemes.

The wind sliced through the basketball court, shaking the two bent rims and bowing a clump of weeds that sprouted through the asphalt along the far baseline. A pair of nervous young men prowled under one of the baskets, shooting junk shots with a faded and bald yellow ball. At the other basket six of us played hooky and three-on-three.

I was being guarded by a light-skinned player with a menacing Oriental moustache (his nickname was Chink) as I dribbled at the top of the key. There I was, dribbling in one spot, twitching and feinting until at last Chink tilted to his toes. Then a sharp spin to my right to release a high-flying jump shot that clanged against the backboard and bounced off the front rim. There's never any "retrieving" in Harlem, so my miss transformed all six of us into offensive rebounders. Snatching the loose ball, I uncorked a fadeaway jumper, but, God damn, I missed again. Worse, Chink bounded from the pack and tipped the ball through the hoop. It's winners' out, and the ball game continued.

Suddenly a fire engine screamed down the street. The men on the benches craned their necks. The junkies tried to hide in each others' shadows. But hoopers know that turned heads allow easy layups, and the game went on.

"Hey, man! It's a fire!" one of the men yelled from the bench. "Look! You can see the smoke!"

But us hoopers persevered.

Then another man turned to the basketball court, cupped his hands around his mouth, and shouted, "Hey, Royce! Ain't that your house burnin', man?"

"Yeah, Royce!" chimed another man. "Your house is on fire!"

I'd just missed still another jump shot, and all the shouting stopped the ball game in its tracks. "Yeah," I snarled. "Fuck it. Ain't nobody home anyway.... It's my ball, man. That cat was yellin' at me while I was shootin'. That's offensive interference."

The men on the bench rocked with laughter. "You hear that shit?" one of them said.

"Yeah," another clucked as he scratched his veins. "That poor nigger. Royce got the worst habit I ever saw."

One summer morning when I was fourteen I stumbled against a chair on my way to the bathroom early on a Sunday morning, waking my father from a drunken stupor. Cursing, Daddy snatched an empty wine bottle from the nearby night table, climbed out of bed, and crashed the bottle over my head.

"You stupid motherfucker!" I screamed at him. "You done cut me all up!"

The sudden gushing of blood instantly sobered him, and he ran to fetch a bath towel for me to press against the wound on my forehead, then hurriedly dressed, grabbed my free hand, and rushed us out of the apartment. I was wearing only slippers and boxer shorts, the kind with an open fly.

Daddy hailed a taxi on Amsterdam Avenue, shouting to the cabbie, "Harlem Hospital. The emergency room. And step on it."

Only then did he speak to me: "I'm sorry, kid. I'm really sorry. You don't have to believe me if you don't want to, but I love you."

I lied when I said, "I believe you, Dad."

We were kept waiting in the emergency room for over an hour, even though Daddy hounded every doctor, every nurse, every white-gowned person he saw. "My wife is Mae Johnson. She works here. My son is bleeding to death. Can't you...? Won't you...?"

But I didn't care about my wound as much as I did the humiliating possibility that my weenie might show through my shorts—so I sat with my legs firmly crossed and took tiny steps when I had to walk. The cut above my eye needed eight stitches.

Later that evening, when my mom came home from work, I overheard my parents arguing:

"The kid was making a racket, Mae. He wouldn't stop when I told him to, so I threw the bottle at him. I wasn't trying to hit him. Just to scare him and make him shut up."

"You're lyin', you drunken bum."

"Ha! Look who's talkin'?"

After that me and Daddy never again went to the park together, and he seemed different to me—more remote, more irritable—and we seldom spoke. All the beautiful experiences we'd shared now seemed to have been fantasies I'd dreamed up by myself. I was confused and also angry.

Several days after he'd smashed the bottle over me, I finally asked my mother this: "How come he hit me like that, Ma? And how come you still huggin' and kissin' with him?"

Then Ma sighed and said, "He's a jazzman. He's a artist, so his love is all mixed up with a bunch of other things."

How could I believe her? "He ain't no artist, Ma. He don't never paint no pictures or nothing like that."

"I mean a music artist."

"What's a artist anyway?"

"A artist is somebody who creates something new. Just

somethin' new."

"Then I'm a artist, too, Ma. Creatin' layups and stuff with a basketball."

"I believe you are, son. Now, c'mere and hug your poor ol' mama."

Me, I was the big cheese in high school. On the court I was godlike—creating something out of nothing, bringing a dead ball game to life, walking on air and being everywhere at once. It was like everybody else was playing in slow motion except me. My coach (his name was Melvin Brooker) just gave me the ball and told my teammates to get out of my way.

In the classroom my hardest task was to stay awake. A bunch of girls looked to please me by doing my homework and term papers, and I studied just enough to stay eligible to play basketball. I cruised to my graduation with a 73 average.

Outside of school the bitches were sighing all over me and saying that I was more handsome than Billy Eckstine, but I was a hooper and I had to keep myself clean. Besides, here's my parents talking about being so much in "love," and Daddy wasn't hardly ever home, and when he was, after two days they were both drunk as skunks and fighting about money.... No, thanks. Me, I get all the loving I need from tip to buzzer.

One time Ma took me down to the Five Spot to see Daddy play. And I was amazed to see my father sweating, straining, and blowing wild sounds full of pain, the notes coming so quickly that I couldn't hear them all.

During the break I was thrilled when Daddy proudly introduced me to the other musicians. "This is my boy Royce. He's gonna be a great basketball player when he grows up and make a lot of money so's his daddy can retire young."

At first my daddy's friends all looked like a bunch of goofs to me, but they turned out to be okay guys. What I remembered most about the musicians was shaking their hands and feeling their powerful, knuckle-crunching strength. I'd bet that they could have all palmed a basketball with ease.

Afterwards I decided that I really loved my daddy even though he cut my head like he did.

More and more, Daddy was on the road. In spite of his self-doubts, his career seemed to be thriving. "Hi, kid," Daddy would say upon arriving, "Ain't no place like home." Then it was, "Bye, kid. Ain't no sweeter music than road music."

After Daddy gave me the Victrola, he got me three of those 78 rpm records—the Nat King Cole Trio, Louis Armstrong, and the Ink Spots. I've got one metal needle, all round and dull at the tip. (Fucking little bitty thing like that costs two bits.)

Sitting up in my bed, I reach backward to the dresser top and crank the Victrola's handle. Then I carefully place the needle on the outer track and lower the volume.

"Sweet Lorraine
Oh, my darling sweet Lorraine...."

While the record spins and King Cole croons, I attend to my schoolwork—reading for the third time a selection from Plato's *Republic.* What is this boolshit and what does it have to do with me? All this nonsense to memorize.... Shadows on a wall in the back of some secret cave.... What does it mean? Why would anybody want to stay in a fucking cave? And there's a picture of this cat on the cover of the book wearing a cape and a little skirt. Talking about *this* is the truth. No, *that's* the truth. And what is truth anyway? Park Avenue truth? Harlem truth?

"Sweet Lorrainnnnne...."

Suddenly I hear a loud thud overhead coming from the upstairs apartment, and then another thud and some loud high-pitched laughter. A small lump of plaster is loosened from the ceiling and falls through my makeshift wire basket. *It's good!* With tomorrow the first day of basketball practice, I can hardly control my excitement. Me, I'm positive that I'm good enough to play beside Otis. *Like Nedick's!* For certain I'll work my ass off, and I'll learn to control my showboat maneuvers—but I'll play so good anyway that Goldberg will have to let me start. *CITY WINS AGAIN!*

I'm more than ready. Ever since school started six weeks ago, several of the C.C.N.Y. players have been scrimmaging four nights a week at the college gym. Goldberg's assistant coach, Dickie Weiss, unlocks the doors at seven P.M. sharp, tosses out a few basketballs and then disappears. Most of the varsity players join the run—Barry Hoffman, Phil Isaacson, Thad Miller. But never Otis. For real, the varsity players are smart and intense, but they also seem kind of grim. Whatever the chosen sides, I always eventually dominate the game, the ball finding its way into my hands because my teammates trust me. My vision. My decisions. Maybe it's because I care more about the game than my part in it.

Sometimes I come upon Otis in the hallways between classes. The big man flashes me a fleshy grin and says, "You better be in shape, boy."

During the first week of classes I tried to contact Goldberg, fast-breaking my way into the Ol' Coach's office in the gym building. Just as quickly, I was chested to a halt by a mousey older woman who said that I needed an appointment. Flustered, I turned tail and fled.

"But ah, the pleasures of philosophy." That's what my "philo" teacher always says. I like that word, "philo." Knowing it, saying it, makes me feel smart, like I really belong there at the college. I'm studying my ass off and taking notes like a motherfucker.

So far I estimate that my grades are like this: C– in both English and philosophy. Trigonometry is a serious problem—I can memorize the formulas, but I'm not sure when to use which ones. I scored a 45 on the only trig test so far. That's an F. The red flag. World History is easiest— maybe a C+ —just for remembering dates, names, acts, bills, battles, reasons why things either happen or don't happen, and everything in strict chronological order. Even so, I'm still confused about the "historical sweep" my history professor is always talking about.

Studying takes so much of my time that, lately, I've even cut my nighttime scrimmaging to Mondays and Thursdays. When will I have time to study once the season gets under way?

Yet I know that somehow I'll find the time. "A college diploma," Ma always reminds me, "is money in the bank."

I wonder how much money the pros make. George Mikan. Ralph Beard. Max Zaslofsky. Harry Gallatin. Whitey Skoog. I can name every player in the N.B.A. Of course, my special heroes are the Knicks' Sweetwater Clifton, and Chuck Cooper of the Boston Celtics, the first Negroes ever to play in the pros. And how much money will I make?

My reveries are blasted by the urgent passage of a fire engine through the Harlem night. Me, I surely do love fires. If Ma wasn't asleep, maybe I'd run outside and give chase to the fire engine... like I used to do when I was a kid.

Forcing my attention back to Plato, I read the small words in the dim yellow light. Reading until the words fall into my lap like dead ants.

Chapter Three

October 15, 1950

—SIDNEY GOLDBERG—

The College of the City of New York, founded as a public trust in 1904, is situated on the western edge of Harlem between Washington and Edgemere Avenues, and bordered north and south by West 129th Street and West 134th. An imposing Gothic urban campus, cut into squares and rectangles by several busy city streets. Converse Avenue with its clanging trolley cars. West 131st Street noted for the various record stores selling jazz, rhythm and blues, and even gospel. The university's gray stone buildings tower above the neighborhood rooftops like castle keeps.

C.C.N.Y. offers no lawns and no dorms—and demands no tuition. Which is exactly why our entrance standards are so lofty: a high school average of at least 85. Almost as hard to gain admittance into C.C.N.Y. as into Columbia University (I never concern myself with the academic status of our basketball recruits. That's Weiss's bailiwick, along with his cousin in the admissions office. What the two of them do is their business and none of mine.)

Including graduate school, over thirty-four thousand full-time students are matriculated at C.C.N.Y., the world's third largest university. For most of these students, C.C.N.Y. reflects the glory of a country that provides a no-cost, guaranteed future solely on the basis of merit.

C.C.N.Y.'s elite young students are the activists, the freethinkers, the artists, the scholars, the engineers, the social workers, and the rabble of their generation. Meanwhile, on the bathroom walls and bulletin boards, they scream at the world in neat graffiti:

"COMMUNISM IS THE ANSWER!"

"VEGETARIANS ARE FRUITS"
"SOCIALISTS EAT SHIT"
"GUNS FOR THE ARABS, SNEAKERS FOR THE JEWS!"

Bully for them, and they'll learn soon enough it's money that moves the world. Yes, indeed. And I pity these youngsters because their world is so safe—no Huns or Nazis to vanquish, only minor skirmishes with endless legions of faceless yellow people. Instead of a red-blooded all-out war to preserve the free and the brave, they have a politically inspired "police action."

Oh, well. I digress.

Yes, the low-income, high-minded students of C.C.N.Y. Deluded young intellectuals searching for glorious causes. Their primary saving grace is that most of them are also basketball addicts. The C.C.N.Y. faculty routinely includes Nobel Prize winners and other famous professional geniuses, yet my boys are still the darlings of the campus.

A silver darkness inside Wingate Gymnasium, and an ancient rosewood basketball court that measures only eighty feet from baseline to baseline, a full four feet shorter than regulation. The gym is therefore called "The Bandbox," wherein I spin my spidery half-court zone defenses, innumerable numberings from 3-1-1 to 1-1-3. "The record," I'm fond of saying, "always speaks for itself."

@ the Bandbox — 221-68
@ road games — 110-89
@ the Garden — 34-21, including one
glorious N.I.T. championship

Framing the dark court, a brace of pull-out bleachers is capable of seating perhaps two thousand fortunate fans. The circular running track overhead can also contain another five hundred latecomers to stand and push and shove one another toward the front railing. During a ball game the spectators scream themselves hoarse with ear-splitting choruses of the famous City College cheer:

Allegaroo-garoo-garah!
Allegaroo-garoo-garah!
Eee-yah!
Eee-yah!
Sis-boom-bah!

A rather primitive rhyming scheme, and altogether meaning-less—but loud as the dickens!

All of my practices (basketball and otherwise) are closed to the public, but today, the first session of the new season, I've graciously allowed the gentlemen (ahem!) of the fourth estate to witness the proceedings.

During practice sessions my habit is to wear a customized purple nylon sweat suit with gold trim. The gold letters scripting **C.C.N.Y.** across the front of the sweatshirt are hidden now behind my folded arms as I stand safely out of bounds and astride the timeline, but they coordinate nicely with the gold chain that I wear around my neck to support my gold-plated whistle. Vanity? Most definitely. But also the trappings of command. "Move it, boys," I shout to my players as they run suicides to tone their legs. "We're anxious to get past the preliminaries."

(So what if the neck that wears the gold is somewhat wattled these days? That's unavoidable. Yes, of course I'm getting old. Yes, the specter of death hides in my shadow. But even if death should overtake me here and now, I have achieved several measures of everlasting greatness. I am the coach of the reigning National Invitation Tournament champions. I am the lord of basketball, and I rejoice in my own excellence.)

On the court the fifteen varsity cagers are divided into two squads, the players and the pretenders. Each of them wears dark purple pants of cotton, and the eight returning veterans have sleeveless purple jerseys. The other seven players are either useless scrubs or ignorant freshmen and wear white jerseys. (My intent here is to establish a natural hierarchy, as well as setting a goal for the younger boys.) There are no logos or lettering on any of the practice gear, only random yellow numbers on the backs of the jerseys. (This is to remind the boys that they are merely replaceable units in a larger entity.)

My assistant, Dickie Weiss, is a devious little weasel, a petite man who wears shoulder pads under his sweatshirt and considers himself quite dapper. It's been years since I relinquished the administration of the basketball budget to Weiss, and I'm sure he's a ganef, making his own shady deals with the sporting-goods suppliers just like I once did before my prudent investments in the stock market made me a wealthy man. Weiss believes that he's pulling the wool over my eyes—but in fact his petty embezzlements are the glittering chains that keep him here as my willing factotum. And I do give the little fool credit for consistently recruiting such excellent players. Yes, the players may laugh at him behind his back, but Weiss's beady blue eyes never overlook a crossed step, a head turned on defense, a zig instead of a zag. And he constantly calls the players to task in a shrill and scratchy voice as he conducts them through my famous Star Drill, a brutal and endless rehearsal of defensive footwork.

"Otis Hill doesn't have his ass down!" Weiss says. "Johnson's hands aren't up and moving!" Except for the padded shoulders, Weiss wears the same purple practice gear as the veteran players.

Occasionally I address a particular player's inadequacies in tones deliberately clipped and snide. "See to your balance, Big Boy. Your weight is too far forward. Suppose the Coach chose to sneak up behind you and kick you in the ass. Why, then, you'd fall on your face."

Nobody laughs, nobody dares speak as the players run through their paces. The muted shouts and the whistles, the slow initial unfolding of an infinity of zones. Today the team will be drilled in the stolid and universal 2-1-2 zone defense. The offense is also traditional, the weaving of men through devious patterns, so deft and precise.

The privileged spectators sit quietly clustered in one section of the cream-colored bleachers: Barney Polan (as usual) in the seventh-row center, flanked by Jimmy Cannon, who (as usual) smells of whiskey, and Westbrook Pegler, who (as usual) reeks of Wild Root Cream Oil. Arthur Daley, a second-stringer from *The New York Times*, is resplendent in a neat pinstriped suit. The oafish Jimmy Breslin from the *Tribune.* Damon Runyon from the *World Telegram-and-Sun.* All the heavy hitters are on hand except for Red Smith. (My sainted father, *requiescat in pace,* believed Red Smith to be a noble writer, who has cheated his own talent by not penning a novel. I know Smith to be even more pompous—and with less cause—than I am.)

The wordsmiths' notebooks are flipped open, their pencils waggle idly in their fingers. Cannon yawns (which I can tolerate because I do recognize his occasional gifts, his flair for metaphor and his boozy Irish poetry). Polan stealthily scratches the inside of his nose (the boob-in-chief, writing lumpish prose for his lumpen readership). Nationally celebrated journalists afraid to speak out loud lest I cast an imperial gaze upon them in dire warning.

Now Cannon fumbles open a squashed pack of Chesterfields, then he glances up at the several **NO SMOKING** signs posted on the walls.

"Shit," Cannon says too loudly, and I laugh lightly and ruefully shake my head to show them what a regular guy I really am.

Now Weiss directs the players through an elementary exercise designed to deflect a ball handler's quick progress toward the basket. White against purple, the younger *shvartzer* (Jackson? Johnson?) is paired with the Italian boy, an olive-skinned senior who is easily the team's best defender. The freshman's task is to dribble the full length of the court, changing direction at prescribed points (marked with plastic yellow traffic cones), with a specified swiveling of his hips and a front crossover. The wily senior is supposed to play defense with his hands clasped behind his back, using only fast footwork to challenge the freshman's every attempt to change direction. The black boy is quicker in his own angular way, but the more experienced player easily anticipates the freshman's every movement, consistently forcing him to give ground.

"Hurry along there," I say. "We haven't got all day to waste on preliminaries."

Meanwhile Weiss hops about and lightly claps his hands as he says, "There's Johnson with a ten-second violation! Good work, Giambalvo!"

Finally, in his frustration, the black boy breaks free of his defender's uncanny pressure by resorting to a behind-the-back dribble, the ball vanishing for a moment, then reappearing in the freshman's right hand. The brazen *shvartzer* laughs as the court lies open before him, beckoning him to swoop hoopward and dunk the ball. But for the first time since practice began, I toot on my golden whistle, a different sound than Weiss's, much more piercing. The players freeze in midstep, then quickly move away from the unfortunate freshman.

"You!" I shout. "Number Thirty-seven! Fancy Dan! What the fuck do you think you're doing? This isn't the fucking Harlem Globetrotters!" Then I nod imperceptibly toward Weiss, who forthwith dispatches the entire squad to run ten full-court windsprints.

"Push it!" Weiss insists. "Move! No stragglers! The last two finishers will run ten more!"

And the players race as if their lives are at stake, as crazed as horses caught in a flaming barn. All of them paying dearly for the black boy's sin.

—BARNEY—

After glancing at my wristwatch, I stand up and whisper, "'Scuse me, boys."

Then I walk into the hallway and find a public telephone. A nickel in the slot, chiming, activating a dial tone, and I dial the number from memory.

"Good morning, this is the Beth Abraham Home. How may I direct your call?"

"Room Two Forty-two, please."

"That would be... Mister Samuel Polanski?"

"That's correct. I'm his son, Barney."

"Just one moment, sir."

The wires hum and spark and my father is on the line, coughing.

"Hi, Pop."

"Who's this?"

"Barney. How're you feeling, Pop?"

"Feeling? I feel old, that's how I'm feeling. What else can I feel at my age? I feel old all the time. I'm telling you, Barney... this advice is the only advice I can give you.... You hear me, Barney?"

"Yeah, Pop."

"So listen to your father, Barney, and don't get old. Ha! That's my advice. Don't get old. That's a good one, ain't it?"

"Yeah, Pop. That's a good one. Are you taking your medicine?"

"*Vot den?* Or else the nurse says she'll have to pull down my trousers and give me a shot *in tochis* with a long needle. When are you coming to see me, *tateleh?*"

"You know how busy I am, Pop. What with college baskets just starting. And football. And next week's the Melrose Games...."

"Busy, busy.... So when're you coming to see your poppa?"

"As soon as I can."

"You know who was here today?" the old man asks in his rheumy voice. "My crazy brother Max was here with another crazy get-rich-quick scheme."

"Pop, what'd I tell you about giving money to Max?"

"It was only fifty bucks."

"For a horse?"

"For a horse, a ball game, the stock market.... Who can remember?"

"Pop. We've talked about this...."

In the background I can hear a man's voice saying something urgent and my father asking, "What?" The man speaks again, louder, but still too garbled for me to understand.

Then my father is back on the line. "I gotta go. It's the TV. Those puppets, whatzer names? The dragon with the buck tooth and the pretty lady?"

"'Kukla, Fran, and Ollie.'"

"Yeah, it's my favorite show on the TV. I love it when the dragon bites the one with the big round nose."

And the line is suddenly disconnected.

—OTIS HILL—

Man, I'm already sick of this tiresome boolshit. Him and his flunky teaching us the same old moves, the same old stupid-ass drills, just to keep us moving, just to keep us busy, just to pass the time and make us think we're really doing something that counts. Shit. Then when the games start for real, we wind up doing whatever the fuck we want to anyway. Goldberg and his sidekick, man. Neither one could coach his way out of a paper bag.

Ready or not, here comes six weeks of practice. Man, I wish I was in better shape. I know I'm gonna be sore as a motherfucker tomorrow. And the old coot won't even let us scrimmage full-court for another two weeks. Maybe I could accidentally sprain my ankle and lay low until right before the whistle blows. No, man. That ain't no good. I gotta be ready to go full-tilt or Gianelli might cut my share or cut my throat. Shit! And with Musberger graduated I gotta be the contact, making all the arrangements, picking up the payoffs, and doling it out to the guys. Fuck it, man. See if I don't take myself a little off the top for my troubles.

Man, I still can't believe I lost all that money on the horses. It's like Gianelli fixed all them races just to fuck me up and keep me on the line so I couldn't quit him even if I wanted to. Which I don't.

The only things I'm happy about? That my ma ain't lived long enough to see me the way I turned out. That this is the last season I got to play for Goldberg.

The only things I'm worried about? That small as I am, I can't cut it as a power player in the N.B.A. And then what? Play A.A.U. ball for some company in the Midwest. Don't sound like much. Shit! I should've spent the summer working on my outside game.

Fuck me.

—SIDNEY—

Weiss is teaching the team's primary and ancient offense, my beloved five-man weave. The most veteran players already move swiftly, pivoting sharply, faking with hips, eyes, and shoulders. Crisp, efficient. How could any defense ever keep up?

I remain unmoving and majestic on the sideline while Weiss barks corrections. "Again! Again, Isaacson! We'll stay here all night until you do it right! No! No! What happened to you over the summer? Amnesia? *Inside* the pick at the foul line extended! Inside!"

This has gone too far and I must intervene, speaking with a strained fondness that reveals my acute disappointment. "Isaacson. What are you? A moron? Morons aren't supposed to get into City."

Now the white team is playing offense—Big Boy is guarded by Lefty, and the younger *schvartzer* is being defended by an upperclassman. Over and over, the same programmed moves, the same choreographed feints. All in the name of discipline.

"Again," Weiss drones. "Hill, open up your right foot before you pivot. Greenberg, fake with your head *and* your shoulders."

Then, just as the young *schvartzer* receives a pass on the wing, his erstwhile defender missteps and falls tumbling to the floor. The freshman is quick to seize his chance—unguarded he dribbles to the basket and scores an easy layup unopposed.

The ball is barely through the net when I trill my whistle.

"You! Fancy Dan! You again? What the fuck are you doing?"

The freshman audibly gulps and dares to answer what he failed to recognize as a rhetorical question. "He... he fell down."

I huff and puff, pretending to be angry. But despite myself, I feel a twitch of compassion for the youngster. Honoring his talent and, yes, his innocence, too, I'll refrain from cursing him for his latest transgression. "Your assignment is to run the pattern, not to go off on your own little tangent. And what would you have done if he hadn't fallen? This isn't the Harlem Globetrotters."

Another nod and Weiss prompts the team through another ten grueling windsprints.

Eventually I mercifully sound my whistle to officially conclude C.C.N.Y.'s first practice session of the season. Then the players give way as I advance to my familiar spot at the very epicenter of the center-jump circle. It's time for my postpractice "lecture," a longstanding City College tradition.

The gathered journalists carefully dismount from the bleachers, not venturing to speak until the nearest door has closed behind them. So they all think that Sidney Goldberg is an asshole. What else is new?

And here I am, my fifteen players collected around me, fifteen fine young soldiers including the three *shvartzers,* my personal army encircled to secure my every flank. And on this very first day of practice, I'll woo my boys with compassion and wisdom.

"That was sloppy, boys. And sloppy means stupid." Revolving in a small slow circle as I speak, I give everyone an equal chance to hear me clearly, to gaze upon my face. "Not good enough, boys. Not by a long shot. We need more precision and that means more concentration and more commitment." I cease my small-footed circlings when I come face-to-face with the young *schvartzer.* "And you! Fancy Dan. Do you think we can win with your frivolous attitude?"

He shrugs, totally confounded.

Good. If I can destroy his own personal concept of logic, of cause and effect, then I can restructure the way he thinks, and eventually he'll be a useful ballplayer.

"The answer to my question is 'no,'" I say, then I smile tightly and nod for Weiss to assume command.

"All right, everybody!" Weiss pipes in his weasily little voice. "Just so's to make sure you'll sleep good tonight, why don't you guys line up on the baseline and give me ten more windsprints?"

Chapter Four

November 29, 1950

—JUNIOR—

Staring at the small yellow flame. The hot light dancing atop the stubby white candle suggests the stump of a finger on fire. I blink and my eyes feel dry and heavy. In truth, I'm much drunker than I want to be. The brief light wavers in the wake of a waiter bustling past the table, the flame bending again as several couples move toward the dance floor. Still, my heavy gaze remains fixed. I barely hear: the sound of ice cubes tinkling in someone's glass, the merry voices, the insistent laughter, the distant pounding of music. Some old familiar song—"I Can Dream, Can't I?"

I hope that somewhere within that slow fire, that sun-colored light, there's a source of healing, of peace. Some hint perhaps of Jesus burning in white glory. Something similar to what my mom sees in all those candle flames she lights at the plaster feet of the Holy Mother at St. Bridget's Church on DeKalb Avenue. Ellie Paluski, who prays every day that I'll see the light and decide to be a priest. (Yeah, right? And become a dickless geek like the teachers at St. John's? No thanks, Mom.)

My mom's favorite passage in her worn leather-bound Bible comes from Luke, where Jesus said, "God is love."

However, according to my dad, neither God nor love have anything to do with anything. "It's all about the feel of a basketball in your hands," my dad tells me, "and your faith that tells you the shot is good even before you release the ball. And the thrill of a dancing net. And the times when the rim reaches out to you and the basket is as wide as the rings of Saturn. That's when you'll find God and love and peace of mind. Not in some dead book."

Dad taught me how to shoot. *Pow!* Hit that bull's-eye. And I grew up believing that I could shoot my way out of any kind of trouble.

My dad taught me other valuable lessons, too. In the fifth grade, when I demanded a weekly allowance, he showed me how to set up a simple betting scheme to entice my classmates' lunch money into my pocket. (Pick three baseball players in today's games, and if they total six hits, you'll win six-to-one on your bet. Go ahead. Everybody's doing it.) When Sheldon Shapiro began offering the same bet at seven-to-one odds, I sought my father's advice, and he said, "Who's the biggest bully in the class? Go make a deal with him to muscle out the kid who aced you."

My dad knew everything about everything, and we were buddies. We'd play H-O-R-S-E in the playground and no matter how many letters he'd spot me, I'd still lose. We'd also compete one-on-one and he'd spot me a diminishing number of points as I got bigger and he got older, and he'd still beat me. We'd sit in the bleachers and root for the Dodgers. We went to football games and basketball games and boxing matches. He called me his "main man," and I loved him much more than I loved my mom. (She was such a nag. "Clean up your room."... "Say your prayers.")

In our neighborhood everybody bet on some kind of sporting event. Everybody had a hot tip on something. There were two bookies working out of the local candy store and another one in the deli department at the A & P. By the time I was twelve, I'd mastered an outlandish repertoire of trick shots at various odds—eight-to-one for a backward free throw; five-to-one for a layup that bounced off my head, off the backboard, and through the hoop; twenty-five-to-one for a hook shot from midcourt. And the suckers couldn't get their money down fast enough.

As far as I knew, Dad worked as a "consultant" for a chain of sporting-goods emporiums (The Athlete's Advantage, Inc.), a job that gradu-ally eroded his wind, his legs, and tragically his shot. By the time I was fourteen, the shot-matching games went my way, and he'd have to rough me up to win his share of our one-on-one confrontations. Once, when he shouldered me into a pole and refused to admit the foul, I went nuts and threw a haymaker that clipped his jaw. Immediately I began to cry, and he hugged me man-to-man, and we forgave each other.

And Mom used to nag him, too.

"That's three times this week, Raymond, that you stayed out all night."

"Just business, honey. Chauffering that congressman around town, then cleaning his vomit off his clothes and getting him safely to bed. Then the other night I had to deal with the teamsters union because some of the drivers've been stealing stuff off the trucks. Then last night there was a fire in the warehouse that I had to check out. When I'm on the job until four or five in the morning, I'd rather find myself a hotel room somewhere than come home and wake you and the boy. You know?"

She knew all right. *"He that speaketh lies shall perish."*

To no one's surprise, I became an All-Catholic League player at St. John's Prep, and even though I was widely recruited, my mind was set on following my father's footsteps to St. John's.

And, sure, I felt guilty about rigging ball games—and I'd rather die than have my dad find me out. Funny thing is, I can't really remember exactly how it all got started. I remember meeting Rosie and Johnny Boy at some big-deal alumni's shindig in Riverdale. And I also remem-ber being impressed by Billy Becker's stories about free money. (Yes, the same Billy Becker who's an All-Star with the Boston Celtics.) But I can't remember which happened first. All I know is this—that I hate it when we have to fix a ball game. Those are the poisonous games, the evil games, that neither me nor God will ever forget. Last season, for the first time even some of the "straight" games seemed to be tainted.

But, I swear to God, I don't know how to stop. I love the money, and I love acting like a big wheel, and I love fucking Rosie, and everybody says that I've got the world by the nuts, but I swear... sometimes I hate myself.

"I'm aware there's much disillusion there
But I can dream, can't I?"

And the small candle flame that now pinches at my eyes offers me no comfort.

"Hey, Junior! What the fuck're you? A fucking moth?"

It's Gianelli laughing at me, the old man's narrow chin stabbing into the candlelight, laughing with his thin lips stretched to show his yellowed and wobbling teeth. It's Gianelli, swallowing his laughter, releasing only a series of dry puffs: "Keh, keh, keh...." Look at that vain old man in his fancy blue suit and his red tie handpainted in a bold Hawaiian design.

If he only knew...

—ROSIE—

The old fuck. With his daily manicures, and his perfect shaves, with the hot towels and ointments that tighten his flesh, even the practiced flashing of his diamond pinky ring, all designed to convince Johnny Boy that at age sixty-seven he's still suave as ever, still the able-bodied he-man.

The fucking asshole. Let him die, right this minute. Let him choke on his fucking drink. Then I'll laugh and I'll dance and I'll piss on his grave.

The decrepit old bastard, he thinks he knows me, thinks he owns me. "Flirt with them," he says. "Promise them everything. Let them get close enough to smell it, but don't give them shit."

If he only knew....

Look at how startled Junior is, like Gianelli just caught him choking his chicken in public.

"What're you," Gianelli says again, "a fucking moth?"

Also seated at the table are two of Junior's teammates: Jimmy McCoy and Shawn Sweeney, both of them drunk and bleary-eyed. I'm sure that these two jackoffs are bragging to all their buddies that they've been fucking me all along. That's because they're too ashamed to admit they ain't.

"A fucking moth!" McCoy bellows, his red crew cut bristling and flashing in the light of a thousand chandeliers. Good ol' half-wit Jimmy McCoy, wearing a red plaid sports jacket that he outgrew in high school. With his hairy red wrists thrust from the sleeves. With his royal blue necktie knotted too tightly and a snot-encrusted handkerchief drooping from his breast pocket. Even when sober, McCoy's pasty pink face seems to be flushed with a beery good time. The six-foot-six-inch, 225-

pound senior is St. John's leading rebounder—and when McCoy grows up, he wants to be just like Junior. "A fucking moth!" McCoy says again. "Look! Junior's gonna burn his fucking Pollack nose off!"

Shawn Sweeney is a dour point guard with quick feet and steady hands. Like Junior, Sweeney is a spiffy dresser, all dapper in his gray gabardine suit. The slick hair. The cologne. The image is marred only by a small overbite that makes Sweeney look like a hayseed. But at five-eight and a tensile 170 pounds, Sweeney is feisty as a cat in a bag. There's Sweeney jabbing a sudden elbow into McCoy's rib cage and saying, "Simmer down, big fella. This ain't the Shamrock Lounge. Control yourself."

McCoy's response is once again too loud and too rude. "Fuck you, Sweeney! You control your own fucking self!"

"Easy, boys," Gianelli says quickly, stretching his wobbling smile ever wider. "Let's remember where we are."

—JUNIOR—

The fabulous Copacabana on Broadway and East Forty-third Street, where the elite meet to eat. The syncopated music and the fancy dancers, the drinking and feasting in merry celebration. The waiters dressed in tuxedos, picking their way gracefully from table to table, painstakingly polite, even calling McCoy "sir." The beautiful showgirls dressed in tailored tuxedo tops and short black skirts who roam through the elegant bustle selling fresh flowers or cigarettes. For fifteen bucks a gorgeous photographer will chirp, "Say cheese," then freeze the moment for posterity. All the Broadway crowd like the Copa late at night. The ritzy high society too, and certainly the rubbernecking tourists. Look, ain't that Walter Winchell sitting at that corner table? Who's the blonde with him? And look over there. Ain't that Perry Como? Sammy Kaye? Ain't that Howard Keel? Paulette Goddard? Ain't that Ray Paluski's son? Fuckin' A! I can't get enough of this!

I drain my latest glass of beer, my ninth, but who's counting? It tastes flat and pissy. So I tap the elbow of a passing waiter and order a double scotch on the rocks. (I wish I had a pinky ring to flash in the candlelight.) The waiter glances at Gianelli, who nods. With the waiter gone, Gianelli casts his tight, benevolent smile in my direction and says, "Easy on the sauce, son. The season starts tomorrow night."

"Don't I know it," I say. "But I'm too nervous to sleep anyway, you know? Might as well have myself a good time. . . . Hey, you guys. Who's got the Sen-Sen?"

"Don't sweat the small stuff," says Sweeney. "Coach Mack's hangovers are always worse than ours. He won't notice nothing."

Suddenly the oafish McCoy pounds the table with a huge fist, bouncing the silverware and making the glasses jingle. "Hey, Sweeney! I don't care how fucking drunk I am. I ain't gonna let you say nothing bad about Coach Mack."

Sweeney just smiles and says, "Me say something bad about Coach Mack? Hey, Jimbo, you're barking up the wrong tree. I love Coach Mack like he was my own father. Ain't that right, Junior? Don't I always say that?"

"Sure thing," I say, happy to be the arbitrator. "Everybody knows that Coach Mack is the fucking greatest. Lookit. He runs the easiest practices ever. He has no curfew on the road. Not even when we go to Philly. And he fixes any of our grades that ain't up to par. Hey, he even puts all our friends' names on the Gate List at the Garden so's they can get in for free. I mean, how can anyone not love Coach Mack? He's like Santa Claus with a whistle around his neck."

Vindicated, Sweeney says, "I just got only one complaint against Coach Mack. After three years I'm getting sick of his flex offense. It's so boring. Pick down, cut across, pop up, pick down, cut across...."

"Boring," says Gianelli, "but effective."

Jesus! I can't keep my eyes off of Rosie. For the evening's festivities, she wears an elaborate orchid corsage pinned to the sleeve of a green taffeta dress. Her party-time makeup makes her look lovely and untamed. And I'm so drawn to her narrow, red-painted, ravenous mouth as she slowly licks the pink plastic stirrer that came with her highball.

Jesus! I've got a boner! What if I came in my pants? A shudder, a sudden yelp, a wet stain...then what? A gunshot?

...And there's that birdbrain McCoy, finally subdued, sitting motionless with his eyes closed. I wonder what he's thinking about. A steak? A glass of beer? A ten-dollar bill? A pair of tits? Then McCoy suddenly raises his head and calmly says, "You know what I really like to do? I like to fuck dames up the shit chute."

Rosie trills a small laugh while me and Sweeney exchange a fearful glance. But Gianelli is also laughing. "Keh, keh, keh.... Don't you worry, boys. My Rosie here is a real modern woman. Strictly up-to-date. She ain't offended. Ain't that the truth, lovie?"

"That's right," Rosie says. "I'm as up-to-date as tomorrow's news."

"Anyway...," I say, sitting up straight and focusing my full attention on Gianelli. Is my tie on straight? Could I walk a chalked line? Could I count backward from a hundred? No matter. The opening game of my last basketball season at St. John's is close at hand and my hands are still empty (not even counting the money I owe that low-life bookie to cover all my dumb-ass bets on the Dodgers). Time out. Time to get down to business. "So tell me, Johnny Boy. What's the deal? We think that since the three of us here are seniors, we should get a raise this season."

—JOHNNY BOY GIANELLI—

Ｗhat children they are. I don't give a shit that they're such wonder-ful, graceful athletes. All I care about is that everybody is always kissing their asses and they think the world was created for their pleasure. Like children, they get excited over trinkets. Like children, they have greedy hands. They're too innocent and too childlike to know good from evil, and that makes them weak. And I ask myself why God created so many weaklings. And the answer is so that sharks like me can eat.

But life ain't always so simple, and here's the kicker: Like these children, I can't tell the difference between good and evil. My excuse is that I'm too old and too corrupt.

I wonder who's feeding on me.

"Sure, boys," I say, instantly agreeable. "I was just thinking the very same thing. Ain't that some coincidence? You and me, Junior. We're on the same wavelength." I pause to swill the ice around in my drink. "Tell you what, boys...."

Sweeney swivels in his seat to look sidewise at me. McCoy looks slowly from me to Junior.

"Last year you got what?" I ask, teasing them. "Two grand each for going under, right? And a grand and a half for going over. Tell you what. This year, because you're seniors, how about three grand for under and two grand for over?"

Junior doesn't blink, I'll give him credit for that. "Three and a half and two and a half," he says.

Bah. He's talking about pocket change. When I've got a game in the bag, I can make anywhere from fifty to a hundred G's.

"You got it," I say, "but only on one condition. That we start tomorrow night when nobody'll suspect anything's amiss. The first game of the season against Southern Missouri at the Garden. Don't you love it?"

—JUNIOR—

Fuck me! I want to win that game! I want to have fun!

But Sweeney and McCoy are nodding like crazy and already counting their money. What would they think if I got cold feet? What would Rosie think?

—ROSIE—

Don't do it, Junior. Tell the old coot to stick it up his ass. Be a man. Don't let him push you around.

I shake my head slowly from side to side, but all the kid wants to do is prove that his dick is bigger than anyone else's.

—JUNIOR—

"That's hunky-dorey with me," I say with bravado. "I don't know about you two palookas, but I could sure use some big money right about now."

McCoy laughs loudly. "Me too," he says.

When Sweeney feigns indifference, I'm quick to say, "So, Johnny Boy...what's the spread looking like and which way do you want us to go?"

Gianelli hunches closer over the table. "For the second game, in case you're interested, it's City minus two-and-a-half over Rhinegold. That's the game everybody's interested in. I'd say it's a firm line, two-and-a-half, 'cause most of the big money's already on board. And in your game? Well, now, why don't you tell me what *you* think the spread should be?"

I'm definitely intrigued. Let's see...last season the Southern Missouri Terriers had a record of 17-and-8, playing mostly a cream-puff schedule, which is why they were never considered for inclusion in last year's N.I.T. This year the Terriers have graduated their starting backcourt, but remain big up front—six-six, six-eight, both juniors, and their high-scoring senior center, Jim Barlow, is a bona fide six-ten. Instead of practicing today, Coach Mack showed us a game film and explained how and why we're easily the superior team, much quicker and certainly more experienced against nationally ranked competition. Then "Big Mack" listed several of our home-court advantages: "We'll all be sleeping soundly in our own beds tonight, and meanwhile they'll all be tossing and turning in their strange hotel beds. Plus, like I already said, we're flat out quicker than them. Plus, I'm better looking than their coach, What's-izz-name? Plus, when I was a kid I had my first holy communion with Father Joseph, the father of one of tomorrow night's referees." Coach Mack also counts on most visiting teams developing "Gardenitis" and suffering nervous hands and clumsy shooting.

Whatever the spread, I always have the opposition well scouted: Southern Missouri hasn't played in the Garden since 1948, when they stunk up the court in losing to N.Y.U. by 78–56.

"My own opinion," I finally say, "is that we should be favored by four-and-a-half points."

"Keh, keh. You wish. The line I got, you guys are minus seven-and-a-half."

"Jesus," says Sweeney. "That's a lotta points to be giving to anybody. Even if we was playing the Sisters of the Poor."

"That's right," Gianelli says with his mirthless grin. "But it's twenty-five fat juicy C-notes for each of you to win by at least eight. I'll make the payoff right afterward in the same place as always. Cash on the line. What d'ya think, boys?"

I laugh, the picture of confidence. "Easy as pie.... All's we gotta do is keep the game kinda close, you know? Just make sure the scrubbies stay safely on the bench. Get it, McCoy? We don't want to let fuckups like Dodge and Rooney get a chance to go out there and play crazy and fuck up our payday. We want to play it just like we did against St. Joe's last year. Remember?"

"Sort of," says McCoy. What a fuckin' dumbbell.

"Look...we get ahead early, see? We kick their asses in a hurry. Show them who's boss. Then we stay maybe ten to twelve points ahead all the rest of the way. That makes sure it's close enough for Coach to keep us out there, see? Then we air it out in the final few minutes just to make sure. Hey, going over the spread against a shitty team is easier than going under against a good team."

McCoy can't remember the question. Sweeney is too busy sneaking glances at Rosie's tits to pay attention. Gianelli laughs, "Keh, keh...you've got a talent, all right. Raymond Paluski, Junior. Just like your old man. Both of you always got yourselves a game plan. Is it a deal?"

Without even looking at my teammates, I say, "It's a deal."

Then Gianelli raises his glass and we all follow suit as he proposes a toast:

"To James Naismith, who invented the great game of basketball. And to Chicago Charlie, who invented the point spread. Salud!"

"Salud!"

"Eh, salud!"

Gianelli flags down a passing photo-girl and pays for a posed picture, all of the celebrants toasting ourselves with half-empty glasses. Always the sport, Gianelli folds a five-dollar tip into the photographer's cleavage.

"Thank you, sir," she says brightly, a leggy brunette. Gianelli supplies the address of his construction company and she claims that the photograph will be in the mail by Monday.

Raising myself from my chair with only moderate difficulty, I say, "Excuse me, everybody. I've got to make a deposit." I locate a public phone in the vestibule near the men's room.

"Hullo?"

"Yeah. It's me."

"It's me? Me who?"

"You know who," I say, already impatient. "Just don't mention my name on the phone."

"Christ Almighty. Don't be so fucking paranoid. Nobody knows and nobody cares. Believe me, people don't believe what they don't want to believe."

"I don't believe you.... Anyway, is your deal still on the table?"

"You bet. Just tell me what Gian—"

"Don't."

"Okay, okay. You tell me Mister G's line and I'll credit your account for another C-note. Just like we said."

"Sure thing.... He has City minus two-and-a-half."

"That's about right. And for the first game?"

"The visitors plus seven-and-a-half."

"Holy shit. That's way too much. I got you guys minus four-and-a-half."

I hear a strange clicking on the line, like a rapid-fire Morse code, then a low-level buzzing. "What's that?" I ask.

"Nothing," Klein says. "There was a fire in the bakery on the corner yesterday morning, and the phone's been fucked up ever since. Either that or the FBI's zeroed in on me. Ha! So who do you think is giving Mister G that cockamamie spread?"

"Who knows? There's still a lot of time before the game starts. Maybe somebody's waiting in the woodpile to make the home team a better offer."

"You know something, Junior? Sometimes I think you're not nearly as dumb as you look."

"Don't call me that, you stupid asshole!... Anyway, listen up. I'll take City minus two-and-a-half for a C-note."

"You got it, pal."

"Where's the spread heading?"

"There's been nothing unusual, but tomorrow's another day."

"All right. See you then. We'll talk some more."

"This is Agent Three-thirteen signing off. You hear me, Hoover? You fucking little runt!"

Back at the table several of the Copa's showgirls have stopped by to greet Rosie. She's their heroine—a high-kicker who married rich. Who cares that her Sugar Daddy is old and dried up? Rosie's legit these days. The showgirls blatantly flirt with McCoy and Sweeney, who're both stunned into slobbering silence and alcoholic flushes.

... And the small candle flame flickers, and its heart is bright and searing.

Chapter Five

November 30, 1950

—BARNEY—

My idea of heaven is my snug three-room apartment—#10B—on Niles Avenue in the Flatbush section of Brooklyn. Whatever the season, whatever the weather, my window shades are drawn for absolute privacy, and also to preserve the mood of whatever I happen to be either reading or writing. Whenever I'm reading at my leisure, I'll sit in the lamplit darkness on my broken-backed green velvet easy chair with my feet propped up on a rickety walnut coffee table that Sarah bought for two dollars at a tag sale over on Avenue X, the table now stained with coffee rings and blots of spilled ink. I'm comforted, too, by my bookcases, black walnut sentries stationed at every patch of bare wall. My guess is that I own about two thousand books, the novels arranged alphabetically from Anonymous to Zola. Of course, I mostly read Shakespeare, but also Christopher Marlowe, Thomas Kyd, and Ben Jonson just to make sure. And the only housekeeping duty that I embrace is a daily dusting of my bookshelves.

Otherwise my dirty clothing is unceremoniously draped on chair-backs. Mismatched socks are gloriously strewn on the floor. Careless piles of magazines are underfoot, and newspapers are randomly discarded. (It's called "freedom," not being a slave to my possessions.) In addition, the ancient, black-blotched linoleum-covered floors in all three rooms are also littered with greasy paper bags, the remains of my favorite take-home meals—hot dogs, kasha knishes, and pastrami sandwiches from a strictly kosher delicatessen over on Barkley Street. Unwashed dishes are stacked in the kitchen sink. The toilet bowl is indelibly shit-stained. Tufts of greasy hair clog the drain in the bathtub.

"Yes, heaven is everywhere at home...."

I realize that my slovenly "bachelor pad" is a belated protest against Sarah's incessant cleaning and dusting. I can still hear her hocking me to "have a place for everything and put everything in its place." She used to follow me around spritzing Pine Fresh deodorant everywhere my cigar smoke touched a piece of furniture. Living with her was like living in a museum.

Nowadays I'm committed to establishing simplicity and comfort in my days and ways (and my Saturday mornings). I just toss off the refuse of my life with no care where anything lands —and every month, I simply pay an agency fifteen dollars to send a "girl" to clean up. They're mostly skinny, unappealing shiksas, but once one of them offered to fuck me for a five-dollar bill. I'm a sport, so even though I declined, I did her a favor and tipped her an extra three bucks. What the hell? Easy go, easy come.

Otherwise it's easy for me to ignore them while I work at my desk composing another small masterpiece.

And oh, how I love to write. Trying to make the words fit just so, to find the epiphany in every home run and called third strike. My beloved typewriter is an ancient Royal that I use carefully, almost tenderly... **DATELINE, BROOKLYN...** with every letter pressed separately and crackling like a gunshot. Also on my cluttered desk, a chipped white coffee cup filled with pencils and pens. Sheafs of yellow foolscap and white typing paper. A box of black, slick-sided carbon paper. On the wall above, a small cork-surfaced bulletin board is pinned with scraps of newsprint, each item suggesting a future column: Ned Garver and his fluttery knuckleball. Johnny Mize and his 48-ounce bat, the heaviest in the majors. Ewell Blackwell has only one kidney. Ted Williams is the big leagues' only active .400 hitter. Preacher Roe's lifetime batting average is .037. Clipped from a magazine in a doctor's office, a chiropractic analysis of Stan Musial's corkscrew batting stance.

For further inspiration, hanging on the wall beside the bulletin board is a single framed photograph of me and Jackie Robinson standing awkwardly side by side in front of the Dodgers' dugout.

Ah, yes.

> *"The poet's eye, in a fine frenzy rolling,*
> *Doth glance from heaven to earth, from earth*
>   *to heaven..."*

I trust that my eternal reward will be the perpetuation of this perfect moment: sitting in my green chair, reading the Bard on a Saturday morning, no column due until tomorrow night at eleven sharp, which is a million years away from now. A moist cigar stub carefully tucked behind my left ear while I intermittently eat huge spoonfuls of old oatmeal from a bowl set on my lap. Relishing the "saltness of time." My Saturday mornings giving spice to the rest of my workaday week. Making my life so peaceful, so bounteous, so profound.

Also, reading the mail when it comes. A letter from Sarah's lawyer asking for more money. (More money so she can have extra cheese on her pizzas.) Inevitably an invitation to speak to Rotarians, Lions, Kiwanians, Elks, and/or Odd Fellows. And always the latest *Sporting News* to study.

So, too, the "Schwartz Pages" in *The Sentinel,* just to see if that asshole Morty Bernard has cut a precious inch or two from my column. (Not to worry, though. I make certain to file all the carbons of my originals so that someday my mortal prose might be published intact in *The Collected Woiks*.)

The subject of today's column is the imminent local college basketball season, and my annual preview thereof: City College is tabbed as the finest team in the East, challenged only by Holy Cross with All-American Bob Cousy. City's biggest drawback is the "unaccountable" inconsistency of Otis Hill, "who, at the top of his game, is the best power player in captivity." At the risk of incurring Sidney Goldberg's displeasure, I further suggest that perhaps Hill is playing too many "backboard-banging, body-smashing minutes." Moreover, Royce Johnson is touted as a future All-American who might languish on the bench for most of the season. The only pertinent quote I culled from Goldberg is this: "Unfortunately the young freshman will have to learn the ropes the hard way. There's no 'Experience Pill' to give him."

After the reigning N.I.T. champs, Rhinegold is definitely New York City's most potent squad. Sammy Goodrich is hailed as a potential First Team All-American. An N.I.T. bid is "to be expected," and the Golden Lions are one of the most "dangerous" teams in the nation.

Out on a limb, I declare the '50-'51 St. John's Redmen to be the school's best group of cagers since the fabulous Wizard Five. They're quick and experienced in the backcourt and powerful (if undersized) up front. Ray Paluski, Jr., is cited as the team's driving force who should "blossom" this year. Historically the Redmen seem to wilt in close ball games, but Junior's "coming of age" will provide "go-to offense in the clutch." Another certain N.I.T. selection.

While I peruse my own pithy words, I absently scratch my bare head and then try to ignore several moist white flakes that fall into my cereal. Extra protein.

The also-rans are St. Francis, N.Y.U., and Adelphi. In conclusion I boldly claim that the college teams in New York City can match the best teams offered by any other "*state* in the Union." And that asshole Bernard hasn't touched a single gold-plated word.

God, how I love Saturday mornings at home.

"For it's jolly old Saturday,
Mad-as-a-hatter-day,
Nothing-much-matter-day!"

And then the telephone rings.

I never pick up the receiver until the fifth ring, to suggest that the caller has just interrupted the composition of another *opus minimus.* "Hello," I say with a cultivated tone of boredom and annoyance. "Who is it?"

"Heigh ho, Barney. It's me, the original Ray Paluski. How're they hanging?"

"Ray! So great to hear from you. Where the hell you been hiding yourself? What'chu been doing?"

"I been here and there. Doing this and that. Say, I ain't got much time to spare. Just called to ask if you'd like to hook up in the Garden later tonight. I got something important I want to ask you about."

"Sure, Ray."

"Terrific. And if we don't find each other, how's about I'll meet you in Toots Shor's about an hour after the final buzzer?"

"What's the big secret, Ray? Gimme a hint."

"No chance. Everybody's phone is tapped. See ya then."

Ah, yes. A peaceable Saturday morning, but not without its intrigue. Still another reason to look forward to tonight's ball games. My guess is that Ray either wants to tap me for a loan, an intro to one of the Dodgers, or perhaps a plug in "Sports A-Plenty" for a buddy's new restaurant.

Peaceful beyond measure. Time passing as slowly as possible. My life as solid as aged concrete.

Looking up from my reading matter, I suddenly glance at the ominous black telephone, half hoping that someone else will call me. Some old friend. Who? Nobody.

If my apartment is heaven, then the Garden is Eden.

Whatever the sport, I thrill when the houselights dim and the opponents first appear on the field of battle. Even the hockey games have a spectacular appeal, the headlong speed and the reckless violence, the players raising sparkling white dust whenever they wheel to chase the puck. Ordinarily boxing is an odious "sport," yet I cannot deny the pleasure of my own cruel delirium when Joe Louis smashed "Two Ton" Tony Galento's face into jelly. Ah, the woody smells of the pole-vault and the high-jump pits when the Wanamaker Games are in session.

As I sit enthroned at the press table, the referees stop by to pay their respects.

"Hi, Barney."

"What d'ya say, Barney?"

"Howdy, boys. What's the buzz?"

"Nothin' much, Barney. May the best team win."

Passing fans pause to tap my shoulder and ask, "Who ya rootin' for, Barney?"

"I always root for the underdog to win in triple overtime."

Jimmy Cannon sits to my left, barely watching the ball game (another center jump, another season, somebody wins, somebody loses). Instead Cannon is jotting down notes for another of his trade-mark columns, "Nobody Asked Me But," featuring his own inimitable punchlines and hard-boiled aphorisms: "The years are not educators; they are vandals who steal from a man the nimble power of his youth." Also: "We have a tendency to persecute the young because we envy their defiance." What a great concept. Several years back I'd even made one futile attempt to imitate Cannon's style. "Gut Feelings," I called it. The highlight was, "Never trust a skinny cook or a bald barber." Ugh.

Guarding my right flank is young Paul Vaccaro from the *Bronx Home News*, a wiseass punk who talks too much.

As the teams warm up, I grandly, and without apology, belch, tasting once more my standard pregame ritual: noshing a hot dog and orange drink at the counter in Nedick's right next door to the Garden's main entrance at the corner of Fifty-seventh Street and Seventh Avenue. Breathing in the delicious scents of fried grease and secondhand cigar smoke. Listening to the bettors trying to hustle each other. Discovering, despite myself, the up-to-the-minute point spreads. Belching again with overtones of sauerkraut.

And here inside "The World's Most Famous Arena," sixteen thousand fans are primed to shriek at every bounce of the ball, at every whistle.

From the opening tip, I know that the underdog Southern Missouri Terriers have no chance: There's Junior at a mere six-three facing off against six-ten Jim Barlow, with Junior much quicker off the mark and controlling the game's first possession...over to Shawn Sweeney, then back to Junior hustling down the lane.

My game notes are notoriously precise.

		ST J	SM
1Q	0:04 PALUSKI, driving lay-in	2	0

As the game unfolds, I also scribble a few suggestive sentences: "St. John's came out of the gate playing at a hundred miles per hour, speeding to an early 11–3 lead.... The visitors' young guards were at the mercy of Shawn Sweeney."

In the pivot Junior fakes and jukes, always with that sweet spin of his, left to right, spinning tightly, coming out the other side ready to shoot.

And despite the hype, big Barlow is a stiff. He has bad hands. Poor lateral movement. A limp dick instead of a heart. McCoy eats his lunch.

And with Sweeney operating like a Park Avenue brain surgeon, St. John's vaunted flex offense repeatedly slices huge holes in the Terriers' defense. Clearly the visitors are getting...what? "...their clocks cleaned...their doors blown off...." Which reads better?

Zip. There goes Sweeney knifing to the hoop, then serving a soft bounce pass to Junior for a "snowbird." *Zap*. Another turnover from the visitors' inexperienced backcourt.

Vaccaro laughs. "The last time I saw so many turnovers I was in a bakery."

Barlow never passes the ball, and ends up shooting only 3-for-14 from the field. When one of the big man's short right-handed hooks misses badly, the shot barely snagging a piece of the backboard, several fans stand up and shout, "Dumper!"

Even Vaccaro smiles and says, "This ball game smells like a dead fish."

But I disagree. "It's only Gardenitis."

Southern Missouri rallies only when Barlow is benched with his third personal foul, and the margin quickly narrows to 21–26. Say, when did McCoy's hands turn numb and Sweeney's sneakers turn to lead?

"Dump!"

Not a chance. Just the boyos losing interest and playing down to the competition.

Sweeney throws a pass into the cheap seats. McCoy fumbles another rebound out of bounds. Only Junior plays with consistency: courageous in the shadow of the hoop. Snapping the net with his high looping one-handers—the ball spinning tightly off his clawed right hand, his shooting arm thrusting forward as though to grab the basket and bring it closer. By my reckoning, Junior has fourteen points with 1:48 remaining in the second quarter— and St. John's margin is fifteen, when Sweeney and McCoy suddenly yell something at their captain, who merely nods, annoyed, but agreeable. Junior then misfires on his next three shots and the Redmen lead 32–24 at the half-time intermission.

I wander through the noisy crowd, looking for Paluski Senior. On my rounds I spot the C.C.N.Y. players sitting nervously in the stands, wearing ties and jackets. Rhinegold's players wear sweat suits. There's Goldberg hiding in the locker-room corridor chain-smoking his Chesterfields and staring at the floor. There's Johnny Boy Gianelli and that tinhorn Georgie Klein walking in tandem toward the men's room, arguing over something, then hushing up when I approach.

But no sign of Ray Paluski, the elder.

Henry Carlson stands near the pressroom door joking with several out-of-town reporters. "I hate practice," Carlson is saying. "The sound of all those basketballs bouncing gives me a headache. I love coaching ball games because there's only one ball bouncing."

The second half repeats the pattern: St. John's starts out with precise plays and ruthless defense, then slackens when their lead exceeds twelve. As before, McCoy and Sweeney are plagued with careless lapses, Barlow can't play dead, and the score gets close only when Barlow takes a seat.

"Dumper!"

"Fixer!"

The Redmen's starting five finally regain their stride late in the fourth quarter, extending to an eighteen-point lead and enabling Coach Mack to empty his bench with less than four minutes remaining. The final score favors St. John's by 73–59. Junior racks up impressive numbers—twenty-five points and twelve rebounds.

And whom do I meet at the beer stand between games? My Uncle Max. We exchange a brief hug.

Max is a lean man with a full head of wavy brown hair. A hearty septuagenarian, Max is never sick. Not a cold, not a sneeze, not even a cough. His trim, ax-shaped face is as smooth as the face of a man thirty years his junior. Only his eyes are old, blue and cloudy.

"Nu, nephew? So how's Schloime? You hear from him lately?"

"Pop's fine, Uncle Max. I just spoke to him yesterday. He's a little absentminded these days, but I guess that's normal for a man his age."

"Normal? Who's to say what's normal? Believe me, nephew. Nothing about my brother Schloime is normal. You know what I'm saying?"

Max likes to display his hands when he talks: His perfect fingernails, like he's just had a manicure. His perfectly tailored gray serge suit, much too sporty for someone who works in a booth making change at the Chambers Street station on the I.R.T.

"Uncle Max. I've gotta ask you to please leave Pop alone. Please stop borrowing money from him. If you're short, ask me. Not him."

"Ask you? An uncle borrowing money from a nephew? *Oy, tateleh.* If Schloime ever found out, he'd have a conniption. Keep your money, Barney. I thank you for the offer, but your money I don't need. Especially not after tonight."

"Don't even start, Uncle Max. I don't want to hear any more of your crazy stories."

"Not so crazy, nephew. Complicated, yes. But not so crazy. Information, nephew. It's worth its weight in gold."

"Tell it to the judge, Uncle Max. Gambling is illegal."

"Ha. Then half of New York should be in the hoosegow. How can you be so blind, nephew? Something stinks to high heaven in the state of Denmark and all you smell is roses."

"You're just speculating. I'm a writer. I need the proof of something to believe it."

"The proof is that the spread in the City College game goes from two-and-a-half to one-and-a-half in about thirty minutes."

"That's just supply and demand. Bookies evening up their ledgers. C'mon, Uncle Max. These are college kids we're talking about."

"Yeah, yeah. Might as well talk to the wall. So, maybe you'll buy your uncle a drink after the game? Or maybe I'll buy you one if City doesn't cover. Only one-and-a-half points, nephew. You want I should put you down for some pin money, maybe?"

"Uncle Max, don't do me no favors. Don't tell me no more crazy stories and don't borrow no more money from Pop."

"All right, *boychik*. Whatever makes you happy. *Gai gezunt*. Be well."

"You too, Uncle Max."

—ROYCE—

I⁹m at the farthest end of the bench, sitting as far away from Goldberg as possible. Even the ball boy sits closer to the Coach, even the trainer and the student manager. Because I hate the air that Goldberg breathes.

I hate him because he only knows three of his players by name: Benny Tanowski, Phil Isaacson, and Barry Hoffman. (All the Jews!) Everybody else is "Big Boy" or "Lefty" or "Shoulders" or "Number Fourteen." . . . I'm "Fancy Dan." Like I'm a faggot or something.

I hate him because Goldberg curses with the devil's own tongue yet always talks about himself like he's talking about God.

That bastard, he even screamed at me during the first week of practice when I couldn't get the hang of some defense or other: "You! Fancy Dan! Can't you follow directions? How dead-brained can you be? Didn't your mother ever have any living children?"

Say what about my mama? Man, if anybody else ever said something like that, I'd go ahead and punch his fucking lights out.

Otis was right all along. "What'd I tell you, boy? Ain't it easy to hate that loudmouth motherfucker? That's why if you ever get invited to join the club, there's no fucking way you'll ever say no."

I only shrug when Otis talks like that. "I don't know nothing about no club."

There's no way in hell that I want to be part of anything crooked that would compromise the game I love. I can still fly! I can still bring those dead-ass motherfuckers back to life! Shit! You should see the lit-up look on Barry Hoffman's face when I set him up for easy shots that even he can't miss. Man, I can still perform miracles, just like Jesus.

Amen. And Goldberg? Man, he's Jehovah! Mean-assed and unforgiving. He's the old and I'm the new.

Hey, Satan offered Jesus the world, but he didn't take it, right?

And besides, nobody's asked me to join nothing.

Shit, man. Except for Otis's constant bellyaching and bullshitting, none of the other guys hardly ever speaks to me. Actually Barry Hoffman once said "pick left" during a scrimmage. And Phil Isaacson once told me to "switch." From what I can tell, the only time these guys ever speak to each other is when they bitch about Goldberg. So it's just as well my teammates ignore me, because I don't like them either.

I do like Otis, even though he always seems unhappy and sometimes his breath stinks from liquor. (Just like my father!) Otis is kind of friendly and almost protective of me, but he's still after me with all those same outlandish stories of fixes and dumps. Naming names—Joey, Phil, Barry and selected second-stringers. Also incriminating himself. Quoting dates and scores, totaling point spreads and payoffs. "It's free money," Otis insists. "And we get to put a hurtin' on Goldberg, too."

Now, I can easily believe that all the other guys, the Jews, are obviously up to no good, always talking in close quarters, always laughing for no apparent reason. On the court, though, I must admit that the Jewish guys are mostly fun to play with. Quick, tough, and cagey. But they're Jews after all, and Mama told me that the "Jews" got their name from "Judas."

Yet despite Otis's testimony to the contrary, I believe him to be a straight shooter. Especially after watching him practice for the past six weeks. Shit, man. Goldberg purposely recruited a bulky six-foot-seven-inch freshman named Tom Glasel just to be Otis's practice dummy, and Otis beats that white boy like a runaway slave. No, sir. Otis is playing some kind of weird fucked-up joke, and I'll be damned if I'll fall for it.

Meanwhile I watch in agonies of envy as the teams line up for the center jump, with Otis facing Sammy Goodrich. Then Otis leaps to touch the sky and deflects the ball to Isaacson, but a whistle tootles and a bald-headed referee claims that Isaacson moved into the jump circle too soon.

The game only started about one second ago, but Goldberg jumps up from his chair as if his pants are on fire. He curls his right hand around his mouth like a megaphone and shouts at the offending referee, "You fucking asshead!"

Most of the other benchwarmers are relieved to laugh at someone else's expense, but I just scowl and pull a towel over my head.

What if I could push an imaginary button that would make Goldberg die? Would I do it? Shit, yeah. Sometimes in shooting practice, I play a little game with myself: "If I make this next shot, he'll have a sudden heart attack...now!... If I make this next shot..."

And I can't understand why everybody makes such a fuss about Goldberg being such a good coach. The way I see it, the players do all the playing and Dickie Weiss does all the real coaching. Just this morning, in Barney Polan's column, Goldberg was wildly praised as a master motivator. What a joke! Goldberg's pregame speech tonight was just plain silly, urging his "boys" to "make your parents and your coach proud of you." Goldberg's only reference to the Rhinegold Golden Lions was this: "Go out there and kill those fucking morons disguised as basketball players. And that also goes for their ass-kissing, son of a bitch of a fucking coach." It was Dickie Weiss who reviewed the strategy and all the Xs-and-Os stuff.

And, man alive, I've never seen a pregame locker room with all the players looking so fucked up. Nobody laughing, nobody busting chops, nobody even talking. The players just sitting silently in front of their lockers like men condemned. Otis never looked up from his sneakers.

The last thing Weiss told us was, "Listen to your coaches. We know what we're doing. Stick with what we tell you and we'll all be heroes."

Fuck that. I want to be a hero all on my own.

Even though I desperately want to be playing, the ball game itself is fun to watch: Sammy Goodrich plays ornery defense against Otis, forcing chest-to-chest confrontations at every opportunity. Forever committing small annoying gestures: two-fingered pokes into Otis's navel, and gratuitous hip bumps. Goodrich sometimes even tugs at Otis's shorts. So many tiny, marginal fouls that the refs never tag one of them. And Otis is frustrated and so pissed that he misses his first five shots. I'm sitting here thinking that Otis might just haul off and clock that white boy in the face. When Otis rims out a put-back layup, Goldberg calls time out just to tear him up:

"I've got a great idea, Big Boy. Why don't you make a fucking shot for a change? What're you, a fucking pussy? God only knows what's going on out there. Bunch of fucking choke bastards!"

According to the scoreboard, however, we're leading 10–4.

Weiss intervenes to quickly review the scouting report and to tell Otis to square his shoulders when he shoots. The buzzer finally sounds, but the players remain motionless until Goldberg dismisses them with a final snarl, saying, "Okay, girls. Go out there and try to play like men."

Coming out of the time-out, the Rhinegold coach finally springs his trapping defenses. Alternating a full-court 1-3-1 with a half-court 1-2-1-1, even adding a three-quarter-court 3-1-1 that totally confuses Hoffman and Isaacson. The two of them begin tossing passes to the wrong team, and Hoffman manages to dribble the ball out of bounds off his own foot.

Man alive! I could beat that Swiss-cheese press with my left hand. Goldberg wants us to overload one area and throw long sideline passes, but that's crazy. All we have to do is get the ball into the middle of the court.

By the end of the first quarter our lead is reduced to 18–15. Goldberg is literally spitting mad in the huddle, and the sullen players quietly towel the spittle from their faces. "What the fuck?" Goldberg keeps asking nobody in particular. "What the fuck?"

As play resumes, Hoffman commits his second personal foul when he steps in front of Goodrich's latest stampede to the hoop.... After the collision the bald ref calls a blocking foul on Hoffman and once again Goldberg bounds off the bench screaming, "What's the matter, you assheaded scumbag? You got a fucking bet on the game?"

Goodrich's shot is off-target, but he seems to be anticipating every bounce and plays a heartbeat ahead of everyone else. What a terrific player he is! Even better than he showed during the summertime. Damn! I want a shot at him so bad.... Goodrich's sticky defense totally neutralizes Otis. Then when Benny Tanowski hits a few buckets, Goodrich switches over to put the hot man in a straitjacket.

The whole team looks confused and poorly coached. When Otis zigs, Hoffman throws a zag pass to nobody. An inbound play is botched when Isaacson and Hoffman run headlong into each other. The crowd laughs, and Goldberg curses into his hands. At the half, Rhinegold claims the lead, 33–30.

Back in the locker room Goldberg goes apeshit, tossing a tray of sliced oranges against a wall and yelling, "Cocksuckers!" Kicking a metal wastebasket until the sides cave in. "Fucking heartless bastards!" Hurling a folding chair at the blackboard. "Shit for brains!" The fit lasts until Goldberg abruptly turns and stomps off into the adjoining bathroom, to lock himself inside a stall and smoke his cigarettes. That's

Weiss's cue to step forth and calmly explain once more the imperatives of our press-breaker offense.

And as the players finally file out into the corridor, Weiss sidles up to me and says, "Be ready to play."

With the second half under way, it appears that Goodrich has totally fucked up Otis and taken away his heart. I never would've believed it in a million years! Maybe Otis is sick or something. Even so, the game remains hard fought and competitive despite our sloppy play only because Goodrich can't piss in the ocean—shooting only 2-for-11 so far. Most of Rhinegold's scoring is created by our various fumblings under pressure.

			RH	C.C.N.Y.
3Q	3:51	GOODRICH 1-2 FTs	46	44

At another time-out, Goldberg demands that we introduce ourselves to each other. For a moment the guys stand mute, sweating, embarrassed. "Do it!" Goldberg commands. "Introduce yourselves, because you're playing like strangers. Go on! Shake hands!"

Finally Hoffman extends his right hand to Isaacson, both of them smirking. "I'm Barry Hoffman. Pleased to meet you."

"I'm Phil Isaacson."

"Hi, I'm Joey Callahan. Glad to make your acquaintance."

"Go on, everybody! Do it!"

"I'm Royce Johnson."

"I'm Otis Hill."

Nevertheless, as the fourth quarter begins, Rhinegold forges to a five-point lead. That's when Weiss whispers into Goldberg's ear and the Coach summons me from the end of the bench. "Get in there," Goldberg orders, "and do something to make your coach proud."

"For Hoffman," Weiss adds. "Run the four-out weave and look inside for Hill."

I nearly trip over the sideline on my way to the scorer's table. "Johnson for Hoffman," I tell a kindly old man who's sitting in front of a microphone, then I turn to join the fun.

"Hold it!" the old man shouts. "Wait till the clock stops!"

Whoops! The game is indeed proceeding and the players race past me. Otis eyes me curiously as the big man halfheartedly trails the action. Goodrich scores a fast-breaking layup, and Rhinegold is ahead 52–45.

Bzzt!

And the huge electronic voice of God booms and echoes throughout the vast arena: "Into the game for City College is Royce Johnson! Number Forty-one, replacing Hoffman!"

My father's out of town and Ma couldn't get time off from work (I think she's not here deliberatley because she'd be too nervous). Instead, Ma swore she'd be listening "hard" to the radio broadcast, playing it at full volume to compete with the loud noise of the hospital's laundry machines.

Hoffman has his back turned to receive the ball from the ref, so he fails to see me approaching. "Barry," I say shyly.

Hoffman wheels about in alarm. "Johnson! What the fuck're you doing out here?"

"I'm... um... I'm in for you. Coach's orders."

"What?" Hoffman is disbelieving until he sees Weiss frantically beckoning him toward the bench. "Oh, shit," Hoffman says. "Now we're in the fucking soup!" Hoffman looks over at Otis, who returns a shrug. Then Hoffman walks slowly to the sideline.

Lining up on offense, Otis tells me this: "Play it cool, boy. Don't do nothing stupid. You hear?"

I nod, confused, even frightened. But I run my defender into Otis's massive pick and receive the inbound pass from Isaacson.... And the ball is warm and pulsing in my big hands, beating like a leather heart as brown as my own skin. And the basket, too, is alive. And here I am at last, moving among so many frozen statues until the path to the basket looms as wide as the parted Red Sea. Nobody can stop me as I carry the ball forward and drop it into the living hoop.

			RH	C.C.N.Y.
4Q	6:23	JOHNSON, driving lay-in	52	47

And, just like that, I take over the ball game—scoring, passing, even boldly dribbling behind my back to outmaneuver a tight double-team. Rhinegold still leads 55–53 when Goodrich switches his defensive attention to me. Hot damn! And Goodrich pokes me and bumps me, then he steps back to make me prove myself a shooter. No sweat. All I have to do is flick the ball skyward and it dives through the iron ring.

			RH	C.C.N.Y.
4Q	3:16	JOHNSON, one hander, 19'	55	55

Before the referee retrieves the ball and play resumes, Otis catches up to me and says, "From now on I want you to give me the ball! Understand? Don't even think about shooting no more! Don't even dribble! Just give me the ball every time! Or else you'll get us killed!"

What the fuck is he talking about? Basketball means life. What does basketball have to do with killing?

With the victory in the bag, Goldberg now shows a smug grin in the huddle. "Don't foul," he says, all calm and reasonable. "It's as simple as that. Just back off and play token defense. Let them drive. Let them shoot. Don't try to steal the ball. Don't try to block a shot. Don't even touch anybody. Don't try to be a hero. Just let them score. Is that crystal clear to everybody? Let them fucking score."

Weiss wedges his nose into the huddle. "We're up three points, guys. There's only seven seconds left and they're out of time-outs. Even if they score, the clock'll run out. Get it?" Then Weiss is suddenly agonized with an appalling possibility. "Johnson," he says. "If they do score, don't even try to inbound the ball. Right? Just let the clock die."

(No shit, Dick Tracy!)

Bzzt!

And Goldberg can't help laughing out loud. "No time-outs left! That stupid moron!"

Rhinegold's inbounds play directs the ball to Goodrich, who's loosely guarded by Otis. Goodrich twitches right and goes left, guarded now only by the happy twinkle in Otis's eye. "Go ahead, white boy," Otis laughs.

Goodrich gathers his legs to attack the basket, not a defender in sight as the clock counts down... 4... 3... 2... and then I'm up there, soaring through the blue smoke, my entire body yearning toward the ball, my long right arm swatting the shot into the stands as the buzzer explodes.

Bzzt!

Some of the fans cheer wildly. Some of them boo. Both Goldberg and Weiss raise triumphant fists above their heads.

"Good job, boys," Goldberg says as he straightens his necktie.

"Way to go," Weiss says to nobody in particular.

As we move quickly off the court, I find Otis and say, "Nice game, man."

The sweat is still steaming from Otis's broad face as he whispers in a raw, red voice, "You fucked up, boy! And if I don't do some real fancy talking, it's my ass!"

The slick-haired Barry Hoffman angles himself into the conversation as we reach the privacy of the corridor. "Great job, kid," Hoffman says with a cold smile. "You fucking idiot. The spread was one-and-a-half."

"Leave him alone," says Otis. "He didn't know."

"Yeah," says Hoffman. "Tell that to Gianelli's goons."

— SAMMY —

After a quick shower I walk westward along Fifty-sixth Street to the uptown corner of Twelfth Avenue where I duck into McCue's Tavern, into a darkly yellow space, long and narrow, dominated by a black mahogany bar and red-padded swivel seats. I watch from behind my game face the faces of the others who boldly track my passage. Jack the barkeep nods in his sly fashion, his right arm outstretched to change the TV channel, from a Tom Mix shoot-'em-up to Gene Autrey serenading a pert cowgirl in the moonlight. *"Sweet Sue, I'd swap my horse and dog for you."* A middle-aged man stands at the bar wearing a wrinkled Saturday-night double-breasted brown suit, staring bleary-eyed and oblivious at the TV. A sagging peroxide blonde ravages me with hungry red eyes. Nobody speaks, nobody makes a sound. Just the gunshots and the black-and-white horses stampeding along dusty trails as I make my way toward the men's room.

Pushing myself through a swinging wooden door marked GENTS, I'm assaulted by the fetid stink of stale piss. Even the dangling light bulb seems to glow a pissy yellow. Along the far wall are two cracked urinals whose basins show bloated cigarette butts awash in small sour puddles. There's also a shitter inside a wooden stall, paper towels in a wall-mounted metal dispenser, a single sink, and a small greasy mirror. Limp cigarette butts underfoot.

A perfect place to conduct my subversive business. A perfect metaphor for the land of the scree and the home of the depraved.

Fortunately I'm too dehydrated to piss. Instead, I stride restlessly around the room, pivoting toward the sink, head-faking my own image in the cracked mirror. Until the door opens and Georgie Klein enters.

The bookie wears a gray overcoat around his puny shoulders like a king's robe. And looking down at Klein's head, I can see the first manifestation of a bald spot. Klein has to tilt his head to try and find my eyes in the yellow shadows.

"Good job," he says. "But you really cut it close."

"I always do a good job, and I like to give the suckers a run for their money."

"Tell me this," he says, reaching into his coat pocket and extracting a white envelope. "You were going to miss the layup, right?"

A good question, one that I'd been asking myself ever since that Johnson kid came out of nowhere to block my shot. In the waning heat of the ball game, I believe that I *did* want to make the shot. Just because of my own frustration. Because, no matter what the rewards are, I'm sick of losing. Of course, I did see the kid once he got there, and my impulse was to lean my body into him to try to draw a foul, hoping to create a three-point play that would send the game into overtime. But then, just as quickly, I came to my senses, so I laid the ball out there for him on a platter, to be swatted into the stands. The fans cheered, the bettors gasped, then the kid flashed me a quick look, a sharp glare full of such disdain that I felt angry and humiliated, and I wanted to speak to him, to tell him what the score really was, to challenge him to play me one-on-one right there and then. But he turned away to skip and dance toward his own bench, celebrating his triumph.

"Yes," I said. "I would've missed the layup."

Only then does Klein hand me the envelope and I quickly stash it in my pants pocket, not even bothering to count the bills like I usually do. Fifteen hundred dollars in crisp fifties. He smiles, thinking that I've learned to trust him.

"You guys are a cinch to make the N.I.T.," he says, "and that's when we'll clean up."

"I understand."

Klein proves his promise with squinty eyes and a toothsome grin. "My money's not as long as Gianelli's, but it's just as green."

"I understand."

"No one will ever find us out," Klein boasts, "because I can spread out the action so no one gets suspicious. You know? And I can play off the artificial point spreads that Gianelli's bets create. It's like I'm an independent agent. A soldier of fortune."

All at once, I realize how much I hate this little shit of a civilian, and, at the same time, how much I hate myself, the self that I've chosen to become.

What happens now?

"Get out of here, Klein. Get the fuck out."

He backs away quickly, his open palm demonstrating that he takes no offense at my harsh words. "Sure, kid. Whatever you say. Enjoy yourself with the money." Then the bookie hustles out of the room.

I linger there for propriety's sake, bending over the sink to wash my hands with a stony bar of brown soap, careful not to splash any water on my expensive Sportwatch. Then I soap up and wash my hands again.

—RAY PALUSKI, SENIOR—

Waiting for Barney at a corner table, sitting with my back to the wall, I note every arrival and departure—it's my business. Off to my right, the long mahogany is three-deep with customers, most of them talking about the ball games, and I can guess what they're saying.

"The kid's better'n his old man."

"Yer nuts."

"The new nigger sure looked good."

"I'll say."

"Yeah, but I had Rhinegold plus one-and-a-half and the black bastard cost me fifty bucks."

"Hey, look over there. Ain't that Barney Polan? Go ask him what he thinks."

"Naw. Fuck him. I'm a Yankee fan."

"Drink up."

"Salud."

And I can't help seeing the skull beneath each passing face. But I'm happy enough, just sitting here in total anonymity, well tanned and immaculate in a brown worsted suit, perfectly content, sipping an aromatic brandy.

Here's Barney now, finally seeing me and making his way through the crowd, all smiley-faced and nodding to his cronies, his contacts, his adoring public. I haven't seen Barney in nearly two years (at the fifty-dollar window at Belmont), and I'm alarmed at how fat and unhealthy he looks. Fuck! Maybe I shouldn't be doing this. Maybe the shock will be too devastating. I wonder if anybody's ever died in Toots Shor's.

Barney seats himself, and we both dip our heads slightly as a silent greeting, refraining from conversation until the quick-footed waiter arrives to take Barney's order. Gin on the rocks, a working writer's drink.

Barney's inclination is to protect himself, to keep our conversation lighthearted and familiar. Remember the St. Francis game in '31? And how's Ellie these days? And how's your bum knee? Ever hear from...? But he can't contain his curiosity, so he finally says, "What's with the secret-spy routine?"

Leaning forward, I fix him eye-to-eye. "What do you know, Barney, about point-shaving?"

—BARNEY—

I move my hand up to my forehead and slowly rub myself there. I feel weary, too weary to resist. "You too, Ray? Christ Almighty. What the fuck is going on here?"

Ray judiciously sips his drink, puckering his thin lips to seal in the flavor. "There's nothing going on, Barney. Nothing that hasn't been going on since Christ had pups."

I shake my head again, more energetically this time, trying to swallow some cold, heavy lump that's suddenly formed in the back of my throat. "I don't want to hear it, Ray. I swear I don't."

"Then get up and walk out the door and pretend we never had this conversation."

Yes, that's exactly what I want to do. Take a cab home to Brooklyn and get on with my life. How strange that I'd been trying to memorize Sonnet 112.

"Your love and pity doth th'impression fill
Which vulgar scandal stamped upon my brow..."

But wait a minute! Why be such a coward? What a colossal story this could turn into! Big enough to win a Pulitzer Prize! So I remain rooted in my chair, fascinated, repulsed.

And indeed, Ray proceeds to tell a tale of such fixing and dumping that I almost wish I were deaf: According to Ray, college basketball players "from all over the country" have been in league with gamblers since the mid-thirties. Among dozens of others, Ray specifies Mickey Gorton, Chris Roberts, and the Foley twins—all of them currently playing in the National Basketball Association. "If they ever gave pro players lie detector tests, then the N.B.A. would be out of business the next morning. Believe me, Barney. The Celtics can still be bought for the right price and so can the Zollner Pistons."

Ray also describes the point-shaving tradition in New York, where the seniors invite skilled underclassmen to join their profitable coterie only when necessary. He enumerates several famous collegiate ball games that were rigged, including half a dozen N.I.T. contests. He also implicates two referees. As for the coaches... "Well, down in Lexington, Adolph Rupp's best buddy is a well-known bookmaker. That pious hypocrite! He once came into the locker room after a close ball game screaming at his players because they hadn't covered the spread and had cost his bookmaking buddy a pile of dough. Hey, I'm sure all the coaches know when something's not kosher. If they don't, then they're either awfully dumb or awfully bad coaches."

Ray further claims that every one of the Wizard Five had been on the take. "I got a grand a game and the other guys got about half that. Which may seem like peanuts, Barney, but back then, remember, it was a lot of scratch."

Back in 1931 when Coach Mack missed the start of the season while recovering from hernia surgery, his assistant, Whitey Foxx, had taken over the team. According to Ray, Foxx called a meeting that first day of practice to say that he'd known most of the players since they were in diapers. "It was Whitey," Ray recalls, "who'd taught us how to play ball in the old Ditmas Avenue Boys Club. So, Whitey said that he knew we were doing business and that despite how much he loved us, if he ever suspected anything crooked, he'd turn us right in to the D.A.... And you know what, Barney? We paid him no mind. We went right on shaving points as if he'd never said a word. And sometimes we were clumsy, Barney. Sometimes we were minus two-and-a-half or even one-

and-a-half and we'd try to cut it too close and so we'd lose a ball game from time to time. Lose a game we should have won. Those were the only ones I still regret. Anyway, Whitey knew we were still turning tricks, but he never said anything or did anything. That's because everybody was doing it. Wherever there was a game on the boards, there were players taking money."

I'm in agony. "Tell me why, Ray. How could you ever do something like that? You must've known it was wrong."

—SENIOR—

How can I get him to understand the way it used to be? The way we used phony names when we played in all of those money tournaments. I was either "L. O. Cash" ("Lots Of") or else "O. Leo Leahy." Or the whole barnstorming routine—keeping the game close enough on Friday night so that the locals would think they had a real shot at beating us. Then "letting" the rubes convince us to spot them points and let them bet more money than they could afford. Finally we'd kick their asses on Saturday and fastbreak out of town ahead of the posse. In those days money and basketball were part of the same tradition, the same action. There were no questions asked about what was right or what was wrong.

"We did it because we needed the money, Barney, that's the first thing. Times were bad back then. And like I said, because so many guys were doing it, Barney. So many guys in so many schools that it almost seemed okay. You know what, Barney? You were a chump if you didn't go along."

The waiter never returns. The jovial Toots Shor himself wanders past our table, ever the glad-hander—yet even he respects the urgency of our close conversation.

"I don't understand," Barney says. "How could you ever face yourself in the mirror...? How could you pretend to be... I don't know what... a good citizen?"

What a dunce this man is. How can he have survived for so long in Sportstown U.S.A. and still be so naive? But his question comes from his wounded heart, so it deserves a considered answer.

"Sure enough, Barney, I knew that shaving points was wrong. And I do have principles. After the Knicks cut me in training camp.... And I do appreciate what you wrote about me back then, Barney, but the truth is that I was too slow to play at that level. Anyway, that's when it all hit me. What I'd done. Who I was. Who I thought I was. It was a painful time for me, and for Ellie, too. I have to give her a lot of credit for sticking by me. Like I say, none of this was easy, but this is what I came up with, Barney. I've been able to live more or less peacefully with myself all these years... by realizing that everybody has his own guilty secrets, Barney. Even you."

Look at him, blushing like a schoolboy caught peeping through the keyhole in the bathroom door while his older sister's taking a bath. He doesn't know whether to shit or go blind.

"I mean, I haven't killed anybody, Barney, or robbed a bank. All I've ever done was to cheat myself. And let me tell you something, Barney... we all do it. Whether we take the path of least resistance, or fool ourselves into thinking we're better than we really are. Every day, Barney, there's a hundred ways we cheat ourselves and lie to ourselves. The point is, Barney, that I forgave myself a long time ago. And every time I fuck up again? I try hard to learn whatever lesson there is to be learned, and I try to forgive myself all over again. Again and again, Barney. Because none of us is perfect."

I slug down the rest of my drink and stare him in the eye. But I still don't really understand why I fixed ball games, why I ruined the thing I loved the most. I might as well try to understand the meaning of Hiroshima and Nagasaki.

"Who...?" he says, trying so hard to make sense of this catastrophe, or at least find somewhere to cast the blame. "Who was bankrolling all of this?"

"Anybody who could put together the right deal. Big-time

bookies and two-bit hustlers. We had to sift through several deals before almost every important ball game. And it wasn't so easy to get the right results, Barney. My God, I can remember five or six games when both teams were trying to lose. What a mess. You had to be a fucking Einstein to keep all the numbers straight. And you know something, Barney? Remember when Howie Scales missed his senior year at City when he supposedly broke his leg in a car accident? Well, the real story is that Howie had his leg broken for him because he made a foul shot he was supposed to miss."

Now look at the poor bastard, sweating like he's been locked inside a steam room with all his clothes on. How can I ease his suffering? What could I ever say? The same lame rationale always comes up. "Everybody was doing it."

"Why would anybody," he asks, "even the most hard-bitten gambler, ever want to fix an amateur basketball game? If you want money that bad, go fix a pro game."

"Not only the money," I say softly, as though talking to a child. "Also for the secret thrill of knowing something that no one else knows. Not even the president of the United States. For the money, Barney. And for the power."

Sipping lightly at my drink, I try to smile oh-so-wisely, but I suddenly feel like I've lived too long. "And you know what, Barney? Some guys just like to fuck things up whenever they can. Just to take something good and turn it to shit."

—BARNEY—

Why is Ray telling me all of this? Why now after all these years?

"Because," Ray says, and a brief salty wave washes against his hard gray eyes. "Because my son is shaving points big-time and the district attorney is closing in. I need you to help him, Barney. In fact, I'm begging you. Please, Barney. Use your connections. If you need to bribe somebody, I'll get you the cash. If you need to make threats, I'll get you the muscle. Please, Barney. I can get you anything you want. Money. Dames. A house in Florida. Name it, Barney, and your best dreams will come true...my God...just the thought of Junior in jail...please, Barney. I'll get down on my hands and knees right here."

"Okay, Ray," I say too quickly, because I have no intention of calling, threatening, or bribing anyone. "I promise to do whatever I can."

I've got to get out of here. I've got to get home to my favorite green chair. I've got to finish memorizing last season's American League batting averages. I've got to memorize a sonnet.

I stand so fast that my chair tips over backward. Ignoring the waiter who rushes over to help, I say, "Phone me, Ray. We'll talk some more about this. I gotta go now. I gotta go home."

As I flee through the crowded nightclub, I suddenly notice how flaccid and ponderous my belly is. People move quickly out of my path, my blind steps lurching as though I were drunk.

Chapter Six

December 9, 1950

—HENRY—

Practice ended an hour ago, yet three of us linger on the red-trimmed basketball court. Sammy Goodrich, me, and a junior varsity player (Danny Simon—good hands, bad feet), whose task is to retrieve errant shots. And there're plenty of these, which is exactly why I've insisted on this after-hours shot-intensive consultation.

"Hell, yes," I say with a grin. "You got to love it, or else you'll hate it."

After our opening-night loss to C.C.N.Y., we've reeled off four consecutive wins, struggling, however, to win close games against inferior competition. A three-point victory against lowly Muhlenberg. Then beating a weak squad at Adelphi by only four. Nevertheless "ugly" wins are vastly preferable to "beautiful" losses.

I'm not going too crazy yet, because I believe we'll get in synch soon enough. It's the holidays that fuck these kids up, all that peace-on-earth bullshit. Too much goodwill toward all men makes for passive basketball players. (The only good thing about the Christmas season is the annual cease-fire in Korea.)

The team's biggest problem is that Sammy's feathery touch has become hard as a jackhammer. Through these first five ball games, Sammy's field-goal percentage is a measly 28 percent, just about 15 percent lower than his career efficiency. Once Sammy starts shooting up to par, we'll truly be a powerhouse team. (Meanwhile we're 4-and-1, which ain't exactly like having hemorrhoids.)

I can see it already in my mind's eye: We're due to play City College again in three weeks at their gym. Sammy shoots the lights out and we humiliate them by twenty—no, thirty!—points, and wipe the arrogant smile off Goldberg's face. (That fucking asshole couldn't coach his way to a free meal. It's that sneaky little assistant who goes out and recruits the best available talent in the city. I wonder what kind of freebies that kid Johnson is getting....) To top it off, the very next day the North Koreans unconditionally surrender and all the fucking nuclear bombs are put in mothballs.

Hell, yes.

In war or peace, I always love working one-on-one with certain players (the intelligent ones) on the more esoteric individual aspects of the game. Rebounding. Passing. Picking. Cutting. Defense. I know every drill from defensive slides to zigzag dribblings, from pivot postures to show-and-recover techniques, but shooting is my specialty. Didn't Barney Polan once call me the Shot Doctor? Hell, old as I am, I can still convert over 85 percent from the foul line with my looping underhanded release.

Anyway, here's Sammy shooting a fifteen-foot banker from the right side—an easy movement of long limbs and graceful angles. Sammy loads the shot precisely at his left shoulder, a classic one-hander, with the wrist snapping, and the hand catapulting the ball so high...and wide and hard right, to noisily bang against the wooden backboard.

As the ball bounces away, I pretend to duck away from a live hand grenade. "Look out!" I shout. "Hey! Anybody get hurt?"

The J.V. flunky ventures a weak laugh, but Sammy's game face remains intact. Jesus, kid. Loosen up. Sure, Sammy works his nuts off, but he's too damn quiet, too serious. If I hadn't personally seen the kid's transcript, I'd swear Sammy was at least thirty-five years old with a wife, two kids, and a mortgage.

"Damned if I can see anything wrong," I say as Sammy misfires again. "You just keep on shooting, why don't ya, and I'll eventually dope it out."

So I scrutinize every aspect of Sammy's stricken one-handers and hooks, even his layups and botched free throws. I study the position of Sammy's feet, the sequential weight shiftings, the anglings of the shoulders. Is Sammy's shooting elbow crooked into the dreaded "chicken wing"? Is the wrist too stiff, or too loose? I observe Sammy's hands. The release point. The follow-through.

Strange. All the parts seem in order, yet most of Sammy's shots are spinning too tightly and falling short.

"Try moving your left elbow a little closer to your body," I advise him. "Yeah. Like that. Now emphasize the follow-through. Concentrate on shooting just the bottom half of the ball."

Another jump shot slams hard off the boards like a cannonball. "Well," I joke, "at least I think you killed a cockaroach that was crawling around up there."

Thus far Sammy's shooting hasn't noticeably improved, but I'm sure having myself a whale of a time.

Thunk!

—SAMMY—

I'm certain that the considerations of late-game score management are what's messed up my shooting stroke. So despite Carlson's annoying tinkering, I know the problem to be more mental than mechanical. A certain tightness of mind and spirit. A certain feeling of vulnerablity.

Swish!

And I'm going batty. My mind feels like a punching bag. What if Klein gets in over his head and rats me out to save his own ass? What if any (or several) of the girls I'm screwing gets pregnant? What if my father dies during the season and I have to miss some games? Everywhere I look, there's disaster about to happen. What if I get drafted and the army doctors say that I'm really six-foot-six?

Thunk!

I'm only shooting twenty-eight-fucking-percent! My scoring average is down to 12.4 points per game. How could any N.B.A. team justify choosing me in the first round of next May's collegiate draft? Or even the second round?

Thunk!

Sometimes the basketball feels soft and shapeless in my hands. Sometimes the ball feels like a leather-bound cannonball.

Thunk!

There's only one consolation: Hit or miss, I still have nearly five thousand dollars credited to "Sheldon Silvestri" in a savings account in a Staten Island bank. Five grand! And I'm thinking (and thinking! and thinking!) that maybe it's time to lay low for a while. Maybe cash in on only three or four really big paydays from here on.

Thunk!

I've already turned Klein down for both of next weekend's ball games—aiming to get my game in order as well as to tease the bookie into doubling the stakes. That would be three thousand dollars per game, times let's say three more games.... Eleven fucking grand!

Plenty, but never enough, even though my current and foreseeable expenses are minimal: During the summers I work in the Catskills and whenever school isn't in session I live in a dollar-a-day room at the Williamsburg Y.M.H.A. My athletic scholarship provides a private dorm room, tuition, meals, books, even laundry money. In addition, the school pays me twenty-five dollars every week for a bogus job—the check says "Student Assistant in the Equipment Room." Also, Carlson occasionally slips me a few bucks, and the day after every one of our victories, there's always another twenty dollars slipped through the ventilation slot in my varsity locker.

I'm living on Easy Street, right? So what the fuck am I so worried about? Like the prodigal son, my shot will return soon enough.

Thunk!

Having five thousand smackers in the bank should generate a certain measure of security. Haven't I beaten the system? Wasn't I smart enough to spend the money frugally? Not like my foolish teammates, arousing suspicion with their fancy new suits and their alligator shoes. My only self-indulgence is the Dumont television set in my dorm room.

Thunk!

Five thousand smackers! That's all that really matters anyway. Right? Soon to be eleven thousand! Enough to buy five cars. Or two houses in Florida. Or five mink coats. Or a small yacht. Eleven thousand dollars! More than twice the salary I'd receive even as a number-one draft pick in the National Basketball Association. In fact, the league's best player, George Mikan, only earned $6,000 in '49-'50.

That amounted to $3.21 for every point Mikan scored.

Chicken feed.

Thunk!

Damn it! What the fuck is wrong with my shot? (And I'm pissed off at myself for being so concerned about my shooting. Shooters are a dime a dozen. Look at Junior over at St. John's. He's a real sharp-shooter, but he's a cardboard player. He who lives by the jump shot, dies. But that's not me! Surely the N.B.A. scouts can see how versatile my game is. Right? Jesus fucking Christ! I don't know anything anymore.)

Right now, my only long-range goal is to finish out this miserable season and then start all over in the N.B.A., testing (and proving) myself against the world's greatest athletes. But there's a catch here, too, because there's only one team I want to play for:

> *"In the first*
> > *second*
> > *third*
> > *fourth*
> > *fifth round, the Indianapolis Olympians pick*
> > > *Sammy Goodrich."*

The Olympians were chartered as the N.B.A.'s newest franchise in the summer of 1949. The team features Ralph Beard, Alex Groza, and Wallace Jones, who'd all been star performers for Adolph Rupp at the University of Kentucky. Another ex-Wildcat, Cliff Barker, is the playing coach, and still one more of Rupp's boys, Joe Holland, is a substitute guard. (Georgie Klein swears on his "mother's eyes" that all five players were turning tricks in college, an assertion that I ardently disbelieve on the hopeful grounds that somebody, somewhere, has to be on the up-and-up.)

And get this—these five players, along with Lexington sports-writer Babe Kimbrough, also own 70 percent of the ball club's stock! The revolution is upon us! Socialism is born in the N.B.A.! Imagine how proud my father will be when I'm playing for the Olympians. Today professional basketball, tomorrow the world!

In the '49-'50 season the Olympians won their division but lost to the Anderson Duffey Packers in the second round of the play-offs. Groza averaged 23.4 points per game and was selected to the N.B.A. All-Star team. Beard scored 14.9 and made the second All-Star team. So far this season Indianapolis is a mediocre team—and I root for them to lose so they'll have a higher draft pick in May. (And if another team were to draft me? I'd sue the league for restraint of trade.)

Swish!

As a sophomore I chose to negotiate my business long-distance with a bookie from Toledo whom I'd met in the Catskills. The payoffs were delivered in timely fashion by courier the day after every game. A bloodless thousand dollars for every close shave. The arrangement turned sour late in the season only when the courier began skimming my cut. "Forget it!" I told the wicked messenger. "I don't work with crooks."

Klein is much better suited to my purposes because he's independent, knowledgeable, reliable, and available. And I'm such a dominant player that, despite the meager efforts of Gianelli's hirelings, I can unilaterally turn a ball game up, down, or sideways.

Thunk!

Holy shit! That's it! My step is fucked! My setup step forward is too short and unbalanced! Step and shoot! Step and...

"Could be," Henry is saying, "that maybe your right hand is on the ball too long."

(Yeah, Henry. Whatever you say.)

I unleash a long one-hander from the top of the key, mindful this time to lengthen my step, and also to push off the floor from the ball of my left foot instead of lifting from the heel. *"Good! Like Nedick's!"*

"That looked great!" Henry enthuses.

And another bull's-eye. And another.

"Feels terrific, Coach. I think that's the trick, what you said about my right hand."

And Henry can't stop smiling.

Chapter Seven

December 10, 1950

—OTIS—

We've only played four games and I already wish the fucking season was over. Goldberg is biting my ass during every time-out and I want to kill the motherfucker. Royce has finally figured out what's what and he's always looking at me like he's some kind of hungry puppy looking for a bone. I know what the kid wants—money! And, man, is he good! The three games we were working, we had to freeze him out to keep everything cool. We let him roll for the other game we played for free, and he was a fucking monster. With a looser coach the kid would be an All-American.

But the game that got to me was two days ago against St. Francis in their gym in Brooklyn. It's a rickety old joint with a dark floor that's just about the same color as a basketball. Damned if I don't lose two or three passes every game I play there. When someone throws me a bounce pass, the fucking ball just disappears. Not that it mattered a whole lot last Tuesday because we were favored by seven-and-a-half and trying to control the score. And it sure seemed like Benny Tanowski wasn't with the program.

Their best player is a six-foot-three blood, name of Vernon Stokes, who can jump like a kangaroo. Tanowski was guarding Stokes because he's our best defender. Tanowski can be a stubborn bastard. A mean streak runs through him, and even though he doesn't say much, I kind of like the guy. He's been turning tricks for three years along with the rest of us and he knows how to take care of business. Tanowski's careful, careful and controlled, but lately he's started to live it up (too much, if you ask me), what with his fancy new Studebaker, not to mention his gold watch, alligator shoes, and spiffy suits. I think the easy money went to his head, made him feel like a big man. So when he was hounding Stokes all over the court and putting the guy's game in a bag, I said, "What's going on, Benny? You know the score, don't you?" So he says, "Fuck you, Otis. You play your game and I'll play mine." So I says, "It's your funeral, man, but you're messing with *my* money." So he says, "Fuck you." And that's that. Meanwhile the guy I'm checking is a big white stiff, name of Walt Adamushko, and I got to let him have a party so's we can squeeze under the spread. And there's N.B.A. scouts in the stands laughing at my defense, and that's why, at first, I was pissed.

But now I'm scared shitless.

That's because I read in this morning's newspaper that Tanowski was in a car accident somewhere up in Throg's Neck in the Bronx. The story said he was drunk and crashed his car into a telephone pole. But I've been with Tanowski for four seasons, playing and partying, and I never ever saw him take a drink. Not even a sip of beer.

So I'm thinking that Gianelli did it. Ain't no other possibility.

Man, oh man. If I had the guts, I'd deliberately sprain my ankle in practice and miss the rest of the season. But I know I won't. I'll toe the line. And when Gianelli says, "Jump," I'll do it. And when he says, "Shit," I'll squat.

Chapter Eight

December 11, 1950

—ROYCE—

At Mister Gianelli's fancy penthouse apartment for dinner, Otis and Barney eat three steaks each, and I have two. Then the (white!) servants serve us free champagne—just like in the movies. Tastes like sour ginger ale. But, man alive, thinking about Benny after that accident, all I have is one little sip. Gianelli's old lady, though, is drinking that stuff like it's water and she's been out on the Sahara for about a week.

Mister Gianelli is real friendly. "You don't have to lose any ball games," he says. "So who's the ones who suffer? The bettors? So what? They're suckers anyway. And there's so much money floating around, Royce. It doesn't seem fair that you guys do all the work and get nothing. Did you know that City College is guaranteed fifteen thousand dollars every time you guys play a basketball game in the Garden?"

Fifteen thousand dollars! I could buy a house for Ma and a car and have lots of white servants. . . .

"So why shouldn't you get a piece of the pie, Royce? And what if you do happen to accidentally lose a game or two? It's no skin off your nose, is it? You can also think of it as a way to get even with Goldberg, that two-faced cocksucker. Pardon my French."

French?

"So what if City College wins sixteen games this season instead of seventeen? Who cares? You'll still get into the N.I.T. And ten years from now it won't make any difference to anybody. Believe me, Royce, shaving points is a victimless crime. And besides, everybody's doing it."

Me, I'm not shocked anymore, and I'm not so scared as I thought

I'd be. I mean, we won't be fixing every game, just four or five. And once the game starts, I can still have fun out there and still be an artist. The basketball will still be round, the rim still ten feet from the floor. Otis even told me I wouldn't have to know anything about what the point spread is. When he gives me the high sign, I'll just pass the ball to him or Barry and then I won't have to worry about anything. Me, I might even be riding the pines when the game is on the line.

So what the fuck? What do I really have to lose? Mister Gianelli has so many cops and judges in his pocket that there's no chance of getting caught. And if we did, we'd have a free pass anyway. And, man alive, I love the idea of making Goldberg bleed.

—OTIS—

The young buck over there, he thinks he's with it now, ready for a shave and a haircut, but he's still a little scared. Wait'll the white bitch goes into her act. Then the poor nigger'll be barking like a dog, howling at the fucking moon and begging to dump every game on the schedule. As if a fine white bitch like that's gonna really give it up to a nigger with empty pockets. Yeah, I went through the same routine with her a couple of years ago. She was playing with me and I was playing with her. I knew all along that I was with the program anyway. Because I'm hooked on easy money and I know it. Man, but I do feel sorry for Royce. He's a real nice kid with a super-duper game. But if he ain't doing business like the rest of us, then it won't work out for nobody. It's all about cash flow. And fuck him anyway. I got to make my own way and he's got to make his. Shit. I ain't his daddy.

—JOHNNY BOY—

Hill and Hoffman won't even look me in the eye. Good! I must remember to send Carmine a little bonus for doing such a good job on that two-timing dickhead Tanowski. Yeah, now they're all scared enough to eat shit and bark at the moon. And the young nigger? Rosie'll have an easier time with him now.

—ROYCE—

Oh, man. I don't like this at all. Dinner's over and everybody else is talking business in the game room except me and Gianelli's wife. She's moved her chair closer to me here a the dining-room table, much too close.

"Catholic school was so stupid," she's telling me. Don't you think that nuns look like penguins?"

"I don't know...."

"You know what the nuns used to tell us whenever we went out on a date and a boy took us out to eat? Well, we were never supposed to order ravioli. Guess why not."

What was ravioli? More French?

"Because," Missus Gianelli says, lighting a cigarette, "the little raviolis might make the boys think of little pillows and then they'd want to take you to bed and screw you. Ain't that a laugh?"

I never heard a woman talk like one of the guys before. I try to imagine my ma saying something like that, but I can't.

"So I ran away from home." Her laughter sounds like frozen champagne crashing on a stone floor. "I hitchhiked my way from Cedar Rapids to New York and that's where I finally found out what it's like to really be alive. You know what I mean?"

No. But I nod like I do.

Then she slides her hand above my knee and squeezes my thigh. Looking fearfully toward the game room, I figure I'm as good as gut-shot.

"That's why I like basketball players so much," she coos. "Because they're so alive." Then she leans closer and I can't help looking down the

V of her nightgown, at her soft white breasts, but in my mind I'm hearing the explosion of a bullet to the back of my head, wondering would I hear it.

—ROSIE—

My God, this one's so young. He's an intelligent-looking kid, but he's so fucking innocent that he sounds stupid. Look how totally helpless he is, with his eyes bugged and his jaw dropped.

Dammit, I'm sick of this crap. What Johnny Boy did to that Tanowski kid ain't right. I do understand that business is business, and that certain people sometimes have to be reminded to keep their end of a bargain. But Tanowski ain't no businessman. No, it ain't right. And here I am in shit up to my eyebrows. Always conning these young kids, like one of those cows they use in the slaughterhouse to lead the bulls through the death gate.

But it does beat shaking my ass on the chorus line, don't it? A dream come true, ain't it? So how come I feel like a two-dollar whore?

Not that he needs any convincing.

Jeez. I hope the old goat drops dead before my ass is around my knees and I'm stepping on my tits.

And what would I do then? Funny as it sounds, I always wanted to go to college and learn to be a schoolteacher. Yeah, I love little kids. My sister in Chicago has three of them, little cutie pies, two girls and a boy. But ever since that scrape-job I had when I was fifteen, I can't have any of my own. Not that I ever wanted any. No thanks. All their squalling and bawling and shitty diapers. Only to grow up and break your heart. Somebody else's kids are the ones I like, and only the real little ones. Kindergartners. Yeah, that's what I would do. Teach kinder- gartners. Must be a German word.

Meanwhile I hear Johnny Boy's dry laughter moving loudly down the hall, so I slug down another glass of bubbly, and I'm already too drunk to think clearly. "Look, Royce. This is what I'm supposed to tell you: That I don't care shit for beans about the color of anybody's skin. That in the dark, everybody's the same color anyway. You know? That I really like you, Royce. That you're cute. That I think maybe we can be friends. Johnny Boy wants me to make friends with all of his boys. Are you gonna be my friend?...That's what I'm supposed to tell you. But this is what I really want to know, Royce: Are you as nice a kid as you seem to be? Or are you just an asshole like those other guys?"

The kid's so confused he doesn't know whether to shit or go blind. "Lady," he says, "why're you talking to me like that?"

"There's gotta be a bottom line in a person's life, Royce, ain't there? And even if you do something bad a thousand times, you can still stop doing it and try to start all over. Not that I'm ever gonna be a virgin again, see? I mean I'll probably do the same lying, sneaky bullshit all over again with next year's crop of freshmen. And that's okay, too. Those are the cards that I dealt myself. But I want to know that maybe I can stop when I really and truly want to. Or that at least I did stop it once. Like if I was smoking two packs of cigarettes a day and then just for one day I didn't smoke any just to prove something to myself. See? Somewhere, somehow, I have to be coming from something true, you know? And maybe you *are* a nice kid, Royce." Jesus, I need some more champagne. "So tell me, Royce. If I promise to let you fuck me, would that be enough to get you fixing games like those other assholes?"

"You're drunk."

"Not drunk enough."

"You sound like a..."

"A what? Say it."

"A whore. You sound like a whore."

"That's me."

"I never heard of a married woman being a whore."

I laugh. "All married women are whores."

Now he bristles. "Not my mama."

"Okay, Royce. A lot of married women, but not your mama." Now he's totally confused and he drops his line of sight down to his knees. My God! The kid's a virgin! "Royce, why do you want to get involved with this shit for? The money? Ha! Benny Tanowski's money ain't doing him any good with him lying there in a hospital bed." He doesn't understand the connection. "It was Gianelli that did what happened to Tanowski, because he tried to fuck up the Saint Francis game."

"You don't know what you're talking about," he says, on the verge of changing his confusion into anger. "You don't know nothing about basketball."

"It ain't about basketball, Royce. It's strictly business."

"Yeah," he says, defiant now. "That's why I'm here. I ain't as stupid as you think I am."

"I don't think that at all, Royce. That's why I'm trying to help you."

"I don't need no help."

"But you do, Royce, because Johnny Boy is a crazy motherfucker. He's mean and nasty. Believe me, Royce. He's got a black heart. Nothing personal."

The poor chump is relieved when Johnny Boy and his two buddies reenter the room, the three of them smoking big black Cubano cigars, their faces almost hidden behind black clouds of smoke. And despite my warning Royce agrees to become one of Johnny Boy's tricks for $250 a game.

213

Chapter Nine

December 12, 1950

—SENIOR—

What the hell did I expect? Jerky-looking kids wearing propeller-topped beanies and necklaces made of dead fish? A ramshackle building with a lawn all littered with used prophylactics and empty beer cans? Naked coeds being chased around the front porch? Except for the sign above the front door, PHI EPSILON THETA, the building almost looks like just another all-American family dwelling with carefully swept walkways, a well-groomed lawn and cultured flower beds. Good. That shows these kids understand the importance of maintaining appearances, a more important concept than they'll learn in any of their classes. The only discordance is the fact that all the windows have been painted a solid white so that no light enters or escapes. How appropriate—my son lives in a white-eyed blind building.

The meticulous Main Street decor changes radically on the other side of the front door. There's piles of newspapers lining the vestibule, along with leaking bags of garbage. (Another good sign, proving that the brothers of P.E.T. aren't Goody Two-shoes.) To get to the staircase, I've got to kick my way through a minefield of empty beer cans, my every step raising a loud clatter. (An ingenious early warning system!)

A side door opens and a bespectacled young man, who'd apparently been sleeping, pokes his head out to say, "Yeah? How can I help you?" Seeing my tailored business suit, the youngster groans, "Crapola! We ain't supposed to be inspected until next week!"

"I'm just looking for my son. Ray Paluski."

"You ain't from the dean's office?"

"No. Ray Paluski. What room is he in?"

The young man breathes an audible sigh of relief. "Second floor. Number One, in the back. Knock twice, then pause, then knock three times. Otherwise he'll make believe he ain't there."

"Thanks."

The stairs creak like a pair of Buster Brown shoes but are clean and dust-free. The second-floor hallway is regally furnished with a nappy red rug underfoot, a matching couch, and a stately secretary table. Four rooms on the floor, each one identified by a single gold digit, and I knock, as directed, at Number One. A familiar voice from inside shouts, "Nobody's home! Go away!"

I execute the prescribed signal once more. This time the disembodied voice says, "What're you, fucking deaf? Amscray!"

I've promised myself that I won't lose my temper, but, pounding my fist on the door, I yell, "Open the goddamn door, Raymond." From within comes the sound of harsh whispers and quick feet, and the door opens a crack, then wider, revealing Raymond wearing a blue velour bathrobe with his initials inscribed in gold on the breast pocket. His feet are bare, his face unshaved, and his eyes look like they're melting. (How long did the party last? Foolish boy, he thinks he's going to be twenty-one forever.)

"Dad! What're you doing here?"

I push my way inside and make a quick reconnoiter. The room is sparsely furnished with a beat-up couch, a loudly humming refrigerator, and a bridge table surrounded by four mismatched chairs. Posted on the far wall are a chest X ray, a pair of black panties, and an authentic street sign (**W. BROADWAY**). Through a partially open door in the rear of the room, I try peeking into what's obviously the bedroom, but all I can see are large cushions spread on the floor.

Raymond hurries to close the bedroom door before repeating, "What're you doing here?"

"Jesus, Raymond. You look like some kind of playboy sheik."

Clearly uncomfortable, he laughs and says, "I wasn't exactly expecting company. So what do you want?"

"Can I at least sit down? Or is there something living inside that couch that'll bite me on the ass?"

"Sure. Have a seat. You want a beer?"

"No."

The couch is softer and deeper than it appears, and I'm concerned that I'll need his help to get up. When Raymond remains standing, I understand that he's trying to gain an advantage. So who cares? I'm the adult here.

"Raymond, we've got to talk about what's going on. No curve balls, no bullshit. Everything straight down the middle of the plate."

Raymond shifts his weight off his right ankle, which is still chronically sore from a high school injury. "Don't start that again, Dad. Like I've been telling you, everything's in the pink."

"Don't be a jerk, Raymond. Listen to me.... The D.A. is wise to Gianelli's whole operation. The crackdown's coming soon."

"Bullshit."

"It's true. There's a judge that... that I know, and he's feeding me the inside word. They've got the goods on players at C.C.N.Y., L.I.U., Rhinegold, and you guys, too. And that's just here in New York. How about the University of Kentucky? How about Bradley and Toledo? Plus there's at least three guys in the N.B.A. that they know were dumping in college. Norm Mager from C.C.N.Y., who's playing with the Baltimore Bullets. And how about Ralph Beard and Alex Groza with the Indianpolis Olympians? There's also about thirty other N.B.A. players that are under investigation. This whole thing is about to explode, Raymond, and you're sitting at ground zero."

He opens his mouth and out comes that insulting laugh that I hate. "Listen to me," he says calmly, intent on impressing me with his version of a rational argument. "What you're saying is exactly why nothing's gonna happen. The whole thing is way too big for anybody to fuck with. If they do, that'll be the end of college basketball. And if that happens, it'll cost too many important people too much money. The promoters, the athletic departments.... Even the guys who sell tickets and hot dogs and beer belong to labor unions. And it's been going on for so long that it's almost legit. Like cheating on your income taxes. Get it?"

"Hey, jackass. Who the fuck do you think you're talking to? I wrote the fucking book."

He blinks his blurry, road-map eyes, remembering the conversation we had the last time we saw each other, on Thanksgiving. That's when I told him I knew he was doing business with Gianelli and that I'd also been a point-shaver. He'd had no clue I was in the bag, and he'd been clearly disappointed in his dad. But I was delighted when he didn't insist on his innocence. That gave me hope that there's more substance to him than I'd always believed.

"What I'm saying, Dad, is that so many guys are involved that when and if the whistle blows, a lot of them are gonna skate free. And Saint John's is too well connected for us to fall."

"That's not necessarily the case, Raymond. The whole political climate is much different than when I played. Kefauver proved that a crime-stopper can make a big splash."

"Lookit, you've called me a dozen times since Thanksgiving, and we've already been through all this from toe to tit."

"You're gonna go down in flames," I insist, "unless you do what I say."

"Oh, shit. Here it comes again.... Quit school, change my name, and go play for some company team out in Palookaville somewhere."

"Rockford, Illinois," I say, struggling to extricate myself from the soft clutches of the couch, stubbornly waving off Ray's helping hand. "The Edmunson Brothers Tool and Die Company. They'll pay you twenty thousand to watch the grass grow and play on their company team. And it's good competition, Raymond. Hell, Bob Kurland's been playing in the industrial leagues with Akron Goodyear for years now and making more money than Mikan does in the pros."

"Is that all you've got to say, Dad?"

"The alternative isn't exactly a picnic, Ray."

He squirms with impatience. "I told you a million times, Dad. I ain't getting caught and I ain't going to jail and I ain't changing my name and moving to Rockfuck, Illinois. So just leave me alone."

"You fucking moron! I'll bet your phone is tapped. I'll even bet there's a bug somewhere in this room."

"Shit, Dad! The only bug in this room is you, man. You're crazy as a fucking bedbug!"

All of my promises to myself are forgotten as I step forward and attempt to grab the front of his robe. But the boy is too swift and too strong, easily shoving me back into a seated position on the couch.

"I'm sorry, Dad. I know you mean well and you're only trying to protect me—"

"And your mother, too. How would she feel if you were in jail?"

"Hey, how come all of a sudden you're worrying about Ma?"

I'm helpless without my brass-knuckle arguments, helpless before my own son. My temper comes on suddenly.

"You know what your fucking problem is, Raymond? You're a shooter, so you never get your hands dirty, and you think you can shoot your way out of any situation. Your trouble is that you can't, or won't, play defense. You can't set a pick. You won't give up your body and take a charge. All you care about is scoring points. Well, I've got a bulletin for you. That's only ten percent of the game. That's your fucking problem. All you want to do is follow the bouncing ball...."

"I've heard all that bullshit before. Save it for the funny pages."

"What about Tanowski?"

"I'm not Tanowski, Dad. Tanowski was stupid and I'm smart. Tanowski's also an asshole and I'm a nice guy. He once low-bridged me in a frosh game. Just took my legs out and sent me head-first into the floor. My fucking ears were ringing for a week. Besides, Tanowski's a double-crosser and he only got what he deserved."

A small voice shouts something unintelligible but petulant from inside the bedroom, prompting Raymond to try to dismiss me by saying, "I'm telling you, Dad, there's nothing to worry about. You know?"

"No, I don't know... how you became such a loser."

The defeated tone of my own voice surprises me. Is there nothing more I can do? Speak to Barney again? Have Raymond kidnapped and sneak him off to somewhere in South America? Make my own deal with the D.A., trading my guilt and my information for my son's future?

"Maybe you'd better go, Dad."

Then Raymond turns and vanishes into his bedroom, slamming the door behind him. In an instant, I hear the carefree sound of youthful laughter, leaving me feeling useless and desolate.

Chapter Ten

December 13, 1950

—JOHNNY BOY—

I hate hospitals, but this visit is a necessary courtesy. Rosie doesn't like hospitals either, but I wanted her to see my compassionate side. And there's Tanowski, lying on his back with his hands in casts and his arms wired upright so that it looks like he's surrendering. There's also pieces of pinkish gauze stuffed into his mouth and his nose doesn't look so good either. Serves the bastard right.

When he sees me, he tries to scream but all he does is honk like a fucking goose. Makes me want to laugh. His wet blond hair hangs down uncombed and plastered to his forehead. Only his eyes are fully alive, bulging like they're going to explode. He's looking around for a nurse to rescue him, but I've already arranged for us not to be disturbed.

This place smells of rotting flesh. Even the nurse I spoke to smelled like she uses perfume made of formaldehyde.

Let's get this over with. I motion for Rosie to come closer so she can hear me say this to Tanowski:

"It's a tough break, Benny, but that's what happens when you try to drive when you've been drinking too much. As you know, I'm a big City College basketball fan so, out of the goodness of my heart, I'm gonna take care of you, Benny. That's right. I've arranged to pay all your hospital bills. And when you do get back on your feet, I'll make sure you get a nice fat-ass job sitting behind a desk somewhere. So all you've got to think about, Benny, is getting well. Okay?"

Then he tries to turn away as I lean forward, but I grab his chin so he can't move and I whisper in his ear. "It's nothing personal, Benny,

I'd do the same thing for any of my players. I forgive you, Benny. You hear me? I forgive you."

Then I stand up straight and turn to Rosie. "All right, toots," I say. "Let's get out of this morgue."

—MAE JOHNSON—

The furnace has been shut down for the evening and the radiator pipes in the living room are cooling and contracting and clanging and that means another long cold night. I wish I had me a warmer quilt, but I don't. In cold weather, the landlord tells Joe the super to start up the furnace at nine A.M. and shut it off at ten P.M. sharp. The last super we had here used to stretch the hours a little, but he got fired.

Even though I'm chilled down to the bone, I can't complain. I like sitting here in my favorite rocking chair after another long shift in the laundry.... Lord, how I hate that job! I always have such a headache by the time I get out of there, what with the noise from the machines and the ammonia fumes. And why do all the supervisors yell and scream at us to get the work done right? I need a miracle to get me free of that job (maybe Kelsey striking it rich with his music—or Royce with his basketball), 'cause I feel like an old mule that's about ready to break down and die. And I'm mad about it, too. Mad that Kelsey gets to do whatever he wants, making his music and traveling all around while I'm stuck here, still slaving over other folks' dirty stuff. Kelsey "plays" his music and Royce "plays" basketball. But I'm always working and hardly get any chance to play. I mean, I ain't no bowing and shuffling upstairs maid. I'm a person, too. I enjoys me a hot bath, and good food, and a nip to warm my belly (which I can't do now in front of the boy), and a little jellyroll with my husband to warm the rest of me. Amen.

I've learned to do without, but I don't have to like it. That's 'cause all my juices is running dry and for the first time in my life I'm feeling like an old lady. And, 'scuse me, Lord, but pie in the sky ain't good enough. Might be I'm going to hell, too, for all my complaining. Amen to that, too.

But I do enjoy sitting here rocking and knitting, a wintertime sweater I've been making for Royce for several years now, white snowflakes on a blue background. And I got him a new Charlie Parker record for Christmas. So I guess I can enjoy this very moment such as it is. It ain't as bad as all that but for how tired I am.

Maybe it's time to count my blessings. Like the big console radio sitting there next to the window that Kelsey got me one Christmas when he came home all flush with money left over from his drinking and carousing. Tonight's one of my favorite programs, *The F.B.I. in Peace and War*, sponsored by Lava soap.

It don't even matter to me that the living room is kind of dreary, with the musty-smelling rug, the Salvation Army furniture, a broken two-way floor lamp that Royce was supposed to fix. I guess he forgot. Lord, but I am proud of the boy for being the first of my kin to ever go to college, and I suppose he's the biggest of my blessings. I just hope he don't wind up irresponsible like his father. Maybe if I hadn't been working all these years I could've been a better mother to him. But I believe he's got a good heart in him, and he's never been in trouble.

At least I ain't thinking about the hospital no more. Just rocking and knitting and trying to stay warm and trying not to let Royce catch me staring too hard at him while he's all curled up on the floor with one of his school books. He says the radio don't bother him when he's studying. And I'm happy to think how good playing basketball has been for him. He's got a grown-up look about him now. No more whining about he don't like this food or that, or he don't want to go to bed, or he don't want to wake up. He just goes about his business, studying, doing his household chores (except for that lamp), taking what comes just like a man. And I do enjoy going to Madison Square Garden (for free!) to see him play and hearing all them people cheering for him. I don't mind that he's a little bit serious lately 'cause I know he's not shirking his responsibilities. And it also means he's not letting all that cheering and the newspaper stories go to his head.

—ROYCE—

Ma's smiling like she's got the world on a string, clicking those knitting needles to exercise her arthritic fingers. But me, I can hardly pay attention to the stupid radio or my stupid school books. I'm thinking about what I agreed to do two nights ago at Mister Gianelli's place.

> *"Spike, it's me. Father Duffy. The G-men have*
> *got you surrounded. You have no chance, Spike.*
> *Release the girl and come out with your hands up.*
> *It's not too late to change your ways, Spike, and*
> *tread the straight and narrow path."*

The telephone starts to ring, and Ma's worried, wondering who it could be at this hour. She's thinking that Daddy's in jail in some godforsaken city (or injured in an automobile accident, or dead!). Or else the brand-new washer is broken down again at the hospital, and she's going to have to go over there and hand-wash shit-phlegm-pus-piss-stained sheets all night long. Or else her great-aunt Sophie has finally died back home in Booneville.

She sighs as she picks up the receiver, then she says, "Hello? Who is this, please?... Just one moment, please." Then she puts her hand over the receiver and holds it out to me. "It's for you. Someone named Rosie."

"I don't know no Rosie," I say as I reach for the phone. "Hello?"

"Royce, it's Rosie. Johnny Boy Gianelli's wife."

"Oh." I'm stunned, confused, embarrassed. Ma's curious look feels hot, like X-ray vision. "Just a minute, Rosie." Then I cover the receiver with my hand and say, "It's okay, Ma."

Ma says she's going to warm up some milk to help her sleep. I watch her grip the arms of her chair and push herself erect to spare her worn-out legs. And only once she is safely out of earshot do I uncover the receiver and say, "Hello." Again, wondering what Rosie wants, hopeful and afraid that she wants to arrange a date.

"Royce, have you been thinking about what I said the other night when you were up here? About staying away from Johnny Boy and staying out of trouble?"

"Yeah, I've been thinking about it. Don't cost nothing to think about something."

"I know you said what Johnny Boy wanted you to say, Royce. But you don't play again until tomorrow and it ain't too late to change your mind."

"No, thanks. I've already seen what happens when somebody crosses Mister Gianelli."

"That's got nothing to do with you because you never made a specific deal and you never took any money."

"But I gave my word to Otis and Barry and Mister Gianelli."

"Listen to me, Royce. Fuck all of them. They don't give half a shit about you. All they care about is what you can do for them. See? I mean, it's all illegal. Shaving points and deliberately losing ball games."

"Mister Gianelli, he said we wouldn't have to deliberately lose any—"

"Yeah, yeah, I know what he said. Between you, me and the lamppost, he thinks that just because he's richer than most, and just because he can make people dance and make people die, that everybody's supposed to believe every stupid little thing he says. I live with the man, see? And take it from me, he don't know as much as he says he does. He can't even fill a fucking bathtub without pissing and moaning that the water's too hot or too cold, and the plumber's an asshole...and then begging me to make the water the right temperature. So you just shut the fuck up and listen to me, okay?"

"Okay."

"It's all illegal and it can't go on forever. I mean, everybody's so cocky that they're getting careless. Johnny Boy too. He's betting too much money. So it's only a matter of time. But the point is, Royce, that you're too young and too naive to get involved."

"But I already—"

"That doesn't matter. What matters is that you don't want to go to prison, do you?"

"No. But Mister Gianelli...he'd beat me up, or—"

"Fuck Mister Gianelli." Now *she's* getting angry at me. What the fuck am I gonna do?! "Now, I'll make you a promise, Royce. Cross my heart and hope to die. If you ever do business with Johnny Boy, if you ever shave points, or take any money from him, then I swear I'm gonna call the fucking cops on you. I mean it, Royce."

"You can't do that. He won't let you."

"It ain't about what he's letting me do. It's about what I want to do. All right? I got enough stuff on the old fuck to send him away for the rest of his miserable fucking life. So don't worry about him. Just listen to me, Royce. I want you to swear that you'll have nothing to do with rigging ball games."

"What do I do instead?"

"Just tell Otis that you changed your mind. And don't let him bully you."

"Yeah."

"And I want you to swear that you won't do business with my husband."

Crossing my heart unbidden, I feel an enormous sense of relief. "I swear that I won't do business with Mister Gianelli and I hope to die if I do."

"It's for your own good, Royce. And it's for me, too. Someday you'll thank me." Then she hangs up without saying good-bye.

Just then Ma walks back into the room, carefully balancing a steaming glass of milk on a small dish.

"Yes," I say into the buzzing receiver. "Chapter Five. That's right, Rosie...no problem at all. Bye. See you in class tomorrow."

Ma is smiling as I hang up the phone. "Is she a nice girl, son? What does her daddy do to make his living?"

"Ma!" I say and we both laugh. Suddenly I'm sinless and happy again, my childhood instantly restored.

I can't wait to tell Otis, so when Ma goes to the bathroom, I dial his number. But Otis only laughs when I tell him the good news. "You're crazy, boy. That old man'd just as soon have you killed as scratch his ass."

"But what about jail?"

"Guys been doing shit like this for over twenty years, so why should we be the ones who get caught? And if we do? That's just our tough shit."

"But Rosie said—"

"Don't pay that stupid bitch no mind. Fuck her if you can, but don't listen to her. If she blows the whistle on you, then she also rats on him. Please, nigger. Do you think Gianelli would ever let her get away with it?"

Which is worse, being fucked up my ass for the rest of my life or being killed once?

"Yeah, Otis. I guess you're right."

"Damn fucking straight I'm right."

"Tonight's episode of 'The FBI in Peace and War' was brought to you by the folks who make Lava soap.... L-A-V-A...."

Chapter Eleven

January 3, 1951

—BARNEY—

Theoretically I love trains. They represent the perfect combination of dependability, danger, and romance, and I often dream of glorious railroad adventures riding the Orient Express or the Trans-Siberia local. I even like the elevated trains in New York and their slow explosions of steely agony as they approach a station, especially at night, when the long headlights reach bravely into the iron-hearted darkness.

In truth I always take taxicabs—$3.75 to Madison Square Garden, $1.10 to Ebbets Field, $2.65 to Grand Central Station, all covered by my friendly expense account.

But here I am, riding the I.R.T., traveling incognito—wearing dungarees and a sloppy green sweater under a soiled red plaid mackinaw I haven't worn in twenty years—and daring to appear in public without my familiar hat and cigar. With the train roaring through the dark tunnel, and the sudden lurchings, and the lights flickering into quick darknesses, I feel like I'm trapped inside a gigantic iron lung. The top of my skull is peeled away to expose my raw and throbbing brain. My mouth is empty and cavernous, my teeth are reduced to tiny scattered pebbles.

I carry a copy of the *New York Daily News* rolled up in my right hand like a baton. Just an ordinary slobola riding the subway on my way to nowhere.

So far my disguise seems to be working—none of my fellow travelers so much as glance in my direction. Several hardened subway riders nap fitfully. Others stare vacantly through the soot-streaked windows. Sitting opposite me, a young man is reading D. D. Gerson's famous critique, *The Quality of Shakespearean Verse*. The student looks up and challenges my stare, compelling me to quickly look away and begin reading the advertising slogans posted high on the walls above the dangling hand-straps.

"I'd Walk a Mile for a Camel."

"Use Wildroot Cream Oil, Charlie."

Most of the other riders read newspapers, the headlines, a short-hand of strife and death.

WILLIE SUTTON BREAKS OUT
OF SING SING
ALGER HISS SENTENCED
FOR PERJURY

RIOTS IN JOHANNESBURG

ASSASSINATION ATTEMPT AGAINST TRUMAN FAILS

Unrolling the "Schwartz" section, I reread the only news I care about: "DATELINE, NEW YORK.... St. John's basketball team lost another squeaker last night, 54–53, when Ray Pulaski, Jr., missed a wide-open layup just before the final buzzer sounded...."

Since last seeing Ray Senior, I've casually canvassed my bookie contacts without confirming any definite scandalous activity among the local college basketball teams. Just the same rumors, and rumors of rumors. Not that I actually required a second opinion—I know Ray's painful confession is on the level. I did discover, however, from a bookmaker in Cleveland, that several players at Bradley University and the University of Toledo are "crooked as snakes."

This fucking nightmare. And I've totally lost my sense of reality, of those parts of my life that I once believed had true and lasting significance. The Dodgers? Those chokers. College basketball? My ass-wipe newspaper columns? More and more these past few days I've taken refuge in Shakespeare:

*"The time is out of joint; O cursed spite,
That ever I was born to set it right!"*

Okay.

Now what?

For the life of me, I don't know anyone who might help me extricate Junior from this mess. I know no judges, no congressmen. I know no lawyers who aren't ambulance chasers. In desperation I finally telephoned Jimmy O'Hara in the Manhattan district attorney's office, a guy I haven't spoken to, or even thought of, since seeing him last summer at Levy's-by-the-Lake. "I've got to talk to you in private," I actually said. "It's a matter of life or death."

According to O'Hara, "There's no such thing as privacy because even the walls have ears." O'Hara proposed that we meet on the downtown AA local, second car from the end. O'Hara would come aboard at East Forty-ninth Street, at precisely 1:45 P.M. on Wednesday, and I was instructed to divert suspicion by getting on farther uptown.

The train staggers to a halt at the designated station right on time, and there's O'Hara, bespectacled, thin-faced, only in his thirties but with faded freckles spotting his high forehead, foreshadowing what he'll look like in twenty years. I'm glad I've taken the time to dig deeply into the *Sentinel*'s files, discovering that O'Hara's three older brothers (along with his father and four uncles) are cops. Also that O'Hara was valedictorian at St. Christopher's High School in Queens before moving on to graduate from St. John's and then St. John's Law School. Yet he hasn't managed to pass the bar exam in three attempts. The inside word is that O'Hara was hired only because the D.A. and one of the kid's uncles are fraternity brothers. O'Hara's official title is Researcher and he's paid $54.23 a week.

The train lurches forward and O'Hara has to grab at a pole to keep from falling. He wears a rumpled gray raincoat over a gray business suit, but his attempt to appear worldly and sophisticated is ruined by his large necktie that's nearly as wide and as orange as Roy Campanella's chest protector. In O'Hara's right hand he brandishes a brand-new well-oiled leather briefcase. None of the other passengers take notice as O'Hara rubber-legs his way down the aisle.

The train picks up speed, careening through the tunnel, the overhead lights fluttering, and O'Hara seems startled by the sudden flashes, or is it by the unwashed smells of these random citizens whose rights he has sworn to uphold? Like me, he's obviously unaccustomed to riding the subway. But O'Hara doesn't recognize me, so I growl his name above the relentless clacking of the wheels. "O'Hara! Psst! Over here!"

The young public servant is startled once more, even as he plops down beside me with undisguised relief. "Barney! It *is* you! Jeez! I had no idea you was a baldie!"

I shrug, already impatient. "Thanks for meeting me here, Jimmy. Now, what d'ya say we get right down to brass tacks?"

But a grizzled white man with smoky-gray eyes that seem opaque is carefully navigating the length of the train, aided by a long thin bamboo cane that taps the littered floor before him. The poor bastard holds forth a tin measuring cup, which he shakes to rattle the coins within. Instinctively I reach into my coat pocket for spare change.

"Don't be a sucker," says O'Hara. "That's just a flimflammer named Zeke Zalacca. He looks like a bum, but he owns three apartment buildings in Forest Hills and he's got better eyesight than Ted Williams. Puts special drops in his eyes to make them look like that. Got a rap sheet for fraud long as your arm."

As the panhandler approaches, O'Hara says, "Beat it, Zalacca. Go get yourself an honest job."

The panhandler blinks once, stands his ground, then says, "God bless you" and moves on only after a black woman drops a nickel into his cup.

Then O'Hara turns his squinty brown eyes on me. "So what gives with the life-or-death routine? Who's dying and what makes you think I can do something about it?"

Moving closer, I want to touch him, to share our humanness, to let him feel my desperation, but the best I can do is to reach out and put my hand on O'Hara's briefcase, saying, "You got to help me out, Jimmy. I need some information. It's for a friend."

O'Hara recoils slightly, pulling the briefcase under his folded arms. "Like what kind of information?"

The train screams into the next station, and I hold my answer until the new passengers get settled and our journey resumes.

"You gotta tell me, Jimmy... everything you know about the college basketballers shaving points."

O'Hara quickly looks around the car. "What?" he yips, his lower jaw hanging open for just a moment, showing a mouthful of silver fillings. "I don't know whatcha talking about." Then O'Hara tries to stand up, and something happens to me that I can hardly explain, some psychological mechanism suddenly clicks, and I'm no longer a spectator watching my own life unfold from a comfortable distance. It *is* a matter of life or death—mine. And I'm compelled to *do* something *now.* I'm frightened and confused, but I grab a padded shoulder of O'Hara's coat and force the younger man to be seated.

"Hey, Barney! Whatcha doing? I could have you pinched for assaulting an officer of the court!"

"This ain't no court," I say. "This is the fucking I.R.T., Jimmy. And right now it's just you and me, man-to-man. So just quit the innocent act and tell me what you know about college basketball games being fixed."

"Are you outta your frigging gourd? This here is very confidential stuff you're asking about. I can't go blabbing to the newspapers and expect to keep my frigging job." With the pointed index finger of his right hand, O'Hara repeatedly nudges his eyeglasses back up the bridge of his nose as the train rocks and rattles through the flashing gloom. The poor kid, he's more scared than I am.

Displaying my most agreeable shit-eating grin, I say, "Jimmy, this is all off the record, you understand? It ain't for publication. Like I already told you... it's for a friend."

O'Hara hugs his briefcase. "I can't say nothing about a case under investigation, Barney. It's a question of ethics."

"I'll give you a hundred bucks, Jimmy. Make that two hundred. Or even three hundred. You just name your price."

"Jeez, Barney. Now I could have you pinched for attempting to bribe an officer of the court."

"What about Dodgers tickets, Jimmy? Box seats behind the dugout."

When O'Hara merely shrugs, I up the ante. "What about four box-seat tickets for next year's opening day against the Giants?" O'Hara wrinkles his thin dark eyebrows in a practiced gesture of boredom. Now I'm getting steamed, but I say, "All right, you win. . . . I'll get your kid on *Happy Felton's Knothole Gang.*"

"And?"

"How about lunch with Duke Snider?"

O'Hara nods once, then removes his eyeglasses and wipes the lenses clean with the broad end of his necktie. "We was taping the telephone of a subcontractor in Brooklyn," he says. "Guy named Paddy Clune—he's using way too much sand in the concrete foundation that his company's pouring for that new courthouse down on Chambers Street. You know the one I mean? He's not following the specifications in the contract.... So the guy's cheating the city and we're recording his telephone calls. And guess who the guy calls and guess what they're talking about?"

When O'Hara pauses, I snarl, "What the fuck is this? Twenty questions? Get on with it."

"Hold your horses, Barney," O'Hara says in self-defense. "I'm getting there.... So this guy Clune is calling up Johnny Boy Gianelli about five times every day. And guess what these two creeps is yakking about, Barney? That's right. Fixing college basketball games."

We both clam up as the train stops at Thirtieth Street. The doors slide open and an old lady enters pushing a wire-frame shopping cart in front of her. The old lady hustles to find a seat before the doors slam shut like the gates of a jail cell, and the train accelerates.

O'Hara is amused. "You know what I can't figure out, Barney? How come old ladies like that one there, they push those shopping carts in front of them? How come they don't pull them behind like they're supposed to? It ain't very efficient, you know?"

My brain is on fire. My words echo inside my mouth. "Listen, you cluck. They push the fucking carts so's nobody can sneak up and steal the old ladies' groceries when they ain't looking.... So cut the crap, O'Hara, and tell me about the fixes."

"I ain't no cluck, Barney. For crap's sake. I already told you way too much. If the D.A. ever finds out—"

"Okay, okay. How about I get you and your boy into the Dodger clubhouse and introduce you to Jackie Robinson?"

"You mean it, Barney? You could do that?"

"Yeah, yeah. Just keep talking."

O'Hara readjusts his eyeglasses for the hundredth time. "There ain't much more to tell.... I mean, one thing led to another, and the circle got wider.... Fixing college ball games is a felony, Barney. Section

Twenty-four F in the Municipal Code.... And we got the goods on everybody. The gamblers and the ballplayers."

"What ballplayers?"

O'Hara hesitates, but I'm through negotiating. "What else do ya want?" I ask. "Carl Furillo to suck your dick? C'mon, O'Hara. A deal's a deal. Spill it."

O'Hara squirms and fingers his eyeglasses. "Well, Jesus H. Christ. You don't have to get so snappy.... Anyways...we found out that everybody's doing it."

"Like who?"

"Everybody...players at City College, Rhinegold, St. John's, L.I.U., N.Y.U., Manhattan...you name it."

"Who are the players? O'Hara, name me the players."

"Like I says, everybody.... Otis Hill, Barry Hoffman, Phil Isaacson, Joey Callahan, Royce Johnson maybe, Benny Tanowski, Jimmy McCoy, Shawn Sweeney, Ray Pulaski...."

"You got any hard evidence that'll hold up in court?"

"Wait, there's more.... At Rhinegold, we got Gary Edwards, Chip Landers, and Charlie Bloom. At N.Y.U. we got—"

"Hold on, O'Hara."

"Hey, you said you wanted the names, so I'm giving them to you."

"Yeah, yeah. Okay. So tell me what kind of evidence you got."

"Well, we have a whole stack of them vinyl records made off the telephone tapes. Very incriminating evidence even if we can't use it in court. We also got pictures of some of the Saint John's players out nightclubbing with Gianelli. Believe me, Barney. We got at least enough to bring them in, and once we get our hands on them? What with the spotlights and the constant questioning and the threats? Believe me, Barney. By the time we're through with them, they'll be dying to sell their own mothers down the river. I'm telling you, Barney, these kids are so frigging dumb. Most of them are spending much more cash money than they're supposed to have... fancy duds, new suits, watches, gold rings. Spending like a bunch of drunken sailors."

"What'll happen, then? I mean to the kids?"

O'Hara laughs. "That depends. Some of them'll get arrested and some of them won't."

"What does that mean?"

"Barney, I swear to Jesus that I really can't say no more. I'm already way out on a limb as it is. Please don't ask me no more."

"How about World Series tickets?"

"No, Barney. This here is extremely confidential material. I swear I can't say no more."

"Joe DiMaggio's a friend of mine. I'll see if I can—"

"Barney. I don't care if you can get Jesus Himself to show up next week at my niece's confirmation.... It's the end of the line, Barney—City Hall. This is where I get off."

Once again, O'Hara tries to stand up, But I reach out and pull him back into his seat. "Listen, O'Hara... I'm getting you box-seat tickets. I'm getting you introduced to Jackie Robinson. I'm getting you the chance to drool all over Duke Snider's fucking hamburger.... And if you don't spill *all* the beans, O'Hara...? I swear to you. I'll go back on my word and plaster your name all over the fucking front page."

"You wouldn't! You said this was off the record!"

"So I fucking lied."

O'Hara drops his briefcase and uses a neatly ironed handkerchief to wipe his brow. "Barney," he moans. "Gimme a frigging break."

"I ain't fucking around with you, O'Hara. And you'd better tell me the straight dope or you'll be sorry. I swear this on my children's eyes."

Even though I've never even been rumored to have fathered a child, O'Hara says this: "The Saint John's kids'll probably beat the rap 'cause they've got some very important friends in very high places. The highest. That's all I can tell you, Barney. I really mean it."

But I'm ruthless. "I already warned you once. Don't fuck with me, O'Hara."

O'Hara picks up his briefcase and uses the handkerchief to wipe off the scuffmarks. Then he speaks so softly that I have to lean forward to hear him say, "The D.A.'s a graduate of Saint John's, right? Everybody knows that. So there's been some funny stuff happening around the office."

"Like what?"

"Like the recording we made of certain incriminating telephone conversations? They're made of vinyl, right? Well, three days ago, somebody 'accidentally' knocked them off the table and the records shattered into a million pieces. And even bigger than the D.A., Barney, somebody else is working real hard to keep the lid on. Don't make me tell you who it is, Barney. Please."

"You got only one more chance, O'Hara."

"Please, Barney. If this ever gets out, I'll be killed. I'll be excommunicated."

"Let's hear it, O'Hara. In for a penny, in for a pound."

So, putting his immortal soul in peril, Jimmy O'Hara says this: "It seems that Cardinal Spellman got tipped off and he's squeezing the D.A. pretty hard. That's why all the kids from the Catholic schools are probably gonna get away scot-free."

I wheedle one last concession out of O'Hara—exclusive and advance word before any arrests are made. Then I finally let him escape.

"Jesus Christ." Look at me—I'm just another twitching lunatic riding the subways and talking to himself. "Jesus Christ." All the way to Pelham Bay Park and back.

Chapter Twelve

January 9, 1951

—SAMMY—

I'm back on the beam. *Swish!* Locked in. *Swish!* And I can't wait for the game to start. *Swish!* Because this is it, the last game I'm ever going to fuck with. The last game that's ever going to fuck with me. *Thunk!* Step and shoot.... *Swish!* And this one's going to be my biggest paycheck of them all. *Swish!* It's a pick-'em game against C.C.N.Y. here at Wingate Gymnasium, their home court. *Swish!* And I'll get four big ones if we win. *Swish!* No shaving, no dumping, no half-assed hooping. *Swish!* And I'm primed to play the game of my life!

Swish!

—ROYCE—

No question that this is the biggest game of the season for us. Our record is only 10-and-6 and this is our chance to turn it around against Rhinegold, currently 13-and-3 and ranked numer five in the polls. Like Goldberg just said in the locker room, "If we don't win tonight in our own backyard, then we can kiss the N.I.T. good-bye."

The joint is jumping. Even Ma's here. (I haven't seen Daddy since Thanksgiving. He's supposed to be playing somewhere on the West Coast.) How do they get so many people in here? Except for a small space around the court, it's like the subway during rush hour. And the fans are already on their feet and screaming their brains out even though we're still just warming up.

Barry Hoffman's out with a banged-up knee, so I'm starting for the first time ever, and I wish I could say that I'm ready to score thirty points and hold the game in my hands. But me, I feel like shit. There's no lift in my legs, no touch in my hands, and no joy in any part of me. Why? Because Gianelli's paying us to lose.

So far I've worked four ball games and made a thousand dollars! (All of it in a paper bag stashed under my bed, and I haven't dared to spend a single red cent.) My first fix was against St. Bonaventure at the Garden, and although I scored ten points, I deliberately missed an easy shot in the last minute of play. On the road against Wagner, I dribbled the ball off my foot in a crucial situation. Against Holy Cross up there, I missed two free throws late in the game. In the other tainted game, a two-point loss to Penn State also in the Garden, I shot 4-for-5 and scored eleven points, but never left the bench in the fourth quarter.

After every loss Ma tells me the same thing: "You tried your best, Royce. That's all a body can do. The rest is up to God Almighty."

Playing the other games straight was a great relief and I've had several outstanding performances. Against Fordham, I had seventeen points and six assists. Against Hunter, it was twenty-one points, four assists, and a load of fun.

Oh, man. Look who's sitting over there at the press table. Joe Lapchick, the coach of the New York Knickerbockers.

Lord. Lord. How'd I ever get into this? How'm I ever going to get out alive?

—SAMMY—

I should've known that my idiotic teammates would be dumping tonight. Assholes! Look at them throwing the ball all over the court. Letting easy passes slip through their hands. Banging easy shots off the backboard. They're so fucking crude. Is Henry just too stupid to grasp the obvious? Or is he also on the take? After a couple of ridiculous short-hop passes bounce off my shins, Henry takes me out of the ball game and claims that my timing is off. What a clown! Good thing my shot is clicking. *Swish!* We're ahead 17–15 after the first quarter.

—ROYCE—

Jesus, both teams are playing like we're wearing handcuffs. What a horrible game. Otis is missing shots he can make in his sleep. Isaacson is throwing passes just an inch or two out of reach. Me, I'm playing better than I'm supposed to, but that'll change. And Goldberg is going nuts in the huddles. Otis he calls "pussy willow." Isaacson is "shit-for-brains." Me, I'm a "chickenshit freshman."

Sammy Goodrich is shooting out of his ass, and at halftime they lead 36–25. Goldberg's sure gonna massacre us in the locker room.

And I feel like I've murdered somebody and gotten away with it. I feel like I've murdered myself.

No matter how much Goldberg insults us and threatens us, we're much more afraid of crossing Gianelli. Me, I'd rather run a thousand suicides than get worked over with a steel pipe.

In the middle of the third quarter Otis tells me to slow down, and I come up with the perfect game plan. I deliberately dribble into heavy traffic, then, when I'm stymied, I just unload the ball over to Otis. Now it's his problem. And he smiles at me, digging what's going on. "That's right," he says.

And Lapchick's taking notes as fast as he can.

But except for Goodrich, who's making the scoreboard explode like Fourth of July fireworks, Rhinegold's playing just as shitty as us. Credit Goodrich for Rhinegold's 48–39 lead after three quarters.

—SAMMY—

As we're lining up for a foul shot, I say something to Charlie Bloom, our senior point guard, who's playing the worst game of his mediocre career. "I know what you're doing, Charlie, and so does everyone else with half a brain."

"Fuck you," he sneers. "You think you know everything, but you don't know shit."

Anyway, I pick up my fourth personal foul with about four minutes left. Since we're up 68–55 and the game seems secure, Henry sits me down to save me for an emergency. And of course Charlie and his playmates now have a free hand to turn every trick in the book. Passes to the back of a teammate's head. Tripping over the sideline and falling out of bounds. And, after all, how many unguarded layups can the City College players miss without risking immediate arrest? So, while I'm cooling my heels, our lead quickly shrinks. Henry, the shmuck, is apparently saving me for overtime.

The crowd is looking eyes-left at the City College basket, where Johnson is shooting free throws (and converting one of two), when I see somebody on the opposite side of the court furiously waving at me. My God! It's Klein. When he catches my eye, he pantomimes drinking from a phantom cup. The score is US–70 and THEM–64 with less than two minutes remaining when I rendezvous with Klein at the water cooler.

"I'm in big trouble," he says. "I had to lay off a lot of money and so did a bunch of other guys. It's crazy, Sammy. I don't know what the fuck's going on."

I hear Henry calling my name, so I say, "Hurry up, Klein. What do you want?"

"The spread changed drastically, Sammy, and I'm in for more money than I have."

"So?"

"So, you have to lose the game or else I'm a dead man. That's for real, Sammy. If you guys win, then I'm history."

I turn and hurry back to Henry, who's shitting in his pants.

"Go back in there," he says in a total panic, "and turn this fucking thing around, will ya?"

With twenty-three seconds to go, our lead is down 72–71 and C.C.N.Y. is set to inbound the ball.

—ROYCE—

The play's supposed to be for Otis, but everything gets fucked up and nobody's in their right spot. So I'm stuck with the ball, hugging the left base line about seventeen feet out, and nobody's guarding me. And Goldberg and Weiss are jumping up and down and yelling at me to shoot. Fuck. So I do, only I flinch when I shoot, like my feet've slipped, or I've hurt myself, and I heave the ball up there, hoping it hits a piece of something so I won't be totally embarrassed, and the fucking thing goes in! Fuck me!

—SAMMY—

ooo Johnson throws up a silly crazy-ass shot from the base line that actually grazes the backboard before nestling into the net, and City leads for the first time in the game, 73–72.

Henry calls his last time-out and here's his play: I'll pass inbounds to Charlie, who's to dribble to the top of the key and then pass it back to me. Meanwhile everybody else moves to the right sideline, safely out of harm's way. "Don't fuck up, Charlie," Henry says, "or you'll never play another minute for this team." (Jesus! Could it be that Henry does understand?)

As Charlie moves the ball across the timeline, I can see Klein sitting in the stands, hiding his head in his hands. And here comes the pass as ordered, and I've got seven seconds to win this fucking game. Otis is guarding me, but a quick fake right loses him and I dribble hard left, moving away from the oncoming double-team.

Fuck Klein! Fuck the money! I want to be a winner! I want to be a first-round draft pick!

So I snatch up my dribble, then I step and shoot, and the ball rolls sweetly through the air, soaring, flying, a flashing synapse where my outstretched fingers and the roundness of the world meet, our path around the sun, beginning and ending, the congress of all things—

"Yes!" I shout, but the fucking shot misses hard right and we lose.

Chapter Thirteen

January 10, 1951

—ROYCE—

Naturally Goldberg and Weiss were ecstatic, shaking my hand and patting my back after the game, but none of the other guys would even look at me....

...Until just before practice this afternoon, when Otis comes over to my locker, just as I'm lacing up my sneakers, and says, "Here." Then he palms me a fifty-dollar bill.

"What's this?" I say. And I notice that Otis doesn't look as rock-hard and cocksure as he usually does. His eyes are nervous and his smile is more grim than disdainful.

At first I think he's going to ignore my question, then he moves closer and says, "After the game I thought the big man was gonna have a shit fit and point his head-breakers in our direction, but he was all smiling and cheerful. None of it makes any sense. You know? I can't put my finger on what the action is. The best I can figure is that there's some other guys involved, guys with bigger bankrolls, trying to make deals with the same players. I've heard rumors about some guys down in Philly. Sounds like a lot of double-and triple-crossing going on. Anyway, the big man, he says he knows that you tried to tank the shot. He told me to give you this as a token of his forgiveness and a gesture of his goodwill. I'm tellin' you, man, you're the luckiest nigger I ever saw."

"Otis," I say, "I'm not doing anymore games. I've had enough. Tell him that from now on he can count me out."

Otis only laughs. "You mean that from now on he can count you dead." Then he walks away.

I stash the money inside the top of my socks and head upstairs to the gym. Me, I'm already dead, so I've got nothing to lose. Right?

Isn't it amazing how quickly grief gives way to hatred? And I hate our practice sessions, mainly because Goldberg can blow his little pipsqueak whistle and stop the action whenever he wants to curse us. *Tweet!* "You! Fancy Dan! Can't you tell the fucking Four-Up play from the fucking Three-Down? What're you, brain dead? God in heaven, why did You ever invent freshmen?" And, barely ten seconds later, the whistle peeps again. "You! Number Eleven! You shmuck! The guy set you a perfectly good pick, so why the fuck did you take the great-circle route around it?"

Suddenly a side exit door opens and two uniformed security cops enter the gym, each one roughly holding an elbow of a sloppy-looking black man as though he were a prisoner recaptured after an unsuccessful escape attempt. The man looks familiar, wearing a cheap blue suit with a split seam in the back. He's hatless and his short black hair is gummed into knots. Judging by his lopsided steps, the man is either injured or drunk. But, no, it can't be him. It better not be.

"What?" Goldberg barks. "What the fuck is this?"

The older of the two rented cops steps forward to respectfully remove his hat and say, "I'm sorry for the intrusion, Coach Goldberg, but this guy claims he's Royce Johnson's father, and he says he has to speak to him about a family emergency. We didn't want to throw him out in case what he says is on the level."

By now everybody in the gym is staring at me. "Well?" Goldberg says. "Is it true? Do you know this man?"

"Yes," I mumble. "That's him. That's my father."

Then Goldberg turns back to his players. "All right! The rest of you lazy asses, what the fuck are you gawking at? Give me three suicides."

The cops release Daddy, who rushes to greet me with a hug and a disgusting boozey smooch. "Royce," he says. "My son. My main man."

Me, my face feels flush. "What do you want?.... Hey, did something happen to Ma? Is she okay?"

Snorting a laugh, Daddy says, "Ain't nothin' wrong with your mama. Ain't nothin' like that."

"What is it, then? I've got to get back to practice."

The cops stand at ease about ten paces away, twirling their night-sticks, waiting to pounce. So Daddy grabs my arm and says, "C'mere, son. We need some privacy."

Huddling against me near the far corner of the gym, Daddy presses his stinky breath into my face and says, "The thing is, son, I been way down on my luck. I'm ready to cry, man. I'm 'bout ready to die. Nothing ain't working out."

I reach out to him and he sighs as he eagerly grasps my right hand between both of his. "I knew you'd be with me, son." His fingers are cold.

"Tell me what happened, Daddy."

"I had a little dispute with Stan because the greedy motherfucker was cheating me outta my money, so I had to quit the damn gig. You know? I just came into town late last night and I got to get myself cleaned up before I can go to stay with your mother. Anyways, I was in this bar last night, see? And I heard some cats talking about betting and stuff. About betting on college hoops. And these cats, they seemed to be in the know, and they was saying that your team right here was monkeying around with some gamblers. You know? And what I was figuring was, if you could tip me on to something, then I could make a big score and really get myself right again. You know?"

But I can't deal with this shit. "You don't belong here, Daddy, and besides, I don't know what you're talking about. Go 'way and leave me alone."

"Royce. Son. You can't cut me out like this. I'm your daddy, your own flesh and blood. You gotta do me a solid, man."

"I told you I don't know nothing about nobody messing with gamblers...hey, man, I got to get back to work."

But Daddy's eyes get big and his mouth is twitching. "You lying to me, Royce. I can tell you lying."

The heat's going to blow a hole in the top of my head, and I'm going to bleed to death. "You believe some bums in a bar before you believe me?" I'm trying to sound stern and definitive, but my voice quavers like there's a small bird caught in my throat. "Leave me alone."

The old man laughs. "Ha! Now I knows you lying. You can't bullshit a bullshitter, son. So tell me who to bet on and when to do it."

I turn away, but he catches my wrist. "Now I'm getting mad," he says. "I can't believe you gonna do me like this. I'm hurting, son. For real. You want me to cry? After all we been to each other? You want me to beg?"

"No. I want you to go away and never come back."

"You fucking little spoiled bitch!" he shouts, and the security cops perk up. "I used to clean the shit outta your ass and now look at you!" Then Daddy steps forward and slaps my face.

Now I can't move a muscle, not even when he hits me again, because this time I deserve a beating. And I'm crying and sniveling wet glop all down my face. Crying for the both of us, our pain and our humiliation.

The cops run over and tackle Daddy from behind, knocking him facedown to the floor, then quickly pinning his arms behind his back. Vaguely I hear Goldberg yelling, "Hey, that has nothing to do with you! Big Boy! Lefty! Get back to work!"

And now I'm pummeling the younger of the two cops, trying to stop him from hurting Daddy. "Let him go, you bastard! Let him go!"

The cop shrugs me off like my body is hollow. "Easy now," he tells me, but he releases his grip on Daddy, who's also crying.

"I didn't mean to do none of this," Daddy says. "I love you, son. You know I do."

"I know, Daddy. It's going to be okay. I love you too." Then I pull the fifty-dollar bill from my sock and press it into his hand. "Go on home, Daddy, and we'll talk about it later."

"That's a good idea," he says, quickly stuffing the money into his pants pocket, then defiantly shrugging off the cops' proffered assistance.

The older cop, a potbellied, pockmarked man, has something private to say to me: "You want we should arrest him? Even if you don't wanna press charges, we could throw him in the tank and let him dry out for a couple of days."

"No. Let him go. Just take him outside and let him be."

"You got it."

As they lead Daddy out of the gym, somebody suddenly grabs my shoulder from behind. I wheel around, ready for a fight.

But it's Goldberg! I wait, expecting him to blast me.

"Listen," he says softly, "You don't have to explain anything, okay?... My own father was a kosher butcher and didn't have any time for me. When he died, I was only ten years old and I thought I hated him.... What goes on with you and your father is none of my business. I never had a child myself, but everybody's got a father."

"Okay, Coach. Thanks."

"Don't mention it. Go on into the locker room and wash your face. You can either come back to practice or else go home. Either way I'll understand."

In the locker room I stare at the reflection in the mirror above the sink. And an old man stares back at me, a stranger. I wait for the stranger to speak, hopefully to forgive me, to give me instructions, but all I can hear are the dull thumpings of basketballs being dribbled upstairs and the tiny shriek of a gold-plated whistle.

Chapter Fourteen

January 18, 1951

—OTIS—

Goldberg tried to frighten us with how "formidable" the Temple Owls are on their Philadelphia home court, a cramped playing area, nearly engulfed by thousands of hooting and howling students. Plus, Weiss spent two full practice sessions going over Temple's adhesive zone defenses and intricate offenses. But the two kikes were shitting in their pants over nothing. That's because Gianelli hasn't made us a pitch since we beat Rhinegold, so we were as loose as a two-dollar hooker's snatch tonight, trouncing those fuckers 95–71. For one game at least, we played like the champs we really are. And, man, didn't it feel good just to let it rip and not have to keep track of every fucking point? Damn straight. And I'm feeling *so* good because I had game-high totals of twenty-seven points and twelve rebounds. I also notched a career best in another category—Goldberg only cursed me *once* when I missed a complicated layup. (I got whacked on the arm, but the ref was a fucking homer and he just kept sucking on his whistle.)

That's why it's such a happy late-night train ride back to New York, and even though everybody's kind of quiet and low-key, we're all feeling great.

Whether we travel by train or by bus, I'm always at a window seat: to watch the shadowy landscape unrolling now as the train speeds through New Jersey, the trackside depots and yards, the tunnels too, where red lights and yellow lights slash the window.

I turn to Royce, who always sits next to me in the aisle seat. "Only one month to the N.I.T. You hear me, boy? I promise you that the N.I.T.'s gonna be the best thing you ever saw. All that publicity and the crowds and everything. The best teams in the country'll be there and they'll all be taking aim at us. Especially Kentucky. Rupp don't like to get beat by a team of niggers and Jews. That's who I figure on for the championship game. Us versus Kentucky. And if we could win ourselves another championship, that would make everything come out just right. So we got us four weeks to get our game tuned up."

—ROYCE—

$\mathbb{M}$e, I'm as happy as a pig in shit. Hoffman's back from his bad knee, but I got to start anyway and, man, was I in high gear! Sixteen points, five assists, and *zero* turnovers. Put that in your book, Coach Lapchick.

Even better, it looks like Gianelli's forgotten about us, and it never felt so good to be left alone. And for the past few days Otis has been especially friendly to me—even bragging about the woman he's shacking up with in the Bronx. The bracelets and silk stockings and crotchless panties he's always buying for his sugar. These days Otis won't hardly talk about anything except love and hot pussy and living happily ever after.

Why, then, do I feel so guilty that I sometimes play like a stumblebum whereas Otis is so casual and carefree about it? And why do I feel guilty about the money stashed in my hidden shoebox? Money that I'm afraid to spend. Otis, of course, spends his money freely—sporting a new gold watch tonight. So why do I worry? "Yeah," I say. "I can't wait to play in the N.I.T."

"And that ain't nothing," Otis says. "The N.I.T. is just the warm-up. Next summer there's the Olympic Games in Helsinki and you can bet your bottom dollar that I'll be there on the United States basketball team. No question about it." Otis is smiling like he's just won the Irish Sweepstakes. "And even that ain't the end of it. Now I'm gonna tell you this because I know you can keep your trap shut."

"No question about it."

"We been talking to a lawyer from Podoloff's office. What'd'ya think of that?"

"Who's Podoloff? I never heard of him."

"Ha. Then you never heard of shit, boy. This here Podoloff is the commissioner of the entire National Basketball Association. And his shyster's been talking to me and Hoffman and Isaacson and even Joey Callahan about us forming a team together for the N.B.A. The shyster even said that Podoloff already has a name all picked out for us. The Brooklyn Golden Eagles. Don't that sound good? Well, the plan is for us to also be the owners of the team just like the Indianapolis Olympians. I'm telling you, boy, we gonna be rich as Rockefellas. You too, if you play your cards right."

How much money would make me "rich"? How much money would I have to have before I could start spending it?

—SIDNEY—

I always sit alone in the rear of the car so I can see who's doing what. Weiss sits two vacant rows in front of me, just in case I need him to fetch me a drink of water, or to summon one of the players for a private chat. And tonight's game was very satisfying. I love beating up on Fred Cofield in his own backyard. Him and his trick zone defenses. Two-two-one or 1-1-1-2 or 3-2 or whatever, sooner or later somebody's got to guard somebody!

Our current record is 14–6 and we have five games remaining. I can safely project home-court wins against Columbia, Bridgeport, and Hunter College. Probably a loss at Villanova, and next week's ball game against Dayton at the Garden could go either way. That would add up to 18–7 or 17–8, disappointing after last spring's heroics but definitely good enough for the reigning champs to gain readmittance into the N.I.T.

Looking out the window, I see a meaningless blur. Then I huff my breath against the cold windowpane and use my right pinkie to etch this message inside the small patch of frost:

NIT CHAMPS??

There's something about this year's team that I don't trust. Some lack of will, especially in the closing minutes of a tight ball game. Although that Fancy Dan has certainly injected some pizzazz into our offense. And Big Boy had a fire under his lazy black ass tonight.

As the train eases out of the Camden station, a stranger has the audacity to settle into the vacant seat beside me. The man wears a brown felt hat that matches his heavy woolen coat. His eyes reflect the flickering lights of the station and his lips barely move when he says, "Hey, ain't you Coach Goldberg? I recognize you from your picture in the newspapers."

"Guilty as charged," I say, barely civil, hoping he'll ask for an autograph, then disappear.

But the stranger reaches inside his coat and produces a silver police badge. "I'm Detective Joe Wittenberg from the district attorney's office," he says. "There's another detective here with me at the other end of the car. We're here because the D.A. wants to ask some of your players a few questions."

Who? What? Finally I manage to say, "I don't understand."

The detective flips open a small notebook and reads several names: "Otis Hill. Barry Hoffman. Joey Callahan. Phil Isaacson. Royce Johnson."

"My God! What have they done?" Perhaps they've broken into a candy machine in the train station? Or stopped up the toilets in their hotel rooms? Or left the water running in the bathtubs?

The detective shakes his head in the most neutral manner possible. "I really can't go into the details, Coach, but the D.A. thinks they might be involved with gamblers."

My mouth moves, yet I can't discover something else to say.

"We don't want a scene," the detective continues. "So when the train gets into Penn Station, the D.A. would like you to take the team aside and talk to them. Tell them to cooperate."

"Of course," I say weakly. "Of course."

And the man gets up and finds another seat, leaving me to gaze out the train window into the incomprehensible darkness, trying to make some sense of what I've just heard.

Gamblers?

Is this thing possible?

How?

Why?

But, yes!

Hadn't I known there was something wrong with this team? Something sinister? Yes, sir. And despite the bad news, I feel somewhat reassured. After all, this unfortunate revelation can only enhance my already brilliant reputation. Imagine winning an N.I.T. championship with a team that was trying to lose!

Summoning Weiss, I instruct him to tell the players to wait for special instructions once we reach New York.

"What's going on?" Weiss wants to know.

"Nothing," I say. "Nothing that concerns *us*."

The train whistles into Penn Station at 1:15 A.M., and even now the depot is swarming with people: businessmen, redcaps, hookers, vacationers, winos, detectives, and a single newsman, Barney Polan. One by one, the players bend through the exit door and step down onto the crowded platform, their youthful faces already furrowed with apprehension. What does their crazy coach want from them now? A Sunday-morning practice? Windsprints and suicides along the platform? As the train steams and whistles and gathers to depart, the young men huddle around me. They take no notice of four burly detectives advancing to seal off the perimeter.

Always mindful that the temper of the times views the invocation of the Fifth Amendment as the last refuge for scoundrels and thieves, I believe that I've devised the appropriate advice for these unfortunate boys. Then I point vaguely into the darkness, and as though every gesture has been carefully choreographed, the four detectives move forward so that they can easily be seen.

"These men," I say, "are here to take some of you boys over to the district attorney's office for questioning about the possibility of illegal involvement with gamblers. But I want you to know this, that I'm talking to you as if you were my own sons. And I'm telling you to go peacefully with them, go without fear, tell them everything they want to know. If your consciences are clean, then you'll be all right and you won't get into trouble. If not, then I'm sorry for you. If there is a mess, the sooner they clean it up, the better."

Then I order Isaacson to phone me at home after the D.A. is through with them. And I instruct Weiss to telephone the boys' parents right away and inform them that their sons are being detained by the police. Then I turn away, believing that I've done my duty, that my behavior will be considered moral and above reproach.

But all at once I'm overtaken by an intimation of the tragedy unfolding, of young lives on the verge of being destroyed.

So I approach the detective in charge of the operation. "Sir, would it be at all possible for me to accompany them?"

"No way," the detective says.

So I watch helplessly while Hoffman, Isaacson, Number Thirty-one, and the two Negro boys are handcuffed and taken away. And before I realize what's happening, I begin to weep because I don't know all of their names.

—ROYCE—

We all sit slouching on benches in the back of the paddy wagon, holding our hands and wrists stiffly to avoid the grinding pressure of the handcuffs. Phil Isaacson's fleshy mouth sags open and his eyes are half-shut. Joey Callahan just keeps shaking his head and moaning softly to himself. Otis stares defiantly at his handcuffs, looking like he might at any moment suddenly jerk his arms apart and free himself like Superman. Barry Hoffman's bony face is screwed into a sneer and he can't stop talking.

"They got nothing on us," Hoffman says. "Not a fucking thing. All's we gotta do is clam up and we'll be fine. I mean, how could they prove anything? Everybody misses easy shots, right? Even Cousy. Even Mikan. So what else could they possibly have? Some telephone conversations with Gianelli? Or with Klein? Or with that fucking chiseling dago from Philly? Please. None of that's worth shit in court. What else could they have? Tell me. What? Nothing, that's what. All's we gotta do is clam up and we'll be free as the breeze."

Otis stirs and looks up. "Shut your fucking mouth," he snaps at Hoffman. "You sound like a crazy man."

"Hey," says Hoffman. "Who the fuck died and made you king?"

"Yeah," Isaacson says. "King of the fucking rock pile."

Nobody laughs except Hoffman.

And Otis comes to a sudden realization: "I heard what you said, Hoffman. About Klein? About the guy from Philly? Who the fuck are they?"

Isaacson glowers at Hoffman, but Barry only laughs again and says, "None of your fucking business."

"I got it now," Otis says. "You guys were double-crossing Gianelli."

Hoffman isn't impressed with Otis's discovery. "What took you so long, you stupid putz? We've been doing it for two years and making more fucking money than you can count. Remember the West Virginia game? We shopped around and—"

Now Isaacson has heard enough. "Shut up, Barry. This place could be bugged. That's why there's no cop in here with us."

Nobody else speaks for a while, until Otis turns on me, saying, "Don't cry, you pussy. Act like a man for once in your life."

And it's true, so I nod and move to wipe my eyes with the frayed sleeve of my winter coat, but the sudden movement cuts the manacles deeper into my wrists. Yet, how can I not think of my ma? And how can I think of her and not cry? This will be the death of her. She'll have a heart attack, the same heart attack I wished on Goldberg. *What ye sow, so shall ye reap.* Oh, Jesus, save me! Save my ma! I'd rather die than have her die.

Straining my imagination, I pretend that none of this is happening. No, I never agreed to become one of Mr. Gianelli's boys. It didn't happen at all. No. And besides, it was his wife who'd turned my head. Yes, that's what it was. That whore! Making believe she was going to let me fuck her. Hadn't she made the same promises to Otis? Squeezing his thigh and sweet-talking him into selling his innocence? But no, Rosie tried to save me. And no matter what else I try to imagine, I'm still right here and bound for prison.

And what's going to happen to all of my money? Maybe I should call Ma from wherever we're being taken and tell her to hide the money for later. Holy Jesus! If she ever so much as touched a corner of one of those fifty-dollar bills, her hands would bleed. Now I can imagine the detectives ransacking my room searching for the loot. With Ma crying, and all the neighbors peeking in through the open door....

Oh, Jesus! I'm sorry! I'm sorry! I repent of my sins! Please come and save me now! Maybe there'll be a traffic accident and we'll all be killed. Maybe the earth will split and swallow me to hell.

We're smuggled into the Center Street Precinct through a basement door, taken upstairs and fingerprinted. I feel like the whole world is watching me! An old white-haired cop holds my fingers firm and rolls them expertly on the forms. Then I'm put on a swivel stool for my mug shots, right and left profiles, then straight-faced. I try to numb myself, to get interested in the procedures, the details, to keep from crying—and it does seem to help a little. That's how I'm gonna have to live from now on—numb from the neck up. "Look up," the attendant commands me. "Let's see your eyes."

Hoffman smiles and says, "Cheese." Isaacson and Callahan are all soupy-eyed and meek. Otis glares at the camera, his hatred almost hot enough to crack the lens.

Handcuffed again, we're led into separate interrogation rooms. Inside Room 103, the gray paint peels off the walls in long ribbons and there are thick iron bars across the only window. In the center of the room, a small square wooden table and three wooden folding chairs. Above the table a hooded light bulb shivers slightly in a phantom breeze. Someone says, "Sit down there," then the door is locked behind me and I'm alone. I can't help thinking that the small space resembles the room in *Furtive Darkness* where the Gestapo interrogated Robert Mitchum.

For a long time I watch the tabletop where a fat cockroach is grazing on a dried coffee stain. Then he'll be the lucky one and crawl into a hole in the wall and disappear forever. Otherwise I'm alone, with the long shadows grabbing at me from every corner. Wishing so hard only to be dreaming, to wake up in the middle of the Sahara Desert, or on top of

Mount Everest, or at the bottom of the ocean. Someplace else, anyplace.

Finally the door opens and two men walk into the room, a heavy man wearing brown pants, and a white shirt opened at the collar with the sleeves rolled up above his elbows. A name tag is clipped to his shirt pocket—"Dan Potter." The other man is much older, gray-haired and almost frail. This one wears tan corduroy pants, neatly shined black loafers, a moth-eaten cardigan sweater, and no name tag. There's a cigarette clenched in his teeth as though he'd rather be smoking a cigar. As he eases himself into the rickety chair that's opposite me, he carelessly tosses a crumpled pack of Camels onto the table. For the longest time neither of them speaks. Maybe it'll stay like this, with all my guilt, all my pain, left unspoken. Even though my eyes are cast down and my chin is pressed into my chest, I can feel them watching me.

Then the older man suddenly reaches out over the table to mash the lazy cockroach with his bare hand. Now he rubs the glowing stub of his cigarette into the squashed cockroach remains, sending up a small putrid puff of greenish smoke. And he clears his throat to say this: "Hello, Royce. I'm Detective Jeter and I have a few questions to ask you." His smile is so earnest and fatherly that I want to trust him. "We're here to help you, son. We want to get this over with as soon as possible so that we can all go home. What we want is the truth, Royce." He fumbles inside a sweater pocket until he locates a small brass key. "Here," he says. "Let me get those things offa you. They must hurt like the dickens."

I lift my hands toward him and Jeter quickly unlocks the handcuffs. Cautiously rubbing my chaffed and bruised wrists, I very nearly smile at his kindness.

"So tell us exactly what happened, Royce," Jeter says. "You might as well, since we already know everything anyway. We know about you and Gianelli and about you and Gianelli's wife. We know you got five hundred dollars a game. We know who gave you the money. We know where and when. So fess up, son, and maybe things will go easier for you."

My first impulse is to confess, to break down and weep. But me, I'm not a squealer, so I just shrug and stare at the bruises on my wrists. (Didn't he just say that I got five hundred a game? If that's true, then what happened to the rest of the money? Or is he just saying that so I'll think that somebody was pinching my share and I'll be pissed off enough to squeal?... Otis made the payments, so it had to be him! That lying, bloodsucking bastard!... But it doesn't really matter anymore. Anyway, I might be a crook, but I'm not a snitch.)

My silence seems to provoke Potter. "Don't you dummy up on us, boy. We've already got enough on you to toss you in the clink and throw away the fucking key. Yeah, that's right. We know what you ate for breakfast this morning. We know what color your dirty shit-stained drawers are. You can't hide nothing from us, boy. So do yourself a favor and come clean."

"Listen, Royce," the older man says. "Let me tell you a little story.... Have you ever heard of Bradley University? Sure you have. You're a basketball player. They're the team City College beat in the first game of last year's N.I.T. I happened to be there, Royce, and cheering as loudly as anybody. It was a glorious ball game. Well, listen to this, son.... You know who Bradley's best player is, don't you? Sure you do. Gene Melchiorre, a little five-foot-ten-inch runt who ain't afraid to work down in the pivot. Eats nails and spits battleships. But I'll bet you the moon against the stars that you don't know where Melchiorre is right now, right this very minute. He's in a hospital in Peoria, Royce, because he was dumping ball games, and when he tried to stop, some professional creeps broke the knuckles on his shooting hand."

Then Potter suddenly moves forward and slams a meaty open palm on the table. "How'd you like me to break your fucking hand right now and save some dago the trouble?"

"Tell us, Royce," Jeter croons. "Tell us when you agreed to do business with Gianelli."

Big sloppy tears are leaking down my cheeks, and I say, "I didn't do nothing wrong."

Now the old man is talking in a low voice and I almost have to hold my breath to hear all the words. "Cooperate with us, Royce, and we'll talk to the D.A. and see if we can get you a better deal. Maybe a bail your family can afford. Maybe easy time in a light-security joint somewhere in the countryside. Maybe an early parole if you behave. All you gotta do is tell us what we already know."

Suddenly I feel brave enough to be pugnacious. "If you already know everything, then you know that I didn't do nothing wrong."

"Royce," the old man says with a touch of sorrow in his voice. "You just don't understand the situation here. The fact is that your buddies already gave you up. That's why we were delayed coming in here to speak to you."

"What? What you mean?"

Jeter pulls a notepad out of his pocket and reads silently for a moment before he speaks. "Hill, Isaacson, and Hoffman. They all said that you were the ringleader. They said that even though you're only a freshman, you were the one who insisted on accepting Gianelli's proposition."

"What? That's a lie. I didn't do nothing."

"It's right here in black and white," the old man says. "They said they were clean until you joined the team and you started agitating for money. They said that you told them that's the only reason why you came to City College in the first place. For the chance to make money shaving points. They put the whole blame on you."

"Otis said that?"

Just to make sure, Jeter rereads his notes. "Yep. He surely did. What this means, young man, is that you're in deep shit. As the instigator, the court would probably give *you* the longest sentence."

"In jail?"

Potter sticks his sweating face in front of me. "That's what we been saying, boy. In jail with a bunch of rednecks hot after your sweet brown ass."

Folding my arms on the table, I bury my head. Jail. With rednecks cracking me wide open. Jail. With Ma in the hospital dying from the heart attack that should've killed Goldberg. (*If I make this shot, he'll. . . .*) Jail. "Oh, no."

The two detectives let me sink to the bottom of my soul before Jeter throws me a lifeline. "Royce," he says, delicately putting a hand on my slumped shoulder. "There is a way out. There is a way you won't have to go to jail. A way to make all of this disappear. All you have to do is tell us exactly what happened. Who convinced you to dump the games? How much money was everybody else getting?"

I see him through watery eyes and stubbornly repeat my refrain: "I didn't do nothing wrong."

Potter laughs. "They've already ratted on you, boy. But, you know what? We're willing to trust your story instead of theirs. And do you know why? Because you're too wet behind the ears to be the ringleader. And we've got much bigger fish to fry. So we're ready to let you off the hook if you tell us the truth."

"What do you mean 'off the hook'?" I say, daring to see a glimmer of hope. "What does that mean exactly?"

The fat man looks to Jeter, who nods. "What we're prepared to do," says Potter, "is to make you the hero. You tell us everything we want to know. Repeat, *everything*. And we'll let it out that you're innocent. Completely innocent. We'll say we just brought you in for general questioning. We'll destroy the fingerprints and the mug shots. Nobody will ever know that you gave us useful information. Nobody. You have my word on that. Hell, boy, you'll be a genuine hero. Don't you want to be a hero? Don't you want to save your family the embarrassment? The heartache?"

"Do it, Royce," says Jeter. "Be courageous and tell the truth. The truth shall make you free, right?"

"What choice do you really have?" Potter asks. "Go to jail? Or walk out of here a free man?"

It sounds so easy, so foolproof. All I have to do is tell the truth.... Then Ma doesn't die. And I'll be a hero. An All-American. An N.B.A. All-Star. And I'll be rich and famous.

So I sob just once, like I've been paroled from death row, like Jesus has kissed my forehead.

But no. I won't be a snitch. And I say, "The truth is that I didn't do nothing wrong."

Then the fat man hunches his shoulders briefly and gestures with his open palms toward the ceiling, surrendering, and looking at Jeter. "That's good enough for me," says Potter.

"Yeah," Jeter says, obviously disappointed. "The kid is straight."

Then Potter turns to me and says this: "Okay, Royce, we know you didn't do anything wrong. We have a transcription of a telephone conversation that you had with Rosie Gianelli where she talked you out of joining forces with her husband. We also know from that same conversation that Otis Hill was the real ringleader."

"Also," the fat man says, "there's that last-minute shot you made to beat Rhinegold when several of your teammates were trying to dump the game. So we know that you're innocent, Royce, but we had to test you, to pressure you, just to make sure."

Jeter snarls and says, "I'm warning you, kid, you better keep your mouth shut, or it's your ass. Now, get the fuck out of here."

"Yessir."

Thank you, Jesus, for giving me another chance even though I don't deserve it. Thank you, Jesus, for Rosie Gianelli. Thank you, Jesus, for making cops so dumb. Amen.

Chapter Fifteen

January 19, 1951

—HENRY—

The first bomb has fallen, detonated without warning by Barney Polan (in a front-page news story and also in his column) in a special early-afternoon edition of the *Brooklyn Sentinel.* And the fallout will devastate college basketball as I know it.

So I sit here, high in the bleachers, alone in my own personal bunker, confused, mourning, waiting for the next bomb to drop. On me.

Practice is scheduled to begin in twenty minutes, but there's an eerie emptiness here. The student managers haven't arrived yet with the basketball rack and the clean towels from the equipment room. None of the habitual early birds are here to shoot around and play their happy games of one-on-one. And where's my trusty assistant coach? It's as though someone has canceled practice without informing me.

Not that I have much stomach for basketball right now. Nor am I completely surprised at Polan's disclosures.

Virtually every college that sports a varsity basketball team is more interested in promoting a money-making enterprise than in fostering amateur athletics. For example—next week is our annual extended road trip with games scheduled in Peoria, Toledo, Chicago, Cincinnati, and Milwaukee. That's five games in eight days with a total minimum guarantee of sixty thousand dollars against 20 percent of the net box office receipts. Despite this windfall to the Rhinegold coffers, our travel itinerary is mostly determined by cost-effectiveness, which means that we're booked on the cheapest flights, that is, the earliest possible departures (usually six A.M., plus or minus thirty minutes). Whatever chartered buses we need are contracted strictly on the basis of competitive bids—this means faulty heating systems, inexperienced drivers, and occasionally (like last season en route from Oklahoma City to Dallas) running out of gas. Our stopovers in the inevitable fleabag hotels are all-night exercises in itching and scratching. At the same time, under the N.C.A.A.'s regulations, the kids are only entitled to receive two dollars per day to pay for their own meals.

Who are the amateurs here?

Under such circumstances, how can the kids play winning basketball? How can they stay healthy? How can they keep up with their academic assignments?

Maybe it's time for me to retire.

A door opens at the far end of the gym, and here comes Sammy Goodrich dressed in civvies. Neither of us offers an immediate greeting as he sits himself beside me. The kid looks frazzled and sleepless.

Finally I say, "I'm afraid to ask, but where is everybody?"

Sammy won't look at me. Instead he rests his arms on his thighs, interlaces his fingers, and twiddles his thumbs. "About fifteen minutes ago," he says, "just as all the guys were coming into the locker room to get ready for practice, the dean of students shows up with four detectives in tow. The dicks fingered Charlie, Gary, and Chip and then took them away someplace. They also asked about Greg, but apparently he didn't come to school today. Then the dean said that practice was called off."

"Jesus H. Christ!" Of course I'm shocked to my socks, but at the same time, I'm not terribly surprised. "You know what I think, Sammy?"

"What's that, Henry?"

He calls me *Henry*? And he doesn't look up from his slowly rotating thumbs. Jesus Himself! Is this kid finally over the edge?

"I think I've known all along, Sammy, that something wasn't right with this team. I just didn't want to think about it. I mean, these kids are too talented and too experienced to make junior-high-school mistakes. All the missed layups and stupid passes. All the fumbled rebounds and missteps on defense. You know what I mean?"

But he's too absorbed in his handiwork to respond. No doubt about it, the kid is loony. I might as well be talking to myself.

"For Chrissake, I played ball with some of their fathers. Like Charlie's old man, Dennis, who was a helluva defender. . . . Anyway, like I said, I had my suspicions. How could a coach not know if his players are deliberately fucking up? Goldberg's full of shit, or else he's so self-absorbed that he can't see past his own fucking nose. So I guess I'll have to bring in some junior-varsity kids to finish out the schedule. And forget about the N.I.T. Stupid fucking kids! But I'm glad that you're okay, Sammy. At least there's that to be thankful for."

I don't like the way he continues to stare at his swirling thumbs. "Sammy? You're okay, right?"

—SAMMY—

I know that I'll eventually have to tell somebody. Holding it in is exhausting me. But who to tell? My father? "Basketball schmasketball." Besides, now more than ever, Henry needs me on the court, so he'd never give me away. And perhaps Henry is enough of a mensch to forgive me. But I can't pull the trigger.

"...Yeah, Henry. I'm okay."

Then I stand up and walk out of the gym without saying good-bye.

—BARNEY—

I t was nearly five A.M. when I phoned in all the info for someone to rewrite. That made the front page —— CITY COLLEGE FIXERS CONFESS —— and the recital of the known facts was featured on page three under my by-line. On the back page was "Sports A-Plenty," *in toto*, the *coup de ma Ótre* of my life's work.

Fixers Come Unglued

As ever, Shakespeare said it best: "Sharper than a serpent's tooth is an ungrateful child."

Sharp enough to tear a sports fan's dreams to shreds. So remember these names well, remember them for all time: Barry Hoffman, Otis Hill, Joey Callahan, Phil Isaacson, and Benny Tanowski. They're a cinch to make Basketball's Hall of Shame.

These point shavers, these game dumpers, had so much for which to be grateful: a free education (provided at the taxpayers' expense!), once they graduated (which hopefully, they never shall) a diploma made of gold, and the once-in-a-lifetime chance to play baskets for one of the sport's legendary coaches, Sidney Goldberg. The beloved "Ol' Coach," who routinely turns stumble-footed novices into polished All-Americans, and instills the discipline and sense of responsibility that, more importantly, turns boys into men.

And how was Coach Goldberg to know that the young men who bore his trust were, in fact, playing to lose? Being a superb ex-player himself, and still a fierce competitor on the team's bench, Goldberg simply assumed that these boys were playing all out. No other possibility was remotely imaginable.

But these fulsome young fixers have betrayed their youth, their innocence, the very game they professed to love, their parents, their coach, and, yes, the fans.

So what shall be done with them? What punishment is appropriate for their heinous crimes? Certainly expulsion from the university. Also jail sentences of long enough durations to induce sincere repentance. Too bad this civilized country of ours no longer countenances the restraining of wrongdoers in wooden stocks.

What else must be accomplished to prevent further incidents? As much as I hate to say this, college basketball should be banished from Madison Square Garden because of the proliferation of gamblers there. In addition the National Collegiate Athletic Association should forbid college basketball players from working (and hooping) in the Catskill Mountain summer resorts—the breeding ground of sarcasm where the seeds are planted by the wily fixers for future harvests.

The only saving grace for the shell-shocked remnant of C.C.N.Y.'s varsity basketballers is the sterling honesty of Royce Johnson. A mere freshman, Royce shines among his crooked compatriots like a rare jewel. One way or another, character is destiny!

Not bad, eh? Especially impressive given that I started writing at four A.M. in an empty interrogation room at the police station. O'Hara sure kept his word, in spades.

There'll be more inside dope tomorrow, too. Namely, the arrests of a pair of gamblers who "allegedly" bankrolled the fixed contests: Johnny Boy Gianelli and his top henchman, Georgie Klein.

I'm happy to see that Jimmy Cannon got everything ass-backward this time! Here's part of what he wrote in the *Post*'s evening edition:

> The tall children of basketball have been consumed by the slot machine racket of sports. They are amateurs exploited by a commercial alliance of culture and commerce. It is not because I am a sportswriter that I have compassion for the arrested players. They have forfeited honor at an age when the dream of life should be beautiful. We should weep when we come upon a boy who has been fleeced of principles before he is a man. What has made them special has also destroyed them. Their youth has been slain. The assassin of youth is the most repulsive of criminals.

What a joke Cannon's turned out to be.

—JUNIOR—

Is it possible that barely an hour ago I opened my copy of the *Daily News* that the frat flunky slides under my door the first thing in the morning? Or have a hundred years passed since then, since I saw the photos of the four C.C.N.Y. players leaving the Center Street Precinct? Hoffman and Isaacson with their open hands covering their faces. Callahan holding a newspaper over his head. Only Otis Hill showed any dignity, glaring stiff-necked and defiant. A jagged thrill of fear ripped through me. Then the telephone rings.

"Hello?"

It's Steve Evans, a lawyer and a jock-sniffer who never misses a local St. John's game and who sometimes slides me a C-note after we win. He reintroduces himself and explains that the district attorney is interested in questioning me, McCoy, and Sweeney. "Wear your best suit," he says. "We'll pick you up in a limousine in about thirty minutes right outside the frat house. Until then, don't answer the telephone and don't say a word to anybody about anything."

Then the lawyer breaks the connection, leaving me straining to grip the receiver like it's a fifty-pound dumbbell. I've cleaned myself up and put on my best suit, just like he said. But then, for a long time, I've been studying the photo in the newspaper and crying. Yes. Because tomorrow morning it's my picture there, covering my face with my hat, slouching and trying to hide inside my own shadow.

The limo is right on time, a sleek black Lincoln, with Evans and two other lawyers sitting comfortably in the backseat while McCoy and Sweeney perch precariously on two of the three fold-out auxiliary seats.

A priest, Father Theo, sits up front beside the driver. As ordered, I keep my trap shut, and I can't find the guts to even look at my co-conspirators.

Evans seems to be in charge, and as the limo starts moving, he starts talking, declaring that we're "definitely not criminals" and that our "innocence can never be disproved." And I myself am genuinely impressed by Evans's bushy white eyebrows and hard granite wrinkles, by his pinstriped suit, his pearl tiepin, even his manicure. In his mid-fifties, Evans still looks fit enough to lead a fast break. I even like the sound of the lawyer's voice—the broad Bostonian vowels and the self-assured, tightly clipped consonants:

"Just do exactly as I tell you, gentlemen. Speak only when I tell you to, and speak only what I tell you to, and I promise there'll be no repercussions from this. I absolutely guarantee that no charges will be filed. Just as long as none of you even farts until I give you the go-ahead."

Then we ride silently until we approach our destination, when Evans has more instructions for us: "Make sure that you don't duck away from the cameras. Don't look ashamed and don't look like you've got something to hide. Smile at the cameras. Be jocular but not arrogant. Just trust me, gentlemen, and you'll walk away from this mess."

As soon as we stop at the curb in front of the station house, the car is surrounded by a noisy mob of photographers and reporters. A quartet of chesty detectives materialize to keep the press at bay, but the flashbulbs pop and smoke as the photographers hold their cameras high above their heads hoping to snap a lucky shot. And the boisterous gang of reporters pepper us with rude questions:

"How much money did you guys get?"

"Was the Notre Dame game one of the ones you dumped?"

"Who was the ringleader?"

"Did you guys really do it?"

It seems even more perilous inside the building because of the numerous cops (with their pistols protruding jauntily from their holsters) and the faint odor of cold steel bars (the scent of justice?).

A skinny, bespectacled man in a brown suit is waiting for us, someone who looks vaguely familiar. The man confers briefly with Evans, then the gray-haired lawyer leads us toward a nearby room that has the words OFF-DUTY LOUNGE printed in gold block letters on the door's pebbled window. Evans says, "Wait for me inside." As we enter, the brown-suited man also disappears.

A cozy room, full of padded colonial-type furniture—several easy chairs, a long cushy couch, all facing a small conference table set in the middle of the room. Against the far wall a large refrigerator hums efficiently and, beside it, a faucet drips softly into a large porcelain sink. An interior door leads to a bathroom. Several self-standing ashtrays are scattered throughout and most of the floor is covered with a brown braided rug.

The priest immediately moves toward the bathroom door. He's a big-bellied man whose black robe hides his feet and gently sweeps the floor as he walks. "If youse gents'll excuse me," he says. "I got to go take me a whiz."

The other two lawyers plop into easy chairs and one of them pulls a pack of Raleighs out of his coat pocket. He carefully peels the cellophane from the back of the package, secures the coupon in his wallet, then lights up with a wooden match that he scratches against the sole of his left shoe.

The other lawyer looks like some kind of Jewish ambulance chaser. And the guy's aftershave lotion smells like exhaust fumes, too.

The room seems harmless. The priest and the two lawyers are so casual, like we're waiting in a dentist's office. Don't any of them care that my future is at stake?

Nobody speaks as the toilet flushes loudly behind the bathroom door and Father Theo emerges, much too soon to have washed his hands.

"All right," the portly priest says, showing a practiced grin and teeth that resemble perfect rows of yellow corn. "Don't youse boys worry about it. We got yiz covered from A to Z. If it please the Lord."

Then the cigarette-smoking lawyer reaches a long arm to snuff his freshly lit smoke into the nearest ashtray. "For Pete's sake," he says. "I gotta stop smoking these things. Goddamn coffin nails."

I turn to look at Father Theo, who's blithely scratching the inside of his nose with a dainty finger.

The Jewish lawyer is a somber man, who cut the tip of his pointy chin while shaving this morning. "Remember, boys," he reminds us. "Don't you dare say a word until we give you the okay."

Just then the outer door opens and Evans precedes another man into the room. It's John Morley, the district attorney himself, a redhead who sports an almost invisible red moustache. In his time, Morley was the captain of St. John's varsity golf team. He looks like a nice guy, and I flash him my best smile, hoping he'll like me better than Sweeney or McCoy. Last through the door is a plain-faced young woman in a man's tailored tan suit, who immediately sits in an outlying chair and positions a stenographer's pad in her lap. All the men seem acquainted with one another, and handshakes are exchanged in various combinations.

"Miss Cetta," the D.A. says to the secretary. "Those present are Stephen Evans, Allan Edmands, and Paul Kurtz. Also the three young men, Ray Paluski, James McCoy, and Shawn Sweeney." Morley's voice becomes less officious as he smiles at the priest. "And, of course, Father Theo. I'm always happy to see you, Father, and I do appreciate your interest. But this is strictly a legal matter."

The priest's flabby face stretches into a forgiving smile. "Ah, how quickly they forget. I am a lawyer, John. Passed the bar in 1920, and I haven't passed another one since then."

After a polite round of laughter, everybody takes a seat, with the D.A. and the three lawyers around the table, and the priest joining me, Sweeney, and McCoy on the long couch. It all seems so cozy. How could anything sinister happen here?

Evans clears his throat and says rather brusquely, "All right, John. Let's get down to brass tacks. What've you got?"

The district attorney slowly rubs his hands together as diligently as a fly on a toilet seat. "Well, Steve, I'm afraid we've got quite enough to hold them for questioning and probably enough to book them. We've certainly got sufficient evidence to present to a grand jury."

"For example?" says Evans.

"Well, we've got a photograph of these three in the company of John Gianelli, a well-known gambler. Here. Take a look for yourself."

(Rosie's smile is sad. I never noticed that before. McCoy's is broad and earnest. Sweeney is careful not to spill his drink. Gianelli smiles tightly to secure his dentures, the lying scumbag. He was supposed to have everything all sewed up. My eyes are blinded and glazed by the flashing bulb. We all look pathetic.)

Evans dismisses Morley with a small laugh. "So they met a basket-ball fan while they were having themselves a night on the town. So what? Gianelli's not wanted by the F.B.I. or anything like that, is he? His picture isn't on a wanted poster in the post office. So the fan bought a round of drinks. So what?"

"Well, it just so happens that we're bringing Gianelli in later this afternoon to quiz him about his involvement in various attempts to rig college basketball games. Gianelli's also got very close ties to organized crime."

Evans isn't unimpressed. "So go call Kefauver and tell him. Look,

John. I just don't understand what's the big deal. Are you assuming that these college kids should know the particulars of Gianelli's rap sheet? So what, then, are we really talking about? A couple of drinks in a public place? Come on, John. If these kids were doing business with Gianelli, would they be foolish enough to appear in public and be photographed with him? If you ask me, the picture indicates their innocence."

Morley brushes his fingers lightly across his upper lip. "Well," he says, "that's your opinion. On the other hand—"

"Don't give me your other hand, John. Give me evidence."

"Well, there were certain wiretaps that were made. Yes, yes. I know they're inadmissible in a courtroom. Still, there were some very incriminating conversations."

(Oh, shit! Now I'm done for!)

The priest interrupts. "And let me ask yiz something, John, my boy. These wiretaps of yours. Where are they? And can the likes of us get to hear them?"

Morley says, "Miss Cetta," and the stenographer immediately rests her busy pencil. "Well," the district attorney continues, "in actual fact there does seem to be a little problem here. It appears there's been some sort of accident and the actual recordings seem to have been damaged."

"Oh?" the priest says, smiling his eternal innocence.

"Yes," says Morley. "Unfortunately the recordings were, uh, damaged before we had a chance to transcribe them."

(It must be an inside job! Gianelli wasn't bullshitting after all!)

Evans drums his fingers on the table and says, "I see."

With much ado, Morley digs into his briefcase and excavates several sheets of paper. "We do have the records of a series of phone calls that Paluski made from his fraternity house to Gianelli's apartment over the course of the last three years. And another series of calls that Gianelli made to Paluski."

(C'mon, lawyer-man. Wipe the floor with this fucking guy.)

Again Evans discounts Morley's suggestions. "So what? A fan calls his favorite player to ask for tickets. Or to set him up with a pretty niece. Maybe they talked about the weather."

Morley winces, the first sign of irritation. "Steve, they didn't talk about tickets or a niece or the weather. Gianelli and Paluski conspired to fix basketball games."

Evans smirks. "That's your opinion."

(I fucking knew it! I'm in like Flynn! Fuckin' A!)

Morley once more investigates the contents of his briefcase and withdraws another sheet of notes. "Here," he says, holding the notes in front of him. "For a bunch of kids who don't have a pot to piss in, they sure spent a lot of money. Here... receipts for watches, suits, shoes...."

The priest frowns and says, "Watch your language, John."

(Yeah, Father! Excommunicate the motherfucker! That'll teach him to mess with us!)

And Evans shakes his head in apparent amazement. "So the boys saved their allowances. So they brought empty milk bottles back to the grocery and saved up the deposits. So they borrowed money from a rich uncle. Listen, John... is this all you have? Do you really believe a grand jury is going to return indictments on the basis of this flimsy, totally circumstantial garbage? I think you're wasting everybody's time here." Evans buttons his suit jacket and gathers himself to stand up.

"Wait, wait," Morley says. "We'd like to question them."

Evans shrugs. "Sure. Go right ahead."

"No, no. I mean privately. Separately."

(Oh, shit! Don't let him do it! He'll work on me with a rubber hose and crack me open like a rotten walnut.)

"You can't be serious, John. If you want to ask them some questions, you'd better do it now. Or else wait until you get a warrant. But question them separately and without counsel present? Never. This is America, John, not Nazi Germany."

"Okay, okay," Morley says quickly. He even looks somewhat relieved. In a gesture of righteous helplessness, the D.A. nods to the stenographer, then he speaks to me and Sweeney and McCoy as the three of us huddle together on the couch.

"Did any of you ever conspire with John Gianelli to fix the outcome of any Saint John's basketball games?"

As one, we all look to Evans, who says, "Go ahead and answer the question, gentlemen. Tell the district attorney that none of you ever conspired with Gianelli to fix games."

"No, sir," I say eagerly. "I know that I didn't, that's for sure."

"Me neither," says Sweeney.

"No, sir," says McCoy. "My mother, she brought me up right."

Morley smiles dubiously. "Did any of you ever conspire with any other person or persons besides John Gianelli to fix the outcome of any Saint John's basketball games?"

"No, sir."

"Not me."

"Nope."

"Did any of you know about anybody else, either on your team or perhaps on some other team, who conspired with any person or persons to fix the outcome of any college basketball games that you know of?"

"No, sir."

"No."

"Same here."

Ten minutes later a plainclothes detective leads us out of the building through a secret basement exit, where the same limousine that brought us is waiting to whisk us away.

Didn't I tell Dad that he had nothing to worry about? Fuckin' A!

—ROYCE—

Ma is waiting up for me and she's obviously been crying. After all the hugging and kissing is over with, after I say "I'm okay" about a hundred times, then I have to sit down with her and explain exactly what a point spread is and what point shaving means. "But that's not me, Ma. I didn't do nothing wrong. Even the district attorney said so." She doesn't quite get the theory and practice of the gambling devices, but she knows that I'm lying.

"I can tell by your eyes," she says. "They get all tight at the edges when you're fibbing me."

"Oh, Ma. That's just because I'm tired. I've been up all night, you know, and I also played a ball game. We won, Ma, and I scored twelve points and I had—"

"I don't care about no ball game. I just care about you telling me the truth, so help you God."

"All right. I'll go get the Bible and swear on it like they do in court."

But she won't let me. "Don't make it worse," she says.

We go a few more rounds, neither of us willing to budge (why doesn't she leave me alone?), until she has to get ready to go to work. For the first time in my life I see her as an old woman, worn out and beaten, her difficult life suddenly kicking her ass. The Bible has always been her comfort, until now. I know she'd forgive me if I confessed, but I can't do it. Except for the tightening at the edges of my eyes, lying is no strain at all.

The telephone rings. "It's been going like that all night long," she says from the bathroom. "Reporters from the newspapers." I let it ring. "Answer it. Maybe it's your father. I ain't heard from him since the New Year."

"Hello?"

"Don't hang up, Royce. It's me, Coach Goldberg." (Oh, man. What the fuck does he want?) "Are you okay?"

"Yeah. I'm tired, man. I got to get some sleep."

"I just called to say congratulations, Royce, for resisting temptation. It must have been a difficult situation for you."

"Yeah. Look, man. I got to go to bed."

"Sure. Of course. I also want to let you know that I had a talk with the president of the college and he agrees with me that it behooves the school to make some sort of gesture in appreciation of your integrity. So there's going to be a rally in your honor tomorrow morning at ten o'clock in the quad."

"No, no, man. That ain't no good. I don't want no part of it."

Then he laughs at me like I'm a fool. "I'm afraid it's already too late for you to refuse, Royce. The announcements are being posted all over the campus and the newspapers have been notified. The president even said he's going to send his own chauffeur and limousine to pick you up at your home. See you then, Royce."

"Yeah."

Fuck me! This gets worse and worse!

As soon as I hang up the phone, the damn thing rings again, and without thinking, I pick up the receiver.

"Hello?"

"Fuck your hello, you boolshit motherfucker! You fuckin' stool pigeon! If I ever see you ever again I'm gonna kick your ass so bad you'll be shittin' outta your mouth!"

"Otis, man! I ain't no stoolie, man. I didn't tell them nothing. I swear to God!"

"Man, you don't know the truth for lyin'. The fuckin' D.A., he told me all about how you fingered me, motherfucker! Sayin' I'm the fuckin' ringleader!"

"Otis, I didn't say shit! Hey, the cop told me that you turned *me* in! That you said *I* was the ringleader! Then when I still didn't admit nothing, that's when he told me he was boolshitting me and only testing me. I swear, Otis. Don't you see how they're playing? They turn us on each other, then all they got to do is pick up the pieces when one of us cracks. Otis, man. All you gotta do is deny everything. I swear to God, man."

"I don't believe you, man. I think they got inside your head and scrambled your fuckin' brains. I know you ratted me out, man. You're a lyin' son of a bitch."

Suddenly I feel calm and brave and I know I can survive. Truth is a joke, and lies are a bigger joke. Love's a pain in the ass. Justice is imaginary. Freedom is a fraud. All that counts is getting by and getting over. Me, I'm a virgin all over again. So let's blow the whistle and start the next game and don't talk to me about nothing but the final score.

"Otis," I say. "You're gonna believe whatever you want to believe, so it doesn't make any difference what really happened. And if you want to kick my ass, then you're welcome to try."

"Fuck you, man. If I wanted to, I could blow your house down with one phone call to the D.A. But I ain't no low-class field nigger like you, man. I got my honor, motherfucker, and that's something you ain't never gonna understand. Besides, they'd never believe me anyway and they'd just put my ass closer to the fire. Whatever. For the rest of your fucked-up life, man, every time you look in the mirror you're gonna be reminded that you ain't nothin' but a little snitch bitch."

"Fuck you, Otis, and fuck your honor. Where I'm gonna live, man, I ain't gonna need no mirrors."

Chapter Sixteen

January 20, 1951

—JOHNNY BOY—

They make me laugh, these children playing cops and robbers. So they arrest me, John Sebastian Gianelli, right? Only that ain't me! My real name is Pasquale Dominick Sforza. That's right. And here's the sixty-four-dollar question: "Hey, Pasquale, are you a citizen here, or what?" And the answer is: "No, thank you." So what can they do to me? Only one thing—deport me back to *Italia*. And I say, "Hurray for that!" Because that's where I send my money every month anyway. So I'll live the rest of my life in my villa in Florence and I'll say "Thank you" to Uncle Stupo and the land of the free and the home of the red-white-and-blue-and-long-green.

So what do I have to worry about? That double-crossing Jew bastard Georgie Klein who I bankrolled to get control of the Goodrich kid? Fuck him. Let him rot in jail, for all I care. The players? Who? Junior with his elevator that don't stop on the top floor? Otis Hill? That's one fucking nigger who's gonna kill somebody someday, only it ain't gonna be me. Fuck him too. I say throw him in jail so at least the somebody he kills'll be another nigger. And what do I care about all the rest of those jack-offs who thought they could get something for nothing? Fuck them all.

That leaves Rosie. By rights I should have somebody throw acid in her face for fucking Junior. And have her nose cut off for tampering with Johnson. But hey, I don't hold no grudges against beautiful women. So I drop a hundred grand in her bank account and say, "Good-bye and God bless." And while I'm at it, God bless America, too!

—SAMMY—

After reading that Klein's been arrested, I know I'm next. So what are my options? I've certainly got enough money to get the fuck out of here and create a new life for myself someplace else. Canada. England. Switzerland. But who am I kidding? As much as I detest this hypocritical one-size-fits-all country, I'm as American as cow pie à la mode. (Are there any real-life hoopers in Europe? Have the Russians got around to "inventing" the two-hand set shot?) No, I'm stuck here, and this is the only life I have. In truth I have no options, only unfinished business.

My father opens the door and doesn't seem surprised to see me. He wears scuffed slippers and white socks. (I forgot about the dozens of identical white socks he owns. If he loses one here or there, he's always got a match.) His familiar blue terry cloth bathrobe is more ragged than ever. Something new has been added to his housebound apparel, though—a faded red watch cap to protect his head from drafts. "You," is all he says. Then, leaving the front door open, he shuffles back to the kitchen and resumes his evening meal—Campbell's tomato soup garnished with crumbled Ritz crackers. His beverage of choice is Lipton tea (in a glass) diluted with a splash of evaporated milk. As ever, he can't eat without reading a newspaper. Does *The Daily Worker* have a sports section? "Sit," he says, jabbing his nose in the general direction of the only unoccupied chair. "Did you close the front door?"

"Yes, Poppa." His cheeks are scratched and poorly shaven, as though he's been using the same razor blade too long. As he spoons his soup, his hands tremble slightly and he anchors his elbow on the table to steady himself. He's stooped, as though something heavy is pressing down on him, or something irresistible pulling at him from below. Even his eyes seem heavy and drooping. He's old and fragile and the wrinkles in his face seem filled with a light gray dust. "The place looks great, Poppa. Nice and clean. I like the new dinette set."

"A piece of crap," he says. "The Formica scratches too easily. I bought it on time at Macy's. Serves me right."

I came here resolved to make a full confession and to ask not for his forgiveness but for his understanding, perhaps his blessing. My son the pariah. Yet he's still wallowing in his own pain and he doesn't really see me. "Here's a good one, Poppa.... Why did the chicken cross the road?"

"I give up," he says quickly.

"Because a turkey he wasn't."

"Ha," he says, chewing his food slowly as though his teeth are aching.

"So how're you doing, Poppa?"

"I work, I ride the subway, I read the newspapers, I eat, I sleep, I shit. If I'm not too tired, I listen to an opera on the radio. What could be different?"

"How's Uncle Heshie and Uncle Simon? How do they like Florida?"

"Who knows? If we speak on the telephone once a month, it's a lot. But two days ago your Aunt Bessie found out she's got cancer of the liver and she'll never see another Hanukkah."

After he's eaten, he scrubs the bowl, the glass, the spoon and the soup pot with steel wool, then immediately dries everything with a dirty dish towel.

He doesn't offer me tea or water or a cracker. Nor does he inquire after my well-being.

"Poppa, I'm probably going to jail."

That gets his attention—he nearly drops the plate he's replacing in the cupboard. Then he turns to face me, and his sadness and bitterness are overwhelming, greater than mine could ever be. "What did you do?"

"A gambler paid me money to deliberately lose ball games."

"For that they send you to jail? How much money?"

Reaching into my back pocket, I pull out an envelope stuffed with crisp hundred-dollar bills which I casually toss on the table. "About twelve thousand dollars, Poppa. Here, it's for you."

With a dish towel in one hand and a spoon in the other, he's afraid to move, afraid to think.

"Take it, Poppa. It's for you. I don't want it."

Finally he says, "You didn't kill anybody for this? There's no blood on it?"

"No."

"The police don't have the serial numbers?"

"No."

"Then I'll take it."

He flips the spoon and the small towel onto a counter, then grabs the envelope before I can change my mind. Moving quickly, he bustles into the next room and closes the door behind him.

Chapter Seventeen

January 21, 1951

—BARNEY—

This morning's *Sentinel* reports that bail has been set for Hoffman, Callahan, Hill, and Isaacson at ten thousand dollars each, and Benny Tanowski is under guard at Bronx Hospital. Hill has been remanded to custody at Riker's Island while the others have been freed by the anonymous beneficence of a City College alumnus.

Also this morning a photo of Gianelli with the St. John's players at the Copa is splashed on the front page of every newspaper in town. The headline in the *Sentinel* reads:

ANOTHER FIX?
D.A. SAYS NO

My latest column features a lengthy quote from the district attorney:

> "I am convinced that these boys from
> St. John's are absolutely innocent
> of any crimes. They told us of their
> social relationship with Gianelli and
> it was one to which any boys of their
> ages would have been attracted. It is
> significant that none of the boys ever
> saw Gianelli again after the party
> during which the photograph was taken.
> Everything we have heard about these
> young men is entirely to their credit.
> I have no reason to disbelieve their
> story."

In conclusion I fearlessly include another Shakespearean quotation:

"Hast thou betrayed my credulous innocence
With vizor'd falsehood, and base forgery?"

Thus far there's been no public reaction, neither pro nor con, to my "serpent's tooth" line from *King Lear.* Is my erudition being accepted? Or ignored?

In any event the sad, scandalous story is beginning to receive national and international attention: Senator Estes Kefauver of Tennessee, a Democrat with presidential ambitions, claims that his Senate Crime Commission has been probing the basketball fix "for some time." In today's *Daily Mirror* Dan Parker (a rabble-rouser and jingoistic patriot) writes that the United States could cure many of its ills by exporting the game of basketball to Russia. Then Parker quotes from a Russian periodical, *Soviet Sports,* which wants no part of American sports: "Student sports in the United States are used as a means of training young boys in the spirit of militarism. Most large American colleges are now directed by former generals and admirals who are primarily interested in educating the future soldiers of America's aggressive armies. New games played in American colleges include races run backward and wrestling in pits filled with rotten fish."

Arthur Daley of *The New York Times* has Henry Carlson responding to an *unattributed* recommendation that college basketball games should only be played on college campuses. "The way things are," says Carlson, "you could play in the attic or the cellar, and the gamblers would still be operating. I guess from now on coaches will have to start sacrificing talent for character. Thank God for players like Royce Johnson."

Elsewhere Phog Allen, the distinguished coach of the University of Kansas basketball team, eagerly defends the hinterlands: "Out here in the Midwest, of course, these scandalous conditions do not exist."

And down in Lexington, Kentucky, that pompous ass Adolph Rupp has this to say: "Gamblers couldn't get at my boys with a ten-foot pole."

More importantly, O'Hara has stopped slipping me inside information. And Red Smith's piece deals with the arrest late last night of Sammy Goodrich. Fucking O'Hara. He'd better not hold his breath until his fucking kid gets on *Happy Felton's Knothole Gang.*

Goddamn it. This is *my* story.

Then the phone rings and I'm on it before it rings again. Turns out to be some cockamaimie car salesman out in Hempstead who wants to know if I'd be interested in a paid endorsement of his new Chevrolet showroom. Twenty-five bucks. An insulting offer. "I'd never be publicly associated with such an obviously inferior vehicle," I tell him. "I'm strictly a Cadillac man."

Chapter Eighteen

January 22, 1951

—BARNEY—

I wake up to find that a small manila envelope has been pushed under the front door. Inside the envelope is a car key and an unsigned note saying, "Thanks."

I'm confused until I go downstairs, intending to treat myself to some bagels and lox at Hymie's Appetizing Store about five blocks over on Yarry Avenue, and I see a brand-new black Cadillac parked at the curb directly in front of the apartment house. On a hunch I fit the key into the door lock. "Holy shit"! I say as the tumblers click and the door swings open. On the front seat is a registration certificate identifying me as the owner. "Holy shit!" I say at least two dozen times as I drive to the appetizing store.

Then I drive all the way to Coney Island to eat a frankfurter at Nathans Famous. Then I drive past Ebbets Field, then the Polo Grounds and Yankee Stadium. Times Square. Central Park. Fiddling with the power windows, the power seats, the Dyna-Flow automatic transmission, AM-FM radio, air-conditioner, speed control, whitewall tires....

While driving across the George Washington Bridge, I discover twenty hundred-dollar bills in the glove compartment.

"Holy shit!"

Chapter Nineteen

January 18, 1961

—ROSIE—

That was nice of the old fart to leave me the money like he did, and I really am happy that he never did any time. So I got myself into Manhattan Community College as a nonmatriculated student and took a whole bunch of courses. But I dropped out after two weeks because it was all so boring, and nothing they were trying to teach me seemed to have anything to do with anything. So guess what I did next? I paid one of Johnny Boy's old-time buddies five G's to make me up a whole phony personal history: a new name—Mary O'Keefe from Baltimore—as plain as a glass of beer, along with a birth certificate (okay, so I clipped a few years off the top), a Social Security card, a driver's license, even a high school transcript. Then I dyed my hair black, moved to Los Angeles, stashed most of the money in a safe-deposit vault, got a job as a waitress in a neighborhood Italian restaurant, and started from "Go."

So I don't say "fuck" anymore and I just work and go to the movies and normal stuff like that. Once a year I take two weeks in Puerto Rico and go bonkers at the blackjack table and fuck whoever looks good and treats me nice.

About four months ago I had a date with one of the regulars at the restaurant, a car mechanic named Pete, a hardworking, straight-shooting kind of guy with grease under his fingernails. The poor bastard did some time for hoisting a car when he was a kid, so he knows what's what. Hey, Pete treats me with respect, you know? And I don't think I'm gonna go back to Puerto Rico this year.

What else can I say? I still got my figure, and my tits ain't too floppy yet, and life is simple but good. I figure I deserve it.

—MAE—

(Died of a heart attack on November 4, 1954, while watching a professional basketball game at Madison Square Garden.)

—ROYCE—

After my freshman season I transferred to Pontiac University outside of Detroit, where I got my illegal cash from the athletic department. The deal was that the school had no dormitories, so the scholarship athletes were allowed to get reimbursed for their "living expenses," which included rent, food, transportation, laundry, and so on. I lived rent-free in a spectacular one-thousand-dollar-a-month penthouse that over-looked the lake in a building owned by the president of Pontiac's Booster Club. Naturally the one-thousand went into my pocket. Even better, a maid came to my apartment once a week to clean and vacuum, to wash my clothes, and to fuck my socks off. Otherwise I mostly kept to myself and tried not to get too friendly with any of the guys. It was kind of lonesome living like that, but I had to protect myself.

The basketball coach, Mike Charles, was a great recruiter and a creative Xs-and-Os man who designed various isolation offenses and otherwise let us run free. I had a perpetual green light and I averaged around twenty-five points and ten assists throughout my career at Pontiac. Good enough production for the Syracuse Nationals to make me their number-one pick in the 1954 N.B.A. collegiate draft (the third pick overall).

An interesting sidelight to the draft: In those days a team called the College All-Stars would tour the country every spring playing straight-up games against the Harlem Globetrotters. Anyway, before the tour started, two N.B.A. big shots (Red Auerbach, coach of the Boston Celtics, and the owner of the Rochester Royals, Lester Harrison) both called me on the same day to make the same request. Boston had the fifth pick in the upcoming draft and Rochester the sixth, so Auerbach wanted me to "cruise," and Harrison asked if I would "play less than your best" to dissuade other teams with higher picks from selecting me. The merry-go-round never stops turning.

Me, I've been with the Nationals for seven seasons now and I've played in three All-Star games because my numbers always look so good—usually around fourteen points and nine assists per game. But the inside word is that I'm a "forty-six-minute player," meaning that I don't deliver when a ball game's on the line. I'd say that's a simplistic scouting report, but probably more accurate than I'd like to admit.

So far my career has also been dogged with injuries. If it's not a hamstring pull, it's a broken finger or a sprained ankle or a hip pointer or something. I'm used to playing in pain, and living in pain. One is public, the other is private.

My teammates are really friendly, especially Dolph Schayes, Hal Greer, and Dick Barnett. (Scorers always make sure they're on good terms with their point guard.) Syracuse is a small town, so I really can't hide, but I make fifty thousand a year and I own a nifty three-bedroom house with a nice backyard in a high-tone Negro neighborhood. Sometimes I run some free basketball clinics for one of the local boys' clubs, but only on the condition that they keep the media away. For relaxation I read a lot of mystery novels (I love Ellery Queen), and lately I've been taking private lessons to learn how to play the tenor sax. As much as I can, I keep a low profile and I don't mind spending time alone.

We're a respectable ball club and we make the play-offs just about every season—usually losing in the first or second round. We have a new coach every couple of years, as the owner (Danny Biascone, who I rarely see) tries to find the right guy to make us play up to our potential. Lately there's talk of trading me, which is fine. But if I do get dealt to New York, then I'll retire.

I saw Otis once in my rookie year when we were playing the Knickerbockers in Madison Square Garden. He looked all slit-eyed and plenty mean, and I don't blame him, but he seemed glad to see me. He was kind of just "hanging loose," he said, but neither of us said anything about what the newspapers had called "The Big Fix." He looked like he wanted to ask me something but was afraid to do it, so I slipped him a hundred bucks and he seemed happy enough.

Of course I mourned when Ma died.... But deep down? I'm ashamed to confess that I was kind of relieved. Every time I saw her, or spoke to her, or thought about her, or sent her money, I'd be reminded of how easily I'd lied to her and I'd get all fucked up again inside.

My father never showed up again, but I half-expect to see him somewhere down the road, saying, "Hi, son!" and asking for a handout. In a way, I miss him more than I miss Ma.

Sometimes I can forget about my life and my lies and expand into the game at hand. Sometimes. Rarely. Otherwise, playing pro ball is pretty much hard work.

I met a girl up here, Patrice Jackson, and we're engaged. She works in her father's soul-food restaurant, cooking and waiting on tables. She's pretty, sweet, passionate, intelligent, all those things. But the best thing about Patrice is that she knows nothing about basketball.

Sometimes, when I daydream, I wish I'm back at Levy's again, and Junior tells me to miss the shot, and I tell him to go fuck himself, and it's "*Good! Like Nedick's!*," and Ma is alive and my life is going to be different, better.

But God only gives us one chance, and I fucked mine up.

—HENRY—

(Died on July 17, 1960, while in Ireland to conduct a State Department-sponsored basketball clinic, when a terrorist bomb exploded in his favorite Dublin restaurant.)

—JOHNNY BOY—

Marie, she loves it when I sing to her in English. *"Marie, the dawn is breaking. Marie, you'll soon be waking. . . ."* Then she starts giggling, and I wish I could fuck her, but I'm too old.

What the hell. A lot of people I know are dead.

"Hey, Marie. Peel me a grape."

Keh, keh, keh. . . .

—SIDNEY—

(Died on March 16, 1959, when he fell down a flight of stairs in Wingate Gymnasium and broke his neck.)

—JUNIOR—

The fucking Knicks didn't draft me until the seventh round, and I lasted only four days in their preseason camp. Sure, I could score, but I rarely got a good look at the basket, with all those niggers jumping in my face. On defense, guys went by me so fucking fast that I caught a cold. But my father knew a guy who knew a guy, so two days after I was cut, I landed a coaching job.

And that's where I am now, in the coaching racket, up here at St. Albion's University in northern Vermont. When I first got here, the basketball program was a fuckin' disaster—three wins in the last five seasons, a total recruiting budget of two thousand bucks, no assistant coaches, and no godfather in the admissions office. Things changed in a hurry.

What I do is recruit in the nigger neighborhoods in New York, Buffalo, and Boston. Fuckin' A. When I first meet the mom, I act like she's the kid's older sister, and guaranteed the fuckin' kid is mine.

I've averaged nineteen wins over the last four years and last season we almost made the N.I.T. Next year we're scheduled to play St. John's in the Garden! Jeez, I'd love to kick their ass! That's because my ambition is to take over when Coach Mack finally packs it in.

Meanwhile I'm married and have two kids, both girls. But don't worry, I'm still a swordsman on the road. Fuckin' A.

So here I am, living the life of Riley. Which proves one thing—that good things happen to good people.

—SAMMY—

At the trial the judge gave all of us (except Otis Hill) a choice—two years in prison or two years in the army. I chose the latter and it changed my life. Because of my size and my quick reflexes, I was recruited into the Military Police. Imagine me, a cop. Dedicated to preserving the status quo. Cracking the skulls of dissidents, drunks, roughnecks, and peace mongers. And I enjoyed the shit out of it!

For six months I served on an army base just outside of Birmingham, Alabama, and then I was stationed in Germany for eighteen months. Making deals and connections with influential people was easy—one-star generals caught in off-limits bars, visiting congressmen nabbed in whorehouses, drunken dignitaries running amok. The opportunities were endless. One particular situation led to my subsequent (and current) civilian employment.

Seems that a certain well-known Hollywood producer was in town doing a documentary film on American G.I.'s at play in the new Berlin. For his own off-camera R&R, said producer loved to fuck little boys. Eventually one of the mothers figured out what was going on and blew the whistle. This happened on my watch and it was my good fortune to catch the bugger in the saddle.

Once my stint was over, I moved to Hollywood. The producer helped out with a few introductions and I've been a bodyguard to the stars ever since. Robert Mitchum, Cary Grant, Burt Lancaster, Robert Taylor, Claudette Colbert, Joan Crawford, and more. My repertoire is much more limited than in the Military Police—a boot in the ass (or the shins) with my steel-toed shoes usually discourages overly zealous fans.

Most often, a mere threat is sufficient.

I do a lot of drinking in the line of duty. Sometimes drugs too. There's also plenty of leftover women to be screwed. I've grown fat. At 260 pounds, I'm 50 pounds over my playing weight.

Basketball? I haven't touched one since the last game I played for Rhinegold. And I don't miss it either.

And, you know? My father was right all along. The American people have a romanticized view of athletics, and they're eager to identify with this fantasy world as a way of diverting themselves from their own pitiful and unfulfilled lives. The fixers broke a moral code that Sports America made sure everybody believed in, so when we were caught, we faced a far greater wrath than our crime alone merited. We had taken from people what no burglar or common thief ever could. In that period of rampant McCarthyism there were a great many self-righteous reactions to our indiscretions (I'm thinking of that dickhead Barney Polan, for example!). All the coaches yelled their innocence from the rooftops. And we were left defenseless. We took the rap, but I don't feel angry anymore—and I never feel guilty.

So, what else? My father's still alive in a nursing home in the Bronx. I pay the bills and call him once a month.

I'm not a hero and I'm not a villain and I have no regrets. My current lifestyle suits me well enough. Above all, time passes quickly.

— SENIOR —

(Killed in a car accident on the Long Island Expressway on August 23, 1953.)

—BARNEY—

I had what the doctors said was a partial stroke five years ago and I've been confined to a wheelchair ever since. In fact I was in the hospital under heavy sedation when Johnny Podres pitched a 2–0 shutout and the Dodgers finally beat the Yankees in the World Series. I had to read about it in the newspapers.

The *Sentinel* folded in 1959, one year after my Beloved Bums skipped town. What's happened to me should only happen to Walter O'Malley, the greedy prick.

My partial stroke completely ended my career as a writer, but nobody seemed to care. Only Jimmy Cannon wrote something about me, resurrecting his "verse of the peepul" line and saying how I would be missed. That's it. No tears, no laughter.

Let's see…. After I got sick, I traded in my precious Cadillac and emptied my savings account to pay a so-called vanity press to publish *The Complete Woiks*. As far as I know, the book went unreviewed and only 178 copies were sold. I've still got cartons of them stacked up to the ceiling in my bedroom.

Yeah, I still live in the same place. The union sends me a check every month and a girl to clean up the place and do my food shopping. Otherwise I can take care of myself, but I do eat a lot of pizza and spaghetti since Luigi's over on Yarry Avenue started making home deliveries.

Oh, yeah. The Big Fix. Turned out the problem was not confined to New York. Exactly sixty-seven players from sixteen colleges were eventually implicated, including Ralph Beard and Alex Groza of the Indianapolis Olympians, who'd been rigging ball games as undergraduates at the University of Kentucky. The real tragedy is that mushy-hearted sportswriters like Jimmy Cannon had nothing but sympathy for those double-dealing bastards. Sure. Why not feel sorry for Benedict Arnold, too?

Ah, but who cares anymore? Who wants to remember? Nobody, that's who.

Except me.

—OTIS—

The motherfucking judge gave me two years 'cause he said I had tried to "corrupt the innocent freshman, Royce Johnson." About as innocent as John Dillinger.

And that motherfucker is playing in the N.B.A. and making more money than the U.S. Mint. So I go down there to see him play his little shakey-ass game and say what's happening and maybe ask if he needs himself an agent, 'cause I know what's up and what's down and I can get him a better deal for next year. But the snotty motherfucker don't even let me say my piece. Then he gives me some chump change to ease his guilty conscience. Boolshit midnight-looking, nappy-headed, flibber-lipped outhouse nigger.

The whole thing was fucked up, man. Instead of doing their right-eous time, all the white guys got to join the army. The Catholic guys from St. John's didn't have to do shit. Hey, the guys doing business at Holy Cross, LaSalle, and St. Joseph's also got a free ride. I ain't no fool. I knew what was what.

When I got out of jail, I worked in a slaughterhouse in Newark, slitting the throats of those motherfucking cattle, then clubbing the heads of the ones that didn't die quick enough. Wearing fisherman's hip boots to wade in all the shit and piss and blood. Now I got me a better job, loading and driving a beer delivery truck courtesy of some old City College ballplayer who was doing business before the war.

On the weekends I used to play in the Eastern League (for twenty-five bucks a game, two games a week), along with Beard, Groza, Hoffman, and some of them guys. Man, we were the star attractions and we built that fucking league. But then, when everybody's flying high and the turnstiles were spinning like pinwheels, the fucking owners kicked us out, saying shit about their obligation to the public.

And I see that Paluski punk's picture in the papers all the time. How he's such a great coach and how someday he's gonna take over at St. John's. And Hoffman's a fucking dentist and driving a big-ass Lincoln. And Isaacson owns a chain of shoe stores. And Callahan works on Wall Street. And even that sniveling bitch Tanowski runs an advertising agency. And none of them cocksuckers would give me a job, or a stake, or the time of day.

It's almost funny, man. The patty-ass motherfuckers slide and the nigger goes to jail.

Fuck this country, man. Fuck this whole country.